Oil and Water ... and Other Things That Don't Mix

Anthology to raise funds to aid the Gulf Coast clean-up

Edited by
Zetta Brown and
Nicky Wheeler-Nicholson Brown

Oil and Water...and Other Things That Don't Mix

Anthology to raise funds to aid the Gulf Coast clean-up

ISBN: 978-1905091-85-0
Paperback Version

Published in the United Kingdom by LL-Publications © 2010
www.ll-publications.com
57 Blair Avenue
Hurlford
Scotland
KA1 5AZ

Edited by Nicky Wheeler-Nicholson Brown and Zetta Brown
Book layout and typesetting by jimandzetta.com
Cover Photos: iStockPhotos, and from the private collection of
Leslie Lomers and Nicky Wheeler-Nicholson Brown
Cover design by Jim Brown jimandzetta.com © 2010

Printed in the UK and the USA

Dedication

This anthology is dedicated to those who lost their lives in the Deepwater Horizon explosion on April 20, 2010 and to their families. It is dedicated to the people living in the Gulf Coast on the front lines of the oil spill and to their communities. It is also dedicated to the many volunteers who cleaned the beaches, the water, and the wildlife and continue to try and protect and preserve the life that remains.

Publisher's Note

The Oil and Water Project

Although we have picked the following charities to benefit from the sale of this book, they will also benefit from volunteers and direct donations. Please visit their sites and learn more about their mission and how you can help.

Bay Area Food Bank
http://www.bayareafoodbank.org

MOBILE Baykeeper
http://www.mobilebaykeeper.org

And to learn more about *She Writes™*, the online community that brought us together, please visit www.shewrites.com

Follow *Oil and Water...and Other Things That Don't Mix*

Blog
http://oilwaterdontmix.blogspot.com

Twitter
http://twitter.com/OilWaterDontMix

Website
http://www.ll-publications.com/oilandwater.html

Table of Contents

Foreword

Mary W. Rowe
The New Orleans Institute for Resilience and
Innovation

ON APRIL 20, 2010 an oil rig, operating "under the radar" of most of the world, the Deepwater Horizon suddenly became the talk of every town, city, and village around the world. For just over twelve gruelling weeks the havoc of open crude spewing into the Gulf of Mexico dominated the agendas of editorial desks, government agencies, Gulf Coast communities, scientists and engineers everywhere. When would the well be capped? What were the imminent dangers? How will lives and livelihoods along America's gulf coast be changed?

Amidst this sea of uncertainty and seeming helplessness, we have witnessed, once again, the resilience of people to craft responses to unforeseen disasters that support those most affected, but also encourage a broader understanding of the implications of this single event. Community groups, professional associations, industry, academia, even politicians have emerged to pose serious questions about the economic, social, and environmental sustainability of our current ways of living. Into the fray stepped *She Writes™*, a collective of women writers, whose response was to commit this moment in time to art, and to recruit from its members contributions to help us all make sense of a world faced with something elemental: oil and water don't mix.

This collection of poetry and prose, reflecting the diversity of styles and priorities and life experience that is present in "the South" and elsewhere remind us that life carries on, joy and pathos side by each, often joined with welcome humor. The editors of this project and their co-creators from *She Writes™* and beyond are donating the proceeds to two community groups active in supporting the Gulf Coast communities cope with the challenges presented by what is locally known as "the BP Oil Disaster": The Bay Area Food Bank and MOBILE Baykeeper.

Your support of these groups, by buying this book, is a timely reminder that the effects of this debacle will continue to be felt for years to come.

Thanks to the efforts of these women and men, this collection celebrates the creative talents of their contributors, and reminds us that in the midst of adversity and challenge, our capacity to tell and receive each other's story remains our path to a more enlightened future.

Preface
"Conflict...Resolution Optional."
Zetta Brown and Nicky Wheeler-Nicholson Brown

DESPITE our names, Nicky and I are not related. In fact, we have never met in person. We met through a social networking website called *She Writes*™ in their Southern Writers subgroup.

When the oil disaster happened, the members in our little group were sad, mad, and disgusted—which is Southern for "pissed off." I had the idea of doing an anthology to benefit charities dealing with the disaster and I approached Nicky because she has deep roots in the Gulf. She came up with the name and we've been running with it ever since.

The major thread running through this anthology is conflict, because oil and water don't mix. The official theme is "Conflict ...Resolution optional," and these authors have delivered. Not all stories are set in the South, but all have the theme of conflict. You will find funny and poignant pieces of conflict ranging from dealing with personal relationships to dealing with the kitchen oven. Some of these tales have a resolution, some are ongoing, and some conflicts may never be resolved...at least not in our lifetime. There is fiction and non-fiction inside. But the amazing thing is that these authors came from everywhere wanting to do something to help the Gulf region. If donating a story to an anthology to benefit the people and wildlife in crisis can help, so be it.

This is a very unique collection of stories, poems, and personal essays written by women and men. Some are established, award-winning authors but there are several talented, newly published authors and a few new authors making their debut. You won't be disappointed.

I'm a native Texan, born and bred. My husband is Scottish and we live in Scotland. We also have a small publishing company. A good thing about being a small, independent publisher is that we can publish what we want—even if we choose to do it for charity.

My memories of the Gulf are limited to the few short visits, decades apart, but like the saying goes, "You can take a girl out of the South, but..."

Zetta Brown
November 2010, Scotland

ZETTA, as usual, has led the way and there are only two things that I would add.

First, what a crazy idea for two women, an ocean apart, who did not know one another, to do something on their own time to attempt a project of this nature. It has been easy mostly because Zetta's "bee in the bonnet skills" have moved us right along. Whatever happens with this project, my life is already richer for being a part of it.

Secondly, this is deeply personal for me. I am a seventh generation Gulf Coastal inhabitant and the only way I can describe how I felt once the oil started gushing is that my heart broke. My mother's family arrived in New Orleans around 1820 and we've been somewhere on the coast between there and Pensacola, Florida ever since. Native Elders often speak of walking on the bones of their ancestors and once you have been in a place for more than a few generations you literally become a part of the earth itself.

The Gulf Coast has been through so much, particularly in the last six years—one devastating hurricane after another, economic difficulties, over-development and now this horrific oil spill. It has affected our entire way of life and will probably do so for some time to come. The charities that we honor in our donations are doing the best they can to help the people and the environment on the coast.

Ours is a unique culture—a true gumbo of Native, African,

and European heritage. A good gumbo consists of the best that the waters have to offer, the plants, spices, and cooking traditions brought from Europe and Africa and the native plants and spices.

This anthology of writing reflects that heritage in the diversity of writing because there is something here that will speak to everyone.

We are all a part of everything. In spite of all our differences, our separations of place and time, of cultures and even that of species—we breathe the same air, walk on the same land and swim in the same waters. Thank you to everyone who has participated for the opportunity to give back in some small way to this beautiful body of water that gives us so much.

Nicky Wheeler-Nicholson Brown
November 2010, The Berkshires, Massachusetts

Acknowledgements
The Editors wish to thank...

Kamy Wicoff and Debroah Siegel, the founders of *She Writes*™, for creating a place where women can share their experiences through their writing and creating a place on the Internet that is inspiring, encouraging, and empowering for women's voices worldwide. And a special thanks goes to our corner of *She Writes*™ — the Southern Writers group.

We thank all of the contributing authors for their talent and their patience because without you, there would be no anthology.

Thank you, Leslie Lomers and Helen E. H. Madden for the photographs and helping to assemble the cover, and Mary Rowe. Special thanks to Connie Whitaker and David Reaney at Bay Area Food Bank, and at MOBILE Baykeeper our thanks go to Erin Reimer, Tiia Carraway, and Lynne Cooper.

And finally, we wish to thank our loving husbands Jim and Jason Brown; two men who are unrelated but have come to learn what it's like living with two Southern women...and what happens when they get a bee in their bonnet.

Three Haikus from an Angry God
By Tynia Thomassie

These are oily times.
What you consume now eats you.
You are your own terrorist.

Cracked, hatched and birthed, what
slouched near Bethlehem now spreads
in your own backyard.

Complacency and
oblivion can strip you
or coat you. Ssshhh. Choose.

BEFORE PETROLEUM
By Patricia Anne McGoldrick

Everyone knows that
Oil
and
Water,
Even if holy,
Do not mix.
This twosome today
Spells disaster
Now,
Unfortunately,
Ever after.

"Sewer" Candy Store
By Amy Wise

Conflict

AUGUST 17TH, 2007, the day my life was "literally flushed down the toilet," or so I thought. This is the twisted tale of what actually brought me to writing and made my marriage and family as strong as they are today.

THREE YEARS AGO I owned a beautiful candy/gift store with a business partner and dear friend. We had a thriving two-family business and went to "work," if you can even call it that, every single day with smiles on our faces. In August of 2007, everything changed, and our world was turned upside down. We found out that the water our building was receiving was not drinking water—but reclaimed sewer water! Yes, that's right...sewer water! We finally realized why we all kept getting sick, and to make matters worse, the media onslaught began, the customers ran far, far away (who can blame them), and we had to close our beautiful store. People actually wanted to know where our kids went to school so their kids would not be exposed to our "sewer sick" kids! Imagine having your children talked about like that. It was horrible! We went from being the "sweetest candy store" to the "sewer candy store." Um...gross! Two things that definitely don't mix: sewer and candy! Not a pretty mental picture!

The Otay Water Department, the city, the contractor, the developer, and all the other parties that had a hand in the negligence, stood in front of the news cameras and said, "This is our fault and we are going to do the right thing." However, once the cameras went away, they ran as fast as they could to their attorneys and have destroyed us ever since. Remember Erin Brockovich? She fought PG&E. Well, that's my life right now. The destruction of our dream, the illnesses, and the financial devastation has, needless to say, been more than we could handle. Three years later we are *still* fighting for what's right. It's unbelievable to me! Justice? I'm not sure what that means anymore. We are now being sued by the very landlord/builder that rented the space to us because we "broke" our lease! The banks are also suing us because the store that no longer exists can no longer pay the loans. They said, "The lawsuit is taking too long," and they want their money." *They* think it's taking too long? Really? Suing the victims? Wow! Can you say, INJUSTICE!

I want to scream from the mountaintops at the "wrongness" of what is happening. I want to call every news station on the planet so people can see what the "big guys" keep doing to the "little guys." They want to hide what they have done and make it seem like it's no big deal. Well, I'm here to tell you—it's a BIG deal to me. My family has suffered, and my business that I worked all my life to create, is gone. So yeah, that's a big deal, don't you think?

When it comes to the attorneys and companies involved in this case, I have a couple of questions: How do they sleep at night? How do they go to work each and every day knowing that they are destroying people's lives? The old saying, "This isn't personal, I'm just doing my job," can *never* be an excuse. They chose their job, they chose their profession, and they choose to destroy people. They are adults and they can say no, but they choose not to. They might as well be in bed with the devil as far as I'm concerned. What happened to doing the right thing? I'll tell you what happened...power and greed. It's no mystery. Doing the right thing doesn't exist in this case. It's a sad picture of our system when the victims are allowed to be destroyed by the very entities that caused the destruction in the first place.

The "sewer saga" as I now call it, just keeps going on, and on, and on. Sadly it has become such a part of our lives that I am now used to it. It's like a part time job and there is always work to do. We live it each and every day and are constantly having to deal with it in one way or another. If we are not going to doctor's appointments, it's conference calls. If it's not conference calls, it's hearings. If it's not hearings, it's someone getting deposed. Recently my husband and daughter had the "fun" experience of being deposed all day by the defense attorneys from Otay Water, Bremco, Seymour Lewis Development, The City of Chula Vista, and more! I already had that lovely experience for a total of two days and sixteen hours on my own. Now, sadly, it was their turn. I had to sit there in silence as my family was questioned about every detail of their lives. It made me sick to my stomach. My daughter missed an entire day of school, and my husband and I both missed work. I just don't understand how this is allowed. Victims badgered over and over...it's just heinous if you ask me! Heinous!

My husband was brought to tears when they asked him how our lives have changed since getting sick and losing our business due to the water misconnection. I have never seen him like this in the eighteen years we have been together. He is six-foot-three and three hundred-plus pounds and this man sobbed like a baby because he feels helpless regarding the destruction of his family from this lawsuit. He is used to being the husband that takes care of his family, but in this case he can't because his hands are tied and there is nothing he can do but sit back and watch the wheels of justice spin as slow as molasses. My daughter and I had to sit there and listen as he cried, and then we cried right along with him. I have never felt more love and more sadness in my life listening to this big, strong, man, literally sob over what his family is going through. He had to leave the room and go for a walk to calm down and to stop from jumping over the table to throttle the defense attorneys. It was so sad, and it just broke my heart to see him like that.

After my husband was done with his hours of questioning, it was my daughter's turn. As a mother, all you want to do is protect your child. There was nothing I could do to stop them from questioning her. They dug into personal details a teen should never have to share with anyone except her own friends, let alone a room full of strangers. They even talked about subpoenaing her journals for God's sake! Hell will freeze over before I let that happen! This is all so they can figure out a way to take the responsibility away from them and put it on something else that may or may not be going on in her life. Disgusting is an understatement. However, little did they know that my child would rise to the occasion like no other. She stayed totally and completely strong. She amazed me, impressed me, and made me so proud. My fifteen year old showed the maturity and strength of an adult that day. Again, the love I felt for her, just like I did for my husband—incredible!

So even though we have to continue to fight for what's right against attorneys and companies that apparently have no soul— the more they take away from us, the stronger we become. Just when I thought I couldn't love my family more than I already do, they showed me more fortitude and bravery then I have ever seen. All I can say is, "I'm so proud of them!"

The tears have now dried up, and the bitterness and anger have turned to determination. I will never stop fighting for what's right! The "big guys" always think they can win, morals be damned...but this time the "little guys" are stronger than they ever realized, and we will never, ever give up!

Resolution

SO WHAT does all of this have to do with my marriage, family, and writing? Well, pretty much everything. When you lose all you've worked for your entire life, have utter financial destruction, health problems, and then have to totally start over, all at the hands of someone's gross negligence, you either make it or you don't. There is no middle ground. My husband has been my rock, heart, and soul. He has seen me rise, fall, and rise again...actually, more like picked me up off the floor and stood me up again! My daughter, bless her heart, has had to adjust to a mom who was home for dinner, who had the freedom to come and go from her business, who was happy every single day, to a mom who has been holding on for dear life while totally starting over. Our lifestyle is completely different now, but the one thing that remains is our never-ending love. Nothing and no one can take that away from our family!

Even though the negativity keeps trying to wiggle its way in to our lives we are determined to live an even better life than before. The lack of money has been replaced with more love, and the lack of "things" has been replaced with creativity that I didn't even know existed. It's actually pretty cool. I have planted a garden. Okay, I've planted tomatoes, but I'm getting there! I'm shopping at thrift/exchange stores, so now I'm not only saving the "green," I'm being green! Not only that, I have found some really great treasures. It's amazing what we all give away. "Waste" is not in my vocabulary anymore.

I'm also painting and writing up a storm. Two things that I love to do and that give me total and complete peace. When I wanted to write a book about the loss of our business due to the water department, my husband suggested I write about our relationship and family. I created a blog called The Many Shades of Love (www.themanyshadesoflove.blogspot.com) and have been writing about "us" ever since. My blog has blossomed into writing for many other projects, and now, once again I have that beautiful feeling of "working" on something I love.

My faith, amazingly, has grown, when I thought the exact opposite would happen. I *do* believe what goes around comes around, even though sometimes it takes longer than I'm willing to wait. Patience isn't just a virtue; it's now my middle name— or actually, closer to my first name! I'm willing to wait and I'm willing to be patient, because as time goes on, I become a better person and more and more of what I was "meant to do" keeps arising from the chaos.

My husband and I have dealt with so much and we keep making it through all the insane trials and tribulations and coming out even stronger in the end. So in a sense, tragedy is turning to triumph as we take all the bad that continues to get thrown our way and turn it into good. I will keep writing, I will keep growing, I will become stronger, and I will never give up. I have even been called "Tinkerbell" because I always believe people will do the right thing. I have seen the worst in people these last three years, but I have also experienced the best.

Family and friends have stepped up to the plate with love, assistance, shoulders and so much more! Karma *is* still on my side—I truly believe it! It's funny because when you take the vows that say, "through good times and bad" and "for better or worse," it's easy to say, but not always easy to live. It's a piece of cake to make it through the good times, but if you can make it through the bad, and I mean really, *really* bad—you can make it through anything. That's what it's all about.

I know from the depths of my soul that eventually the right thing will happen and we *will* be made whole again. By the time it does, it will be icing on the cake because by then we will have created a truly authentic life. Little did I know this was the beginning of a whole new way of living, a whole new way of thinking, and a whole new way of life! That's what I call the *real* meaning of resolution. The rest will come in time.

Recipe for Disaster
By Lissa Brown

THE COMBINATION of a novice baker and a new oven can produce interesting results. I admit baking has never been my favorite pastime. As a matter of fact, the kitchen is a venue in which I have never been completely comfortable. I do, from time to time, feel inspired to bake a birthday cake for someone, and lacking the experience and the know-how, I am scrupulously careful to follow directions on the cake mix box.

One day, about three weeks after moving into a new home, a wave of domestic inspiration wafted through the kitchen window. By the way, that's new home as in "still finding sawdust in corners." It was a log cabin we'd had custom built. I had all brand new appliances and I figured the virginal wall oven and I could tackle the task.

I began reading the directions on the Betty Crocker box and started to assemble the ingredients. It never fails. There's always something in the foolproof directions that begs explanation. A third of a cup of oil, it said. But what kind of oil? I was reasonably sure I couldn't use 3-in-1 or WD-40, but that still left lots of options.

Trying not to sound too stupid, I called my other half, who, mercifully, is more adept at such things. I casually worked into the conversation that I was baking a cake for our friend Lyn. "What sort of oil works best with a spice cake?" I queried.

"Vegetable oil, of course," was the answer. This was followed quickly by, "Are you sure you don't want to wait until I come home from work? I can do it then."

"No," I replied. I can do this. My confidence had been restored once I verified what kind of oil I needed.

I hung up the phone and went to the pantry to get the oil. Our new larder hadn't been fully stocked yet, but I did see a jar of olive oil. Great, I thought. I took out three eggs, measured a cup and a third of water, and emptied the contents of the box into a mixing bowl. I'm not sure why a pang of doubt grabbed me just then, but before I added the olive oil to the cake mix and eggs, I began to wonder if olives were really vegetables. I wrestled with this for a few minutes and decided I needed to consult an expert.

The neighbor I called sounded a bit incredulous when I asked if olives were vegetables. "Why do you want to know?" she asked. I explained what I was planning to do with the olive oil. "Oh, my goodness," she said. "I'll be right over." And then she threw in a "Bless your heart," and I knew I was in trouble.

The doorbell rang and I found my neighbor with a bottle of Canola oil in hand. "This is what you need to use," she said. "You can bring back what you don't use later."

It's easy to assume that everyone is savvier about baking than I am, and even though I had never heard of a vegetable called a canola, I took her word for it and poured the oil into the bowl.

I added the eggs and water and mixed the concoction until it looked like cake batter. Meanwhile, I'd preheated the oven to 350 degrees and it signaled it was ready. I set the timer for thirty minutes and vowed to refrain from opening the oven door to check on it, as I am inclined to do. I poured the batter into the greased pan and placed it gently on the middle rack of the oven.

After fifteen minutes I couldn't stand the suspense and broke the promise to myself. I opened the oven door and looked at the cake. It looked pretty liquid but I figured that was because of the 3,700 foot altitude of my new home. I'd moved here from sea level. I closed the door and managed to stay away from the oven for another ten minutes.

That was easy to do because the plumbers had arrived to fix the leak in our new basement. I showed them where the problem was and left them to do their work. One of the guys mentioned they'd have to shut off the water for awhile and I said that was fine.

I climbed upstairs to the kitchen and went to check on the cake. It was still very liquid and I began to suspect something was wrong. Then it hit me. There was no heat coming out of the oven. It had shut itself off. These new, high-tech appliances require a bit more intelligence than the old ones, but I really believed I was operating it correctly.

Out came the 62-page oven manual in three languages. I pored over the instructions until I was certain I'd done everything right. I even checked the troubleshooting section and ruled out everything on the chart except the last one that said to call the repair service.

I turned off the oven and restarted it. It started up just fine and I breathed a sigh of relief. From the look of it, I guessed the cake had actually baked for about eight to ten minutes before it shut itself off. I set the timer for twenty minutes and resolved to stand and watch the oven this time.

After about five minutes, the oven beeped and shut itself off again. "Oh fine," I shouted to nobody in particular. "Now what do I do?" I'd already invited people in that evening for cake and coffee to celebrate a friend's birthday.

With all modesty, I must say that I'm a pretty creative problem-solver. For the heck of it, I tried the broiler and it worked fine. I waited ten minutes and it still was working. If I put the broiler on low, it surely would heat the oven enough to bake this cake, I reasoned. I put the cake back into the oven and set the timer for fifteen minutes. I had a deadline to meet for an article I was writing and walked down the hall to my office to work on it.

After about ten minutes, something started to tickle my nose. I sneezed a couple of times and suddenly realized I smelled smoke. I jumped up and ran into the kitchen. Smoke was pouring out the sides of the wall oven. I shut the broiler off, retrieved the charred cake, and rushed it out onto the porch. Of course, on my way I'd managed to set off the smoke alarms.

Now I'm not a religious woman, but I had some pointed questions for our Creator that all began with "Why me?" My questions for the oven company involved God, too, but were of an entirely different nature. They had more to do with the origins of the oven and the parentage of the people who built it. As I went back into the kitchen, I remembered the water was shut off because the plumbers were working downstairs. Luckily, the cake was the only thing that caught fire.

It was beginning to look like my friend was going to have a store-bought cake. Getting to the store was a challenge, however. The nearest store was thirty minutes away, and I couldn't leave the plumbers alone in the house. Since they were the ones who did the original plumbing when the house was being built, I knew the leak they were fixing was due to their own ineptitude. I'd already had a fire and didn't need a flood to contend with.

I swallowed the little pride I had left and picked up the phone. "Honey," I said, "would you mind stopping at the bakery and picking up a cake on your way home from work?" I tried to sound calm although my adrenaline was flowing as I contemplated what I was going to say to the oven company when I made the next call.

My faith in the Almighty was restored when the only answer I got was, "Sure. Did you change your mind?" I hoped to avoid further discussion, but I wasn't getting off so easily. "How about if I make the cake when I get home?"

"No, even you can't make a cake in our oven. It's broken," I reported. "Without going into gory details, let me just say I'm about to contact the manufacturer and let my frustration out on them. Be glad you're not home."

OVER the next several weeks, the repair service visited my home twelve times, each time, except the last one, fixing the errant oven. Fearing what might happen the thirteenth time, I insisted on a replacement oven.

This could not possibly happen twice, I was sure. I was also wrong. The second oven was shutting itself off too. I searched the Yellow Pages for an exorcist and finding none, I decided to call a different repair service.

My prayers were answered. The nice man figured out that the wiring on the oven was installed incorrectly. "You're lucky it didn't burn down the house," he commented as he put it together correctly, the way it should have been done at the factory.

When I called the department store from which I purchased our appliances, the owner informed me "There wasn't nothin' wrong with that oven I took back."

"Oh?" I said. "And how do you know that?"

"I sold it to somebody else and I haven't heard nothin' from 'em." he reported.

I've scoured the local newspapers to see if anyone has either murdered the store owner or had their home burned down by a defective oven. My guess is that the poor people who ended up with that oven have done what I should have done and resorted to buying store-bought cakes and cooking everything else in the microwave.

An Ordinary Difference
By Karen Pickell

ATLANTA sprawls out in every direction. There is no water or mountain or desert to stop it. When we moved here eight years ago, the main road to our subdivision had a speed limit of forty-five miles per hour and no sidewalks. A car could have easily driven up onto the grass or into a tree on this narrow two-lane road without shoulders.

Our nearest store is a mile down the main road from our house. It sits next to the school my son attends. A bus picks him up directly across from our house every morning and returns him every afternoon. The bus route was approved because the hazardous main road was too dangerous for our kids to walk on. And buses are more environmentally friendly than cars—although when it rains, our bus is mostly empty. Parents drive their kids the mile to school so they won't have to wait out in the rain for the bus to come.

Recently our town built sidewalks all the way down to the school and lowered the speed limit to thirty-five miles per hour. There is now a traffic light at the busy intersection the kids have to cross to get there. A couple of times a year the school holds a walk-to-school day. I walk the mile with my son, kiss him goodbye, and then turn around and walk the mile back home. We wave to his bus driver as she passes us on the way there. This is just a symbolic walk after all. No one imagines that walking to school will ever become the norm for our kids. I never walk my son on any other day, and I don't allow him to walk alone. I've never once walked to the store next to the school. The round trip takes me almost an hour.

And I was one of those fabled kids who walked miles to and from school through hail storms and blizzards. What happened to that girl?

I'm one ordinary person. I depend on my car. Our nearest relatives live over 650 miles away. Still, it is important for my children to spend some time each year with their grandparents, aunts, uncles and cousins. We can drive to see them or we can fly in an airplane. I've never looked into whether buses or trains would get us there. We'd rather spend most of our precious vacation days with the people we love than on the road. One way or another, we need gasoline to see them.

Just like we need gasoline to get around Atlanta. Maybe if we lived in the city there would be places we could easily reach on foot or on bicycle. But then my husband would drive farther to get to his job here in the suburbs. We can't all work in the city. We're lucky to have any job at all in this difficult economy. We've chosen to live close to my husband's place of business to maximize the time we spend together as a family. The trade-off is needing a car to get to parks, stores, and restaurants.

If we lived in the city, maybe we could take the train more. Maybe a bus would go down our street. There are few buses nearby here and there aren't any trains. We have to drive just to get to a train. Again, gasoline.

Of course, living in the city is hypothetical fantasy. We can't afford it. Well, maybe we could, if we could stand losing a thousand square feet of living space and most of our yard.

We're not villains. We're ordinary people. We drive five hundred miles to vacation at a beach on the Gulf of Mexico every year. We've fallen in love with the clear, calm water of the Gulf. Someday we want to move to where we can swim in the Gulf every day if we choose. This isn't just a fantasy. We've started researching home prices, schools, and hospitals in a location we can afford just fifteen minutes from the beach. How wonderful our life will be when we can regularly enjoy fishing in the bays, eating fresh Gulf seafood for dinner, and spending date night watching the sunset from a beach blanket. A play date for my kids will be spent building sand castles and marveling at the passing sting rays.

Too many mornings when I walk on the beach I'm disgusted by the trash people left behind the night before. I pick up bottles and throw them into nearby trash cans. I probably don't even walk a mile of the long Gulf shoreline. Does it make any difference that I pick up a few bottles? I know it's a small effort but I feel better picking up those bottles.

Our hometown provides us a big trash receptacle for recyclables. Last year we just had a little box that fit in the pantry. The new one is so big it has to stay outside. Before we moved here, I didn't recycle at all. I never heard of recycling as a kid. Now my son learns about it in school.

Now I carry reusable grocery bags made of cloth back to the grocery store every week. When they first appeared in our local store I thought I would hate them. I thought, sure they may be good for someone in the "12 Items or Less" aisle but not for someone like me. Turns out five bags hold a week's worth of groceries for a family of four. I get my carload of supplies into the house in no time now. The bags are heavy though. My arthritis-ridden mother could never lift them being that full. Nothing is perfect. My husband is happy that we no longer have a pantry full of used plastic bags that I intend to take back for recycling but never do.

Don't get me wrong. I'm not an environmentalist. I'm not willing to leave my family to travel to Louisiana to wash oil off of pelicans with dish soap. I'm one ordinary person. I'm not an engineer. I don't know how to stop oil from gushing out of a ruptured well into the Gulf of Mexico. My job is to make the choices that are best for my family. Sometimes the choice is the lesser of two evils.

An Ordinary Difference – Karen Pickell

We ordinary people love our cars. For a second after I heard about the oil spill, I wanted to ride my bicycle everywhere. I wanted to make my kids walk with me in 90-degree heat every other day to get groceries. I felt the weight of blame on my shoulders for participating in our gas-guzzling culture. Of course, it's not practical in our society of shopping malls and strip centers to walk or bike everywhere. I need my car. I wish I had a choice about how to power my car, but my car only takes gasoline. In a few years when I need a new car, I'll learn about the hybrids. I'll research any alternative fuels that are available. And I've vowed to choose the least of all the evils, if I can afford it.

I'm not a lobbyist. I'm not a politician. Does anything I do matter when there are conglomerates controlling governments? My husband tolerates my boycott of British Petroleum gasoline though he smirks every time I make him drive past a BP station to find an alternative. Happy wife, happy life is his motto. He doesn't think the boycott will make any difference in the grand scheme of oil company greed. After all, we are still buying gasoline. He may be right. But I feel better not giving my money to the company that polluted all over our dream.

What can I do? I'm just one ordinary person. I'm just trying to live my little life as best I can. I chastise my husband when he absentmindedly throws a box in with the garbage instead of with the recyclables. I teach my children that cloth bags are better than plastic, that school buses are better than carpools. I vote for candidates who want to minimize our dependence on fossil fuels.

Does any of it make a difference? I have to believe it will.

Keeping Up with the Coles
By Angela Elson

I ADMIT IT: *I* was the one who wanted to buy the push-reel lawn mower when my husband, Brady, and I went to Sears last spring. "Are you nuts?" he asked, wiping his fingerprints from the John Deere tractor he'd been pawing all afternoon. "Have you ever used a push-reel? They're awful, and unless you're going to help with the mowing..."

I swore I would, because there was something cute and kitschy about a push-reel mower that lent itself well to my romantic ideas of homeownership and marriage—ideas that originated when push-mowers were high technology, ideas that involved frou-frou aprons and homemade piecrusts and other things I'd never seen in real life. "Fine," Brady surrendered. "But you're going to regret this. You'll see."

A month later and drenched in July sweat, I stumble through the yard like a man through the desert and curse Brady for being so indulgent, because all this is clearly his fault. "How do you like that push mower?" He laughs from the shaded porch.

"You're a dick!" I fire back, even though I know he's not and I deserve every moment of this. I see our next-door neighbor step out to get his paper, and, not wanting him to think we're a dysfunctional couple, I amend my previous statement with a "Just kidding, sweetie!"

"I love you too," says Brady. "Now *mow!*"

IT'S TIMES like these when I wonder if Adam and Brit fight about their lawn, but then decide against it since I've never seen them fight over anything. These are friends of ours who live up the road—tan, gorgeous people who subsist on hair gel and Pinot Grigio, and who are so in love that yard work probably turns them on. They have a kind of cloying, ass-grabbing relationship that makes hanging out with them an exercise in averting your eyes.

"And it's all because of you guys...," Brit sniffles when we go out for drinks. Tears trickle down her face like the condensation off her margarita glass. "If you guys hadn't gotten married, then we never would have."

It happened like this: Adam and Brady were best friends when they were kids—in *Tasmania*, a place I didn't even know was real until I met Brady while teaching English in Japan. But while I had to cross an ocean and endure months of hardship and raw fish to find true love, Brit bumped into Adam when he came to Louisville for our wedding. They met at a bar. At two in the morning. On a Sunday. After a few nights together, Adam confessed to us at our rehearsal dinner, "Guys, I think she's The One...Can I bring her as my date?"

"I think it's too late," Brady said, and I loved him for it. "The caterers already have the numbers. Sorry, mate."

I'd like to think I wasn't much of a fussy bride. I was pretty laid back when it came to the flowers and the cake. "But if he thinks," I growled into Brady's ear, "that I'm going to let some girl he's been nailing for five days into *my* wedding he's got another thing coming."

When Adam went back to Australia, we assumed we'd heard the last of Brit, but she went to visit him—twice. A few months later, he took a year-long leave of absence from his job and moved in with her down the street on a tourist visa so they could be together, making our neighborhood now home to *two* Tasmanians in love with two Louisville girls. This has ruined my outlook on love. Every time I think Brady's and my romance is special and destined, all I need to do is look up the road and remember that this kind of thing happens every day.

If Brady and I strive for a hardworking, home-bodied marriage from the fifties, Adam and Brit are looking to resurrect the eighties power couple. To have dinner with them, you must book months in advance. Ask them what they did last weekend and they'll shrug. "Oh, not much." They say it so offhandedly you'll believe them, too, until one of them continues: "On Friday night we went to a wine tasting, and then on Saturday we jogged around the park and went to a football game—"

"No wait, baby. The football game was the weekend before last. After we went for a jog we had a picnic on the river..."

"*That*'s right, sweetie. And then we did the art gallery hop downtown."

"And then Sunday we went to church..."

"And then we had lunch at Brit's parents' house..."

"And then we saw a movie and—"

"And then we went home, and opened a bottle of wine and—" Here's the part where they pull huge, mischievous grins, leering at each other, dropping their voices an octave and giggling. "And, well, we can't tell you the rest."

"Like I'd even *want* to know," says Brady on the drive home. "*Gross.*"

Last weekend Brady and I cleaned all Saturday and fought about the lawn on Sunday. These two events were punctuated by a night of drinking. "Oooh!" said Adam. "Where'd you go? Fourth Street? Irish Row?"

"We had a few beers at my brother's house," I say, and though I consider this a very satisfactory weekend, I still can't help but feel a little ashamed at how lame we seem. But I take comfort in knowing it doesn't really matter what we did last weekend. We could have sung karaoke with Frank Sinatra's ghost or had a foursome with Brangelina, but it would have never been as good as what Adam and Brit got up to. This isn't to say they're pretentious or social climbing; Adam and Brit are just really this fun. They are wonderful, genuinely happy-go-lucky people whom everyone adores. They deserve every nice thing that happens to them—they really do. Theirs is a champagne life so full of joy and adulation it makes me want to barf.

"*ANOTHER* wedding shower?" Brady sighs, opening an envelope with our names misspelled on the front.

I inspect the loopy, Catholic-school handwriting: "It must be one of the bridesmaids."

Brit has lived in Louisville all her life and has amassed an army of acquaintances who are equally tanned, weepy, and well versed in the paler Zinfandels. Since she and Adam have decided to become Mr. and Mrs. Cole, each of them feels the need to throw her a party, and as Brady is Adam's only home-grown friend in town, we are invited to all of them.

It sucks to have your marriage reduced to a footnote in someone else's, but that's what's happened since we started going to these parties. "Oh, so *you're* the folks who had the wedding!" bridesmaids will say to us. "Well, if it wasn't for you guys..."

"Yeah, everyone says that *now*," I reply. "But wait until they get divorced. We'll never hear the end of it!" This is obviously a joke, but not all of Brit's friends find it funny.

Brady and I will stand in a corner with our beers while everyone drags around comically large wine glasses filled to the brim with blush. We eavesdrop on conversations about college classmates or the most recent basketball lineups—topics of which we know nothing. I'm not even sure why we're invited to these things since we don't know anyone besides Adam and Brit. "It's nice they wanted us to feel included," Brady says, and

39

I look over at the aneurism of drunk girls clogging up the bar and say, "Oh yeah, I really feel like a part of things."

Brady and I don't have memberships to tanning salons or dozens of friends who look like they live in Abercrombie catalogs. We don't have picnics or weep over how in love we are, which makes getting together with Adam and Brit difficult in terms of shared interests. But whenever we *do* have dinner, it's like looking into a funhouse mirror, the kind that shows you what you would look like if you were thinner or taller or better. On one side of the table, a Tasmanian and a Louisvillian, cooing and feeding each other spoonfuls of dessert, goading, "Come on, sweetheart. *You* have the last bite."

On the other, a Tasmanian and a Louisvillian, dueling for the last crumbs of cake. "I have a lawyer on speed-dial," I say. "So *drop the fork.*"

Brady and I love each other infinitely, but you'd never know it by looking at us, and it's hard not to feel threatened by Adam and Brit's visible obsession for each other. Here they are, the hot-and-heavy fiancés, and here is Brady and me: the old married couple. I feel like we should be gumming tapioca through our toothless maws. When the meal's over, Brit runs her hand along Adam's cheek and says, "That was a fantastic meal, snookums."

Not to be outdone, I turn to Brady and say, "Oh yes, pumpkin." I pinch his cheeks for good measure. "It was almost as yummy as you."

"I'm glad you liked it, my little double-glazed donut," he replies, before laying the world's longest French kiss on me. We look like assholes, but it's better than looking like we're *married.* "Do you want me to bend you over the dinner table now?" Brady asks, "Or should we save it for the hood of Brit's car?"

ADAM AND BRIT plan to get married at Churchill Downs. "And we stole your idea for the wedding date."

The "idea" in question involves how Brady and I had our wedding on June ninth, which was ninety-nine percent due to the fact that it was a Saturday and the venue was free, and one percent caused by how funny I thought it would look on the invitations. "Sixty-nine," I chuckled to the printer. "Get it?"

Adam and Brit have decided on July 11: "Seven eleven!" they announce in unison and fall over themselves laughing. It's bad enough that they've stolen our love story, but now they've run off with our wedding shtick. And when the wedding invitation arrives monogrammed with a huge A&B at the top, I scream, "Goddamn it, Brady! They even have our initials!"

I'm happy for Adam and Brit; I am. My dissatisfaction stems from the fact that everyone we know collectively (on two continents, mind you) will forever compare us as couples, and Brady and I will always look duller, sadder, colder than them. If I could have had my pick of matrimonial doppelgangers, I would have chosen pudgy, stupid, troll-like people so that everyone would see Brady and me for the winning, loving couple we are. But we got stuck with a real-life Barbie and Ken, which is why a mean little nugget of me is annoyed to have had my thunder stolen, my love story plagiarized by more worthy, more beautiful people. I feel like I should make this humiliation complete and lend Brit my wedding gown so she can look ten times better in it than I ever did.

It's a strange thing to find yourself envying what you don't really want. And trust me when I say I don't really *want* to be Adam and Brit. Just thinking about all their jogging and party-hopping and tailgating and wine guzzling makes me want to take a nap. But still, I feel like theirs is a life I *should* want, a young, exciting, beer-commercial life of looking good and having fun. "We should be *out*," I tell Brady.

"Out where?"

"I don't know."

Bars are loud and restaurants expensive; neither of us dance, so clubs are no good, and I maintain that picnicking is just too lame to be done in earnest. Besides, the laundry has to be done and the lawn mowed, and we're tired from working and the economy is bad. And where else in this town is as nice and quiet and comfortable and free as our own front porch?

"No really," Brady says, "Why would we go anywhere else?"

"But we don't have any friends," I pout. "And don't even say we've got Adam and Brit, because clearly we're too *married* to hang out with them."

"Oh, give them a few years," Brady says. "Eventually they'll be married enough for us."

It's comforting to think that Adam and Brit won't be this way forever; that one day they'll get tired of only eating halves of desserts, realize there are other things to do in life besides each other, and—I don't want to say "cool"—but congeal, perhaps, into subtler, mellower people. Maybe then, when Brady and I are not so threatened by the lava of their infatuation, we'll be able to realize how remarkable it is to have a matrimonial twin. After all, no one else we know cares about cricket, or likes to grill year-round, or finds Outback Steakhouse offensive but tolerates it only because they serve familiar beer. No one else we know has our visa troubles or culture clashes or appreciation for large Qantas airplanes. No one else besides Adam and Brit knows quite what it's like to be in what I once thought was our singular situation, and even though I whine about them constantly, it's nice, when I think about it, not to feel alone.

I take a moment to imagine the four of us in a few years when we're all in our thirties with our kids and dogs and white picket fences, with our barbecues and Cascade beers and backyard cricket matches. Adam and Brit will probably have a sexier minivan than us, but hopefully by then I will have come to grips with this very ugly jealous streak of mine and bring peace to this colony of New Tasmania we've all created. This future excites me, not only for its gentleness and charm, but also—and perhaps most satisfying of all—for the possibility of driving past Adam and Brit's house on a Saturday afternoon to see them standing on their front lawn. They'll turn when we honk our horn in salute, and we'll catch them with their brows furrowed, highlighting the wrinkles and sun damage they've developed over the years, their fists clenched, lips snarling, arguing over whose turn it is to mow.

Where Luck Lies

By Mary Larkin

HAD HIS LIFE BEEN A MOVIE, Josh Jordan would not have gotten the role—he was all wrong for the part. Too tall, too handsome, with eyes that had too much light in them; he didn't look like a man with no luck at all. But he was. Josh Jordan was unlucky in life and unlucky in love.

His father had been a doctor so he had gone into medicine, or at least had tried to, but had had no luck with the chemistry—the organic or the inorganic. *Gray's Anatomy* had left him cold with its technicalities, but he found the illustrations beautiful when viewed without any intent of medicine, so kept the volume on the coffee table. There had been a brief stint trying to sell cars after college in the spring of 1952, the year following his first marriage, but he hadn't actually sold one, so was let go. He almost achieved semi-success as a banker, but in the sixties, made too many loans to too many unscrupulous developers. It had taken him years to crawl out from beneath the shadow of bankruptcy, a shadow that no longer had him in a half-Nelson, but that trailed after him and would be discovered years later still clinging to his lungs. He had had other professions, but for the past nine years, he had endured a very unaccomplished career as a marine insurance assessor. His camera jammed frequently as he photographed hurricane-tossed yachts along the Gulf from Bayou La Batre west and going on out to Dauphin and Gasque Islands, and east along the shore to Perdido and all the way to Lillian, or wind-sheared Chris Crafts and their once-harboring boathouses on the lakes and waterways of Alabama—

Lake Purdy, Inland Lake, the Coosa River, Logan Martin, Smith Lake, Lake Lanier. He was good at assessing damage, and luckily for Alabama Allright Insurance Companies, did not overvalue it.

AS TO LOVE, his high school sweetheart, a dark beauty (my mother, Olivia, for whom I am named), had dumped him for his best friend (my father) whom she married after college; his first wife became alcoholic in the midst of giving him four children and sharing his luckless life but discovered herself as a lover of women after their divorce and was the happier for it; the second, more stylish wife–"Anyone would be, after the first one," Mother had a habit of saying, not realizing that it was clever only once–relieved him of any and all assets he had either inherited or accumulated; and more recently, a third wife died of cancer, shrivelling up like a fresh-cut poppy brought indoors (they won't last a day once they're cut–put them in sugar water, singe their stems–it doesn't matter, they always wither). Josh Jordan had found no empirical truth in the old adage "Third time's the charm."

The hapless of the world are often the romantics, as is Josh. In a poetic and dreamy voice he will tell you, "If you look at a map of Alabama, its bodies of water, its rivers and lakes, alongside an illustration of the heart with its veins and arteries, you will be amazed that their major and minor arteries almost correlate, right down to their lesser meandering tributaries. Just look!" And then he'll pull out his *Rand McNally Alabama State Map* and hold up his old medical text, opened to a surface-view plate of the heart. It is amazing in itself that he can still be amazed at anything at all.

My mother is beautiful the way an icy, dark planet is beautiful: both are dishearteningly desirable, but ultimately, unobtainable. I thought the fact that Josh and Mother were involved in an affair was truly unlucky and that perhaps this would turn out to be what he would later perceive as his worst bout of luck yet if he ever got far enough away to look at it from a distance. The trouble is, he has always been in her orbit. It can only be a matter of time and gravity before he is pulled in to a tighter circle around her. He'll never even make it to the cooled-off inner core of her heart. Eventually, he is bound to plummet past her lovely atmosphere right into her five-mile crust.

Mother is not a sympathetic woman, and even though she is obviously sleeping with him and loves him in her own way, she refers unkindly to him, his three marriages, his children and his life in general as "Lightning-struck once and snake-bit twice." She has no idea that she is not even a variation on a theme, but a continuation of his run of luck. He has nothing material for her to latch on to and abscond with anyway (besides, she has her own assets), but his heart is in danger of being stolen and mishandled, misappropriated. There are worst things to lose than money.

A year and a half after his third wife, the sweet and young one—too young, Mother says—died, her cancer filling and emptying her at the same time, Josh himself was diagnosed with the stuff. But by then he and Mother were in love, seemingly very tight, and had been taking boats and planes and cars to places everybody else had already been—to Ochos Rios, or little excursions to Isle of Palms, or running off to Cozumel.

VISITING him at Mother's was like watching Hurricane Camille hit Mobile Bay. Downstairs I said to Mother, "I wonder if he even knows how bad his luck is. If he does, he doesn't let on."

"Believe me, he's oblivious—totally clueless," she said.

"It must be awful to lose your wife to cancer, and then get it yourself." This reference to the young wife he'd loved so dearly didn't suit mother. She turned her back on me, but I had already seen her face. She started up the steps and I followed.

Mother had gotten Josh's old textbook for him from his home and had set it on the bedside table. Nothing is consistent with the woman, though, and she had blotted out her own kindness by leaving the book open to an illustration of a pair of healthy lungs.

She sits at the edge of his bed and announces, "You should have seen that lung–it was the most disgusting thing I've ever seen in my life." No one but Mother would have wanted to see it.

"Show me where you and Mother went on your trip," I say, trying to steer the conversation to things other than cancer. I hand his maps to him, and his eyes catch light.

"This is where we went last spring, and here is where we're going in June." Josh puts his finger on the places they've been, places that he's highlighted in a hopeful neon green.

Mother, who has no patience with his maps, rolls her eyes and says, right in front of him, "Spare us the maps this time, Josh. We've seen them. You and I won't be going anywhere anytime soon, and you know it." And she goes downstairs.

There's a low in the air. The barometric pressure has plummeted. She's in and out of there like Hurricane Camille, swiping one way, and then coming around and hitting from the other direction. I look at Josh. The damage is done.

His hand pats at the empty place Mother made. I go over and sit, happy to be close to a good, albeit unlucky, man.

"You look like your mother, Olivia."

"A little bit, I guess. Josh, I still want to see the maps. Show me the rivers."

With his finger he traces the Tennessee River flowing into the northwest corner of Alabama where it bulges out to become Wilson Lake and later Wheeler. "It goes all the way across the top of the state like a borrowed blue garter on a bride's leg," he says, and I know he is thinking of Mother's leg. He goes on in a voice that widens, pools up, and overflows. "The Coosa comes in from the east, winding south past Gadsden and Pell City, flanked by the Talladega National Forest a good way. Then it runs on to Wetumpka before it marries the Alabama River, which flows all the way down to the Gulf of Mexico. Lake Tuscaloosa's waters empty into rivers named Black Warrior, and Tombigbee, ending up at the mouth of Mobile Bay. Towns with names like Chickasaw, Mon Louis and Daphne rest on those rich shores, waiting for the waters from the rivers of Alabama to flow and rush and commingle with the warm Gulf."

His words rise and fall like soft waters lapping against us, and for the moment, we are carried.

I lean over and flip the pages of his book until I come to the one I know he likes, the one of the heart. I'm not good at lying, but I try anyway. "She's just worried about you."

"She's not a cartographer," he sighs, and sets the map aside.

"No, never was." I take the map from him and prop it beside the illustration of the heart.

MOTHER does her best by him, nursing him for two weeks before tiring of it. "If you don't control it," she tells him, "it will control you!" To hear her talk, you'd think she believed cancer was a choice.

"Mother, cut him some slack—he just had surgery. There's no such thing as snapping back from cancer. It's not like a bout of the flu."

"He has to try," she says.

A FEW months after his surgery and the radiation treatments, just when his luck was turning, Josh slipped on dew-slicked grass in Mother's yard while walking back up to the house for iced tea. He had been planting a flowering vine at the foot of her mailbox to show his love, a clematis (that mother later dreamed had wrapped around the mailbox post and squeezed until the box popped off before overtaking the yard like ravenous kudzu and devouring the house, covering every entry and every exit, its tendrils lacing delicate but insidious lattice work across the windows so there was no looking in and no looking out, no light from sun or breeze from sky, but it was only a dream), which of course he shouldn't have been doing she told him later, when he fell, fracturing his leg not neatly, as a luckier man would have, but so that the bones protruded from the skin.

Mother saw him from her dining room window, but was sure he was embarrassed about falling. "The radiation has sapped every bit of manhood out of him! He's like a child," she had complained. "It's like caring for an infant." So she did not rush to help him. It was not that she knew about men and their pride, but that she felt he should have some, and get back on his feet. "I can't keep playing nursemaid—he's taking forever to get well. He's got to pull himself up by his bootstraps!" she had told my sister who had called from Texas to ask how he was doing since the radiation. Later, when my sister phoned me, I gave her my own diagnosis of the situation. "Boo, he's a slow healer everywhere but the heart."

Fifteen minutes after Josh's fall when Mother was bringing out the freshly iced tea with lemon and sugar and two cookies from the store for him, he was still on the ground, but had pulled himself closer to the house.

Luckily, Mother saw at once that something was clearly out of place and that he was in some sort of trouble again, that he needed her help one more time.

"Josh?" She could see the blood and the torn flesh and the very bones of his leg, a leg that had been entwined with hers.

"Call 911," he said and fainted dead away.

Oil and Water ... and Other Things That Don't Mix

I HAVE to admit that Mother was kind enough to insist he return to her house when he left the hospital, just as she had when they had taken out his rib to get to his cancerous lung. "I have to bring him here–people will talk if I don't. But I'm sick to death of it all. If I had wanted to be a nurse, I'd have gone to Nursing School."

It was true that there was no one else to take care of him. His son, the one who was tall and handsome and looked the most like him, but who was alcoholic like the mother, had died the previous year in a single instant when his horse spooked and reared and he fell and his neck snapped. His three remaining children were in places far-flung from Birmingham, Alabama; places such as Washington, Montana, New Mexico. Mother would point this out to him as well as comment on it to anyone who would listen, and most people would. "His children don't seem to care. They live far away on purpose. There's bad blood between them...and drink, you know." And everyone did know. She had kept none of his secrets to herself.

Before Mother brought Josh home to recuperate this second time, she explained to him that she felt they needed to re-examine their relationship, that they could still be friends (he would always have a place in her heart), but that she was worn out, and that Perry Livingston, someone they had both gone to grammar school with, had asked her out and that she was tired of taking care and would like to be taken care of instead, and that she had been to the Seafood Buffet at The Club atop Red Mountain, next to Vulcan's statue with him and had said yes when Perry invited her to join him for a week at the end of the month on Bogue Island. "So you can't take too long getting better. Besides, you can't get your strength back lying around in bed all day."

On the phone I ask her, "How can you dump Josh? He loves you, Mother."

"Well, Perry loves me too. Besides, his children don't cause

50

problems, his wife is remarried, and he doesn't have cancer. If it weren't for bad luck, Josh wouldn't have any luck at all."

"People's luck can change," I tell her, meaning Perry's, meaning Josh's, maybe meaning hers.

WHEN I visited him in the hospital to sign his cast, Josh said something strange to me that I still remember. He said, "My heart has been folded like a written-on piece of paper." He was on Demerol and I didn't know if he was talking nonsense, or if he was trying to tell me something important. I have considered what he said, and this is what I think he meant. He meant that the heart is like a piece of paper and that its secrets—its desires and loves, its injuries and vagaries—are written indelibly across it. Mother had held his heart in her hands, practiced her signature, and then wadded the whole thing up.

"The mind might forget, but the heart keeps and ponders. Some things just can't be erased," Josh had said to me, and I had understood that well enough.

When I think about Josh and what he has been through, I imagine his heart literally covered with his joys and sorrows— and the name "Olivia" scribbled all over it. If Josh ever has a by-pass, the cardiologist will have a lot to read.

IT TOOK time, but what I said to Mother about luck changing came true. Lady Luck has at long last smiled her winsome smile on Josh: his broken leg has mended, his cancer is in remission, and he has escaped Mother's orbit (now she only has eyes for Perry). Josh has introduced me to the travel editor for *Southern Sojourns*, his new ladylove. His heart has opened to a new page. I think this may be where Josh's luck lies. She is gentle and kind, and frequently travels with him along Alabama's waterways. She likes maps. "Did you know that the lakes and rivers flowing across our state and down to the Gulf are like the vessels of the heart, carrying blood back to its source?" he asks. Her eyes light and she smiles. Then he reaches for his maps and *Gray's*.

Out of Space – Out of Time
By Kelly Martineau

8:00 a.m.

A WOMAN sits on the other side of my desk in the claimant chair. Thin brown hair lies against her pale skin. Her eyes are tired but earnest as she lists her symptoms.

"Fatigue," she says slowly. "Pain in my hands and feet so bad I can't drive myself anymore." She tells me a friend brought her today. A gnarled cane leans against her chair. She tries to read me letters from her doctor—the diagnosis, the plea for disability benefits.

I let her speak for a minute; I can't bear to cut her off. But she builds her case as though I have some part in this decision, which I do not. Her voice is thin and high, and her pleading words cause my shoulders to slump forward, my posture to mirror hers. My stomach begins to ache. I have to stop her before I take on the emotional weight of her failing body. And I have another interview scheduled in ten minutes.

"Ma'am, excuse me. We don't make the medical decision here. Doctors review each case to determine eligibility." I hate the way I sound—so technical and bureaucratic. But it's the truth, and I haven't figured out a better way to say it.

I ask for her recent pay stubs, and she hands me a neat stack of papers in chronological order. I want to thank her for being organized, for making my job easier, but I say nothing. As I enter the amounts in the computer, I already know that she is making too much money. The dull ache in my belly tightens into a knot. I tell her the maximum amount she can earn to be eligible for benefits.

"But that's not enough for me to survive," she says, her voice faltering. "As it is, I can barely pay my rent and have to borrow money from my daughter to eat. Working even that much makes my pain so much worse, but I don't want to get evicted." She stares at me.

How do I respond? I want to get up, walk around my desk, and sit in the vinyl interview chair beside her. I want to place my hand on her arm and tell her what to do. But I honestly don't know.

What I do know is that her claim will be denied on the basis of her income. Even if she made less than the maximum amount allowed, the medical panel would most likely deny her benefits—they deny most claims the first time. Many people don't try to fight the decision.

I tell her that she can apply again if her income falls below the required level. Her eyes fall to the floor. I squirm in the thick silence between us.

She gathers her things and rises to her feet, her face wincing as she leans on the cane. I walk her to the door and send her back into the world even more hopeless than when she entered. This is my job.

I work for the Social Security Administration. Every morning, I arrive to find six appointment sheets on my desk. Each lists the name and contact information of a disability or retirement claimant, the type of benefits for which the claimant is applying, the interview time, and whether it is by telephone or in-office. Every day's burden is the same—six people to interview and six additional claims to monitor for however many weeks or months it takes to get the supporting documents. No matter how many claims I complete, there will always be more to process.

I walk back to my desk and read my nameplate: Kelly Theurer, Claims Representative. I think about the absurdity of the title. I represent claims—not people or stories or even the government. I am a servant to the claim itself. But I cannot build an argument as in a research paper or essay. I merely transcribe the stories and answers from claimants into tiny computerized boxes. I turn human suffering into a cut and dried claim.

Slumping into my chair, I hastily review the one I just completed, making notes about what needs to be done before I forward it to the medical panel. I check the schedule for my next appointment—Vernon Williams, in-office disability. My belly aches. I clear my desk and wait until the clock reads 8:59. I always wait until the last minute.

9:00 a.m.
OPENING the waiting room door, I announce, "Vernon Williams?" I slide my eyes quickly over the crowd of forty people crammed into the waiting room designed for thirty. I avoid eye contact. No one gets up.

I return to my desk and double check the form to verify the name, the time, and that the appointment is in-office rather than by phone. I wait until the clock reads 9:09, walk back to the door, and repeat. Still no Vernon Williams.

I check one more time at 9:20 before returning to my desk to call the phone number on the claim sheet. When no one picks up the phone, Vernon is officially a no-show. Maybe he had the wrong date on his calendar. Or maybe he was too sick to come in or answer the phone. All I know is relief—one less interview and one less claim to process. I glance at the clock again: 9:24. I've managed to fill almost thirty minutes without doing any actual work.

Oil and Water ... and Other Things That Don't Mix

9:30 a.m.

"I TOLD YOU," exclaims the man in the cubicle next to mine. "I'm not working at all. I CAN'T!" The Claims Representative, Cindy, purses her lips and tells him to calm down with a clipped, "Sir." Her condescending tone makes my chest constrict.

Cindy's cubicle is a mirror image of mine; all that separates my space from hers is a three-foot walkway. About ten years my senior, she talks to me often during the day, and, while I appreciate her assistance and friendliness, sometimes I just want to be alone.

Each morning when I arrive at work, Cindy is already sitting at her desk. As I set down my bag, thinking, *didn't I just leave this place*, Cindy whines, "Can we go *home* yet?" in a rounded Texas twang. She asks the same question every morning with the same friendly sarcasm. I grit my teeth and offer her a weak smile.

No one is smiling now over in Cindy's cubicle. She and her claimant continue to squabble about income. To distract myself, I review my emails. The newest message announces training on a policy update. At first I am thrilled: *a whole morning without interviews*. But my relief fades when I consider three hours spent dissecting a policy I care nothing about.

Social Security training is nothing like the engaging undergraduate curriculum I encountered during four years at the University of Texas from which I have recently graduated. I loved the spark of a fresh semester: a new syllabus with a complex subject broken into manageable topics, the expectations spelled out in neat print across the page.

In college, I read everything assigned, always alert for the connections that bridged even my most divergent classes—the use of a physics concept to illuminate a dynamic in literary tragedy, the creative manifestations in art and literature of the rapidly changing field of modern science. Papers were an arduous task, but I lived for the moment when my ideas crystallized into something deeper than I had originally conceived. The edges of the essay crisp, framing the perfectly pieced jumble of ideas.

The only text I consult now is Social Security policy, printed and stored in binders behind my desk. Some of my co-workers seem to relish these binders, thumbing through their curled pages, certain that every answer they seek is contained within. The plain language abhors rhythm and poetics, yet the sentences are unnecessarily complex and confusing. Searching through policy makes me feel both anxious and numb. I want ideas from books; however, there is no possibility in these pages, just prescription.

9:45 a.m.

I STILL have a few minutes before my last morning appointment. I scan the sheet and sigh when I see it's another in-office claim. People with complications usually come to the office—to make a good impression or present their case in person. Some of these interviewees are simply social creatures. They want to talk; I want them out of my chair.

I decide to refill my water bottle before my next appointment. On the way to the drinking fountain, I glance into my co-workers' cubicles, each one identical to mine. Each space has a desk and two guest chairs. Behind the desk is a second work surface containing the policy binders. Six-foot carpeted walls border the impersonal eight by eight foot cubicles. The office is an even grid of homogeneity.

I miss the wide expanse of the UT campus, rolling up and down hills, pushing the boundaries of its urban setting. Stately limestone buildings topped by warm terra cotta roofs front the paths. Shaded by live oak trees, the grassy malls radiate from the Tower Building, its rise into the expansive Texas sky a quiet reminder of all the things accomplished there.

During college, I walked my favorite routes between the hallowed halls of campus, feeling a pulse at certain spots, the energy concentrated as at acupuncture points or the focus of a parabola. The lacy stonework of the Flawn Academic Center, the colored tiles under the eaves of the architecture library, the east mall tree under which I lay and recognized the web-like interlacing of branches that led artist Piet Mondrian from stylized nature to perpendicular lines encapsulating squares of energy.

Now a walk leads me nowhere but back to my cubicle, only distinguishable by the nameplate and subtle décor. Unlike my co-workers, I have no spouse or children. Where they display family photographs and crayon drawings, I hang art images. As I sit down, my eyes find a postcard that used to hang by my college desk, now taped to the cubicle wall. Mist and snow-coated trees rise above frozen tundra, fronted by a rushing river. An Edgar Allen Poe quote reads, "From a wild, weird clime, that lieth sublime, / Out of Space – out of Time." I stare at the image, stare into it. I begin to feel the cool mist brush my cheek and hear the groan of melting ice. Energy seeps back into my mind.

"Well, here we go again, right?" Cindy's drawl breaks into my head as she walks by my desk on her way to the waiting room.

"Yeah," I mutter and follow her numbly to the door.

10:00 a.m.

WHEN Cindy announces a name, a carefully coiffed woman in her sixties sashays toward the door. Her buttery bone flats match her creamy taupe purse, and she greets Cindy with a wide smile.

As I call my claimant's name, I hope for someone like her: a relaxed retiree who aims to please. No one rises, and I become overconfident in another no-show as I walk back to my desk. Cindy's retiree answers each question succinctly and provides her birth and marriage certificates. I can tell Cindy is pleased because she smiles at the woman and asks about her retirement plans.

I return to the waiting room at 10:09 and 10:19, but the trips yield no claimant. It's my lucky day. As I return to my desk, Cindy and her redheaded retiree are walking towards me on the way to the exit. As they pass, I hear the woman tell Cindy how much she enjoyed teaching.

Back at my desk, I wonder if I should look into education, if I would feel the same energy as a teacher that I did as a student. College suited my work ethic. I worked hard and gained knowledge. I toiled over papers that coalesced. Each step quantified and qualified by a professor's pen. I could always measure my progress. I just didn't know where I was going.

I thought little of life beyond school. My friends majored in practical things like education, math, and biology in preparation for careers. My intellectual interests never aligned with a profession. After graduation, I combed the want ads daily. As a humanities graduate with a minor's worth of knowledge in modern art, I wasn't sure which part of the employment section applied to me. I circled non-profit jobs and submitted a few applications, more for a sense of accomplishment than any confidence that I was qualified.

After a few weeks without a prospect or interview, I received a letter from the Social Security Administration. It claimed that my "superior academic achievement made me an excellent candidate for a Claims Representative position." I swelled with pride, an easy mark for their blustery praise. If interested, I should contact the local office to discuss the opportunity.

So here I am. Now, every weekday morning as I drive to work, I stare at the Tower Building and dream of flying past the downtown exit and heading to campus instead. I crave its familiar structures and paths, hoping they will lead me somewhere unknown and exciting. Somewhere far from the dim cubicle to which I am headed.

11:15 a.m.

I HAVE survived the morning—lunch is in fifteen minutes. Having finished my appointments, I can relax and enjoy a few minutes alone.

I look up as Hal, one of the Service Representatives, steps into my cubicle. The Service Reps work at windows open to the waiting room. They deal with the public all day—answering questions, making appointments, and issuing Social Security cards.

"Kelly, your ten o'clock showed up."

My stomach tightens. If I take the interview now, it will run into my lunch break. I won't get the full forty-five minutes before my 12:30 appointment, and I might not have time to go buy a baked good for the afternoon. But I don't think Hal will care about my dessert. My mind spins as I try to determine which is worse: losing part of my lunch or asking Hal to make a new appointment.

As I'm about to speak, he says, "I told him it was too late and rescheduled him."

I let out the breath I didn't realize I was holding. "Oh, thanks—great."

He turns and walks back to his desk with a taut wave.

11:30 a.m.

LUNCH, the halfway point! I grab my book—Mary Shelley's *Frankenstein*, my favorite from college—and walk to the break room. In school, I ate alone, curled into a comfortable chair in the student union with a book. Other students studied and dozed, expecting nothing from me. But here, people talk if you don't eat in the lunchroom. Besides, there is no private spot to be found.

I pull my leftover stir-fry from the refrigerator and sit at the small round table. Hal works through a bologna sandwich while talking about his recent vacation. "Yup, two weeks in the RV driving around the Southwest." At work, Hal and the other Service Representatives are stuck at their windows all day with only two fifteen-minute breaks and lunch. I wonder if he wanted to keep driving the RV west and never return.

"My vacation is just three months away," pipes up Pauline, the Service Representative supervisor. Her newly permed hair clings to her head in tight gray curls. "We're going to Hawaii this year—three weeks," she adds.

"Three weeks is the way to go," says Hal. "Takes you two weeks to unwind. By the third, you finally begin to enjoy it."

I sigh into my stir-fry. I won't get three weeks for five years. I reread the first page of my book. The naïve narrator, about to embark on his journey to the North Pole, writes to his sister: "This breeze...gives me a foretaste of those icy climes." I picture the postcard image by my desk as I continue reading, "Inspirited by this wind of promise, my day dreams become more fervent and vivid. I try in vain to be persuaded that the pole is the seat of frost and desolation; it ever presents itself to my imagination as the region of beauty and delight." Longing for passage of my own, I underline the quote.

"Kelly," says Pauline, "What are you reading?"

"Oh, uh, *Frankenstein* by Mary Shelley." I look up to see both Hal and Pauline staring at me.

"Is it good?"

"Yeah," I respond, anxious to get back to it. When neither of them says anything else, I offer a close-mouthed smile and lower my eyes to the book. Silence hovers over the room.

They begin to talk about their grandchildren. I read for a few minutes, and then gather my stuff. As I scurry out of the room, Hal asks, "Did we drive you away?"

"What? No, I just have to run an errand."

"Oh, I'm just kidding," he says with a crooked smile.

"Oh, well, um, have a nice lunch," I offer as I back out of the room. I stash my book and lunch bag at my desk. Twenty minutes remains of my break—we are allowed exactly forty-five minutes (by staff vote), and it seems like people keep an eye on how long you're gone. I have just enough time to run a quick errand.

The October sun warms me as I walk to and from the deli. On the way back, carrying a chocolate muffin in a paper bag, I wait for the traffic light to change and stare at my building. The upper floors cantilever over the westbound side of 9th Street, creating a recessed first floor occupied by the Social Security Administration. No natural light enters the office.

When the signal changes, I cross the street and walk toward the entrance. For just a moment, I pause to enjoy the light and warmth a little longer. Then with a deep breath, I plunge into the shade and swipe my security card to enter the building. The cold air blasts my skin, which breaks into goose bumps as I walk one hundred feet back to my cubicle.

I glance at the clock—12:14—just in time. I rush back to my desk and slip the chocolate muffin into my top drawer, saving it for later.

12:15 p.m.

WITH a few minutes before my appointment, I retreat to the supply room for paper forms. The straightforward claims can be entered into the computer, but more complicated cases require paper documentation. The quiet room filled with neatly stacked forms and office supplies is my favorite in the office. No cubicles, no claimants. I pretend I am in the library stacks, searching the book spines for the right call number.

Thinking of the library reminds me of the movie *Party Girl*, starring Parker Posey. Her character is a twenty-something with little ambition whose discovery of the Dewey Decimal System brings order and logic to her life. The rigid rules and numbered policies of the Social Security Administration do not appear to offer the same solace to me.

12:30 p.m.
BACK at the door, calling another name, "Troy Truckman?" I say it twice, but no one moves. I let the door swing closed and return to my desk, hoping that Mr. Truckman will not show. He is still not there when I try again at 12:40.

I didn't feel like showing up when I woke this morning. I considered taking what a co-worker calls a "Mental Health Day." He says it's okay to take one "every now and then." I could use one every week.

Considering the two no-shows, today would have been a good one to miss. Had I stayed home, I would have spent the morning on a project, maybe a piece of jewelry. On my "sick days," I always feel a creative impulse, an urge to make something of the stolen time. After getting out my supplies, I'm usually unsure what to make, so I consider each set of beads, filling the coffee table with miniature plastic bags and boxes. I stare at the beads and findings, but the overwhelming possibility paralyzes me, curdles my creativity. Eventually, I return the beads to the case, careful to organize them in a new way to create the illusion of change.

In the afternoon, I usually try writing, at first comforted by the hum of my computer and the memory of words streaming from my fingertips in college. Again, I wait. Each empty minute makes me feel smaller and smaller in front of the screen. I produce only fragments about the act of writing, the way my college mind dug into an idea and wound itself up for a home run pitch. I write of the fevered finish, the place I can no longer find.

On particularly bleak days, I resort to "the letter." One of the few jobs for which I applied after college was a coordinator position with the Texas Council for the Humanities. I received a standard *Thank you for applying but you're not being considered* letter. I'm not in the habit of keeping rejection mementos, but this one had a handwritten note: "You wrote a lovely and thoughtful cover letter—it was the best we received. Thoughtfulness and good writing will take you far! Take care, Monte Young." For a few minutes, I steep in Young's kind words and cling to the implication that I am something other than a representative of claims. Then I slide the letter back into the file and close the drawer.

12:50 p.m.
I WALK casually to the door to check for Mr. Truckman. Since he probably won't show, I plan to call my last two phone appointments early, and then have a few hours to myself. But this time, Troy Truckman stands slowly when I call his name. I exhale a loud breath; forty minutes is not enough for a disability claim. Mr. Truckman is young—in his thirties—but he walks slowly and with great difficulty. I force myself to walk at his pace so he can follow me back to my desk.

As we sit down and begin, Cindy finishes her interview and walks her claimant to the door. When she returns to her desk, I can tell she is listening to us. Mr. Truckman fidgets and rarely makes eye contact. He seems to be in real pain, but the interview lasts nearly fifty minutes because he keeps going off on tangents about his symptoms. When I finally show him to the door and return to my desk, Cindy clucks her tongue and shakes her head. She thinks he's faking it. I can always tell when she doesn't believe her claimants; her voice cools, and she responds with a terse "Sir" or "Ma'am." I haven't been in my job long enough to read people well, but I think Cindy's been here too long.

1:40 p.m.

I RUSH back to my desk, ten minutes late for my 1:30 phone appointment. Mavis Anderson picks up on the second ring. I apologize for being late, explaining that my last appointment ran long. Miraculously, she responds with a cheerful, "No problem, dear." She tells me she has everything in front of her, and then answers all my questions in the same prompt, efficient manner. In fifteen minutes, I have filled all the required boxes in the application program and secured a promise from Mrs. Anderson that she will mail her certified birth certificate. When I hang up, I remove the hands-free headset. I make a note on my calendar—what the other Claims Representatives call "a tickle"—to follow up with Mrs. Anderson next week.

With my real job out of the way, I open my email and begin composing a message to my co-workers regarding the Thanksgiving luncheon. I have the dubious honor of serving on the "Sunshine Committee," which plans holiday events. Responsible for the Thanksgiving and Christmas potlucks, holiday decorations, and the adopt-a-family gift program, the winter committee does three times the work.

At first, I resented the responsibility. I thought, *shouldn't the new employees be exempt?* Shy with my co-workers, I volunteered for email communication. Composing the first message, I felt the old surge of energy as I tinkered with the sentences in search of the right tone. Now I tend to my duties with gusto, fiddling with phrases to make the content more compelling. A casual compliment from another Claims Rep about my emails means more to me than any word of praise or positive review from my supervisor.

2:30 p.m.
I DON the headset and dial Willis Brandon's number. He picks up on the third ring with a gruff "Hello." I can hear the television at high volume in the background. When I introduce myself, he interrupts, "What? Can't hear you. Speak up." I take a deep breath and repeat my name and affiliation louder and more slowly. "Is this for my retirement?" he questions. Sirens wail on his television. I want to tell him he could hear me better if he turned down the damn volume, but I just answer, "Yes, sir."

We stumble through the interview. It's a simple claim—he's quitting the month of his 65th birthday and doesn't plan to work—but it takes nearly forty-five minutes to work through the questions because I have to repeat each one multiple times.

When I glance over a Cindy, I mouth, *TV.* She rolls her eyes and grins at me. I smile back, for once grateful that she pays so much attention to my interviews.

3:20 p.m.
WITH my appointments completed, I finally have a full hour of unscheduled time. I look forward to this late afternoon respite when I don't have to ask or answer any questions. Most importantly, I can finally consume the chocolate muffin tucked in my top drawer.

Every week, I try to hold out until Thursday. If I give in too soon—Tuesday or Wednesday—it is sure to be a two-muffin week. I'm allergic to wheat, and my beloved baked good turns my belly into a swollen rock. But it's worth it for the hour of pleasure I can wring out of that muffin.

I observe a careful ritual. I have followed the first policy by letting the muffin sit in my drawer for a few hours, indulging my penchant for delayed gratification. The longer I wait, the less time I will have to work after the treat is gone. At the advent of muffin hour, I walk calmly to the pop machine and exchange my sixty-five cents for a cold Coke. I set the can on my desk and unwrap the muffin, its cloying scent rising toward my nose. I open the Coke with a satisfying *dsssshhhhhh* that fades to a whisper. I am ready to begin.

Unwrapped, the muffin is nearly as shiny as its plastic packaging. This unsettling shimmer is due to the volume of margarine that keeps the muffin unnaturally soft and moist. The jumbo pastry has a chewy, ridged top that spills over the neat edges of the pastel paper muffin cup. I gently separate this crown, saving it for last.

I pinch the first half-inch bite and pop it into my mouth. As the muffin melts over my tongue, my tense shoulders release. The flavor leans more chocolate than sweet with a chemical tang that deepens its artificial bouquet. I continue to break the muffin into spongy pieces studded with soft chocolate bits that yield gently to the teeth. I alternate each bite of muffin with dainty sips of cola.

During muffin consumption, I delve into paperwork, opening mail and associating documents with nearly completed claims. I have to wipe my fingers after handling the muffin to avoid leaving greasy fingerprints on a claimant's official birth certificate or marriage license. I process any completed claims on the computer and place the documents in crisp, clean envelopes on which I print the return address in precise letters. I like putting together the pieces of the puzzle and crossing claims off my list.

Once I consume the body of the muffin, I return to the more preferable top. With gentle pressure, it breaks along the fault lines in its upper crust. The smooth surface seems to taste different than the interior with a slightly more bitter and complex cocoa flavor. I relish these final pieces, holding each morsel in my mouth as long as possible. When the muffin finally disappears, I sweep the crumbs into one final bite. I let it glide slowly over my tongue and savor the lingering flavor. And with that, the joy of muffin hour is over.

4:30 p.m.

THE CLOCK hands finally mark the time for which I have been waiting all day—time to go home. As I wait for my computer to shut down, I think of the retirees who stream in and out of my cubicle every day. Some worry about how they will fill their newly acquired free time. More than one person has confided, "I've worked all my life. I don't know how to do anything else." Such admissions make me sad, as if these people age from twenty to sixty-five before my eyes. After only a year of work, I feel myself turning to a fossil.

Whether they plan to work part-time or retire completely, they are done with forty-hour work weeks. I envy the retirees as they rise from my guest chair and leave the office forever. Watching them walk away, I plead in my head: *Take me with you!*

The computer turns off with a sigh, and now it's my turn to leave. But every day completed is another one begun. I know I will be back here tomorrow, staring into the same postcard image, conscious that within its dramatic scene are forces more powerful than inspiration—the invisible violence of the world slowly ticking by.

Call Out

By Maureen E. Doallas

The surface shroud is laid, oxygen leaching.
It's still gushing, this fire-fueled eruption,

this pulsing wound of oil no amount of pressure
stops. Sticky as blood is the ooze, the way it turns up

on shore in viscous little tar balls on hermit crabs' backs,
a sand-gritty clog between the fingers of white-beached

islands that cut the Gulf apart in all directions, coagulating
around red and blue booms like vaccine-resistant bacteria.

Top kill fails and another spill of life rises to attention.

A pelican's tea-brown-stained wings begin the last dance,
flapping rhythmic beats against the red-rust hull of a tanker.

Bottlenose dolphin do their endless rolls on slicks
of waves, served up for the day's pickings ashore.

Northern gannet wither in seaweed, their feathers a totem
of surrender. Ever-circling, gulls bleat alarms at the cache

of shrimp in delicate marsh-reed nets, baking in noon-day sun,
and fish by the thousands rot, their stink fixed in the grasses

Oil and Water ... and Other Things That Don't Mix

where dragonflies, their see-through wings stuck shut
with oily glue, while away a lifetime in minutes. Thick-legged

sea turtles and Portuguese man-of-war wear rescue patches
of dispersant, their arrival too late for the terns and cattle egret

and roseated spoonbills joining slow-breathing tri-color heron
in the mangrove, their quietening plaint become the final call

in the silver sheen of moonlight over Deepwater.

Black Waters
By Nicole Easterwood

TWO WEEKS. Two weeks here and I could see the oil making its way towards my home. The shore was the same, full of people, but they were all there for different reasons beside recreation and sun baking. I felt like my lungs were collapsing inside of my chest knowing that I was back here because a villain was overtaking my home turf.

The people came in droves; some coming in cars, some walking, some flying. They cared, even if they weren't originally from this area. The policemen tried to move everyone off the beach, but all eyes were planted on the water. Everyone was staring out at the murky depths. When their feet starting moving back towards the parking lot, their minds and prayers were with everyone there on the Gulf.

I stood in the quiet of the setting sun and marveled at what it took to begin to destroy the beauty I once took for granted. Now the shore, which had been insignificant land, was ready to be eaten by the advancing muck and the water was turning from crystal clear blue to a devilish, thick black.

WHEN I was seventeen I left Mobile. I hadn't been back to this place in ten years. As soon as I graduated high school, I'd been out the door and off to New York City to pursue a career in modeling. It's like I hadn't even really stopped to marvel and take it all in before turning my back on it completely. It's so different from the hustle and bustle of the city life I'm so accustomed to. It's so laid back and relaxed, but not anymore. Everyone is in a frenzy, panicked beyond belief; looking out at the water and watching the waves roll in for the last time. What used to be a serene vacation spot and hang out, is now morphing into, what looks like, the pits of hell—black muck mixed with red flames of the now-setting sun.

All of the volunteers had spent days wading through the corpses of sea birds in knee length rain boots. My hands were shaking uncontrollably. My home was being invaded and there was absolutely nothing I could do to stop it. There was no magical wand or baseball bat to make all of it go away and even though it had been so long since I had set foot here, I couldn't shake the truth—you cannot ever be taken completely away from the place you were born. It was happening, and with my knees hugging the sand, I started to pray, silently.

"Marcy! Come on! We can't stay here!" John yelled at me, pulling my arm. Like a captain wanting to go down with his ship, I wasn't budging. I was becoming entrapped in the beach, entrapped in my home, once again. I didn't want to have to leave this place again. After all of the years I had spent in resentment, hating this place because I had believed it would always hold me back, I realize that I had loved this place all along. Now, it may be too late, Alabama the Beautiful.

I DON'T know if Mom can forgive me for what I've put her through; the leaving, not calling, not coming home when Dad died from melanoma, all of it. The water's fading fast with the mucky oil. How much time is left before everything fades underneath the black?

I think about the fishermen, the ocean side hotel owners, and the people who count on the Gulf for their families' survival. I don't know what I would do if it were me. Then I think of Mom and the Holiday Inn she owns right on the beach. I wonder if she's okay or if she's on the brink of having to sell her house to pay the bills. With Dad being gone, she only had one income, and with the way things now looked out on that vast waterscape, I feared the worst for her. But I've been gone for so long, so how am I supposed to know if she even owns the hotel anymore?

THE TELEVISION is blasting CNN and from across the room I can see images of the oil gushing into the ocean. It replays again and again and the news anchor repeats herself ten times before moving on to the next subject.

"John?" I scream from the table by the door of the suite.

"Yeah?" he hurls back.

"What do you think is going to happen? I mean, it's not getting any better and it's been months now and no one has found a sure fire way to stop it. We've only been here two weeks and haven't seen the brunt of it. What if we were one of the people whose livelihood was on the coast? What if it doesn't end?"

I hear staggering footsteps and I look up from the glaring trance of the television to a half-asleep John trying to maneuver his way through the room. "Hun, they'll find something. It's going to be fine. Trust me," he coaxed and staggered back into the bathroom, with his toothbrush hanging out of the side of his mouth.

"Why should I take advice from someone who can barely stagger back and forth from the bathroom?" I joked, flicking off the television and walking over to the bathroom, wrapping my arms around his waist.

"Then who are you going to get your advice from? *O Magazine, Cosmo*, oh, oh, oh, I've got a better one!...*The National Enquirer*! There's always a good article about some washed up celebrity giving birth to an alien baby or Elvis being alive, or there's the great who's a tranny and who's not debate! That's always fun!"

"I'm being serious though, John. I'm watching my childhood be destroyed by some greedy ass people who don't know how to fess up to what they did wrong and fix it before it gets worse! It's like they're being babies about it and there's only so much the government can do about it before it becomes an act of Congress—and we know how long *that* would take."

"I think I know what you're really worried about, though. Your family. After not seeing them for this long, you think they may not want you in their lives anymore."

"That's part of it, but I still swear up and down that my parents always hated me. They favored Caroline over everything else. Nothing I ever did was good enough for them. I got a modeling gig in NYC and they didn't even say anything when I left—they just let me go. It's like they didn't even care if I was gone."

John swung around and faced me, taking hold of my waist. "Honey, they cared, even if they didn't want to show it. Pride can kill just as badly as a shotgun can. Plus, I'm here to defend you if everything goes to hell," he smiled looking over at the car keys that were lying on the table. "Ready to go?" he asks. And we turn for the door.

I MET John the first year that I was in New York. He was working as a freelance photographer and he was hired onto the *Vanity Fair* shoot I was hired to do. We hit it off from there; dinners in the city, nights on the couch with Chinese on the coffee table and weekends away.

Now, looking back on all of the time we've spent together, I know why I jumped straight from my old life and into John's arms. It was easy exchanging one for the other, like you do with items in a department store. I decided that I didn't like the looks of the old and I exchanged them for the bright and shiny new life. He offered me what everyone else was blinded to, a new beginning. And so we began our life together—got married, bought a penthouse apartment in the city and showered it with all of the nice things you would see on MTV's *Cribs*. That was that and he was my home. Until the utter shock of gallons upon gallons of oil started to spill themselves on the old garment. Then, I wanted both. I decided what to wear, pondering that the thrift store vintage piece could offer my outfit just what it needed—a thread of familiarity. So, I brought John here to see what I was talking about. When I told him he hadn't ever seen a sunrise or sunset—I meant it.

We sit in front of their house with the motor still running, and I can see Mom's shadow against the kitchen curtain at the front of the house. I am fiddling with my fingers and lightly fraying skin off the sides of my thumbs. I look over at John, and then back at the window, feeling the beginnings of beads of sweat forming on my forehead and my hands becoming clammy. More time, I thought, maybe if I gave myself more time this would somehow be easier and maybe I wouldn't be sweating because of nervousness.

In a lot of ways the oil spill mirrored the relationship I now had with my family. The black waters that were killing all of the wildlife and contaminating the water were exactly the same as the muck that had wiped its poison all over my family. There had been a black layer laid in between them and me—me being the air above that could no longer freely touch the deep blue underneath. I wonder if my mother even knows what I look like now, if she ever bought one of the magazines that I was in. I still wanted to be resilient, but I knew that I couldn't stay like this forever. I had to step out of the car and it had to be right now. With John's hand brushing reassuringly against mine, I clutched the metal and pulled and pushed outward, stepping out onto the curb and slowly walking up the sidewalk.

CAROLINE was always the smart one—the child who seemed to do everything right. I, on the other hand, was the complete opposite. I would doodle in my notebooks and play paper basketball with the notes I was supposed to be using to study for a test. She was Mom and Dad's favorite. It showed in their faces and in the way they treated us. I stayed cooped up in my room mapping out drawings for the clothes I wanted to make, while they were all congregated at the game that Caroline was cheering at. It seemed as if I was the outcast of the family, the black sheep who disappointed everyone and I took it out on them with every call they got from the principal's office or from the police for my incessant, vigorous behavior at a protest that I wasn't supposed to be at.

I've got to give it to her though; she did a really good job at becoming the favored sibling. Turns out, I never really gave a damn in the first place. I was my own person and I didn't need anyone else's approval. I didn't need to put on a tutu, tiara, or uniform to define myself; although Caroline never really knew who she was, but I do. She was what Mom wanted her to be—a frilly, blonde haired, blue-eyed princess.

TWO light knocks on the large, red cedar door and I can see the doorknob turning. Mom is standing right in front of me wearing the usual light sweater and linen pants. I can see the news is on behind her and hear a faint sound—a special report saying that BP is committed to doing all they can to shut off the leak in the oil rig and finish cleaning up what they had caused.

Her face brightens as I look her over and smile. She looks more gorgeous than I remember. I try and speak, but my throat is dry. The laugh lines crease across her face and strands of gray hair fall against her temples. She smiles and so do I, as she opens her arms and tears begin to roll down her face.

This is home, again.

The Scent of Dreams

By Jarvis Slacks

THE FIRST TIME, it was in the early morning. That moment right before you know you need to wake and you actually wake. It was a dream. But was he forming the dream? You can do that. Sometimes you can force a dream to do things, force a dream to exist in a way that it wasn't originally going to be. He was standing on a beach. He was standing there, his feet deep in the sand, his toes and the tops of his feet were covered. They were hot. Burning. And the ocean. It was dark. Black. It didn't know. It was dawn, so the sea was reflecting the sky and the sky was black and so was the ocean. So he walked into it. It was the ocean. That is what you do. You walk into it and welcome that cleansing, cool feel that the salt water gives. So he walked into it and he got to it and he was thigh-high into it and he put his hands into the ocean and he pulled his hands out and they, too, were black. They, too, were the color of the sky. But there was something else. A film. A coat. His hands were coated. He rubbed his hands together and he wiped his hands and he tried to get the film off but there was no getting the film off. It was the color of the sky. The sky was black and so were his hands. But when the sun finally peaked over the horizon, when he could finally see the truth of all things, the sky was a brilliant blue but the ocean was still black and so, too, were his hands. He pushed himself awake, like a boy trying to get away from the class bully. He ran from his own dream.

"You watch too much television," Roy said.

"Not really," Jon said.

They were both at Duffy's, a bar poised as a coffee shop. No one ever bought the coffee, they bought the beer. Drinking became this thing that you did during the daytime. Just like it was anything else.

"You open up a newspaper and there you see it," Roy Wilson said, lifting up a newspaper with a picture of the oil spill on the front cover, that metal piping and mechanic with brown, fluffy ooze steaming out, that black background. People knew what it was once you just said the words, knew exactly what you were talking about and how you were talking about it.

"Fucking horrible," Roy Wilson said. "Just an all around shitty shit. How are we supposed to live our lives this way?"

"No clue," Jon said, taking down his beer and raising his hand to order another one.

"I'm serious," Roy Wilson said. "How are we?"

"We just live it," Jon said. "We do the best we can. That's what we do."

"We who?"

"We," Jon said, opening up his arms. Spreading the fingers of his hand out wide. Moving them quickly so that his arms and fingers and hands were like fans. "Us. Humans."

Roy leaned back, looked at the table. Roy Wilson and Jon Filmore knew each other since high school, old friends bound by the number of years they'd know each other and by the fact they neither one of them get on each other's nerves too much.

"How's Rachel?" Roy Wilson asked.

"Rachel's Rachel," Jon said. "Mad at me."

"You still haven't asked her to move in?"

"Why should I ask her to move in?"

"That's what girl's want," Roy Wilson said. "To be appreciated. To be loved."

"Coming from Roy Wilson. The guy who made out with his first cousin," Jon said.

"It was a confusing family reunion, motherfucker," Roy

Wilson said, his eyebrows straight. "And I didn't know she was my cousin. You know that."

"Still. Your cousin," Jon said.

"Stop changing the subject," Roy Wilson said.

"What's the subject?"

"Your dream," Roy Wilson said. "We should find out what it means."

"Dreams don't mean anything," Jon said. "Dreams are just dreams."

"That's not true."

"Yes, it is true."

"There has to be a way," Roy Wilson said, putting his hand to his face, staring off.

"You're thinking," Jon said.

"No," Roy Wilson said, looking down.

"I don't even want to know what you're thinking," Jon said.

"There has to be a way," Roy Wilson said.

JON stayed at Rachel's house that night. Her bed was softer and her room smelled like shampoo and flowers. He thought he would have better dreams. The dreams were worse. He was in the middle of the sky, now. He was in the air, floating in the air, his feet towards the ground, his head next to a cloud. He stared at the cloud for the longest time, the cloud floating and it being this massive object, the size of skyscrapers. Jon found it odd that they called buildings sky-scrappers when they don't even come close to scrapping the sky. And why such a violent name. Jon woke himself.

"Rachel," Jon said.

"Sleeping," Rachel said.

It was a sticky night. Steamy. Uncomfortable. Jon tried to touch Rachel's back and she let him do it. He enjoyed that, the ability to use her to comfort himself, the ability to relax with her. How long would that last, Jon thought? He liked her, but couldn't relax with her, thought about leaving her because she might leave him one day. That was the dilemma of the modern man. Pre-empting disappointment.

"You're hot," Rachel said, pulling away a bit. Jon rolled on his back, stared at the ceiling until the ceiling and the bedroom blended to a grey haze. Dreaming. In his dream, he was in the clouds still. He looked up and he was so high up that the sky was black, the stars as bright as close candles. He looked down and the ocean was black to. All the ocean. The ground was black. All was black. Black like soot. Then he began to fall.

His cell phone rang. Jon woke up almost like he expected it. How long was his phone ringing?

"Ummm," Rachel stirred. Jon put his hand on her back, to ease her. He answered his phone. It was Roy.

"Yeah," Jon said. "Where are you?"

"I found a guy," Roy Wilson said. He sounded manic on the phone, too excited.

"What?"

"Are you up?" Roy Wilson asked.

"I'm talking to you," Jon said.

"I found a guy down off of Cavil Avenue," Roy Wilson said. "I'm headed to your house now."

"I'm at Rachel's."

"Fine. I'm headed to Rachel's house now."

"Roy. Calm down. Why are you coming here?"

"I found a guy," Roy Wilson said. "It's about your dreams. I found a guy."

JON barely had time to pull on his jeans when Roy rolled up and hooked his horn. Rachel opened her eyes, annoyed.

"It's Roy," Jon said. "You know how he gets. I'll be back."

"Don't come back," Rachel said, lying back down. "You'll

wake me up if you come back."

"Can I call you later?" Jon asked.

"I'll call you later," Rachel said.

"When?"

"Later," Rachel said. "Much later."

"Much later?" Jon asked.

"Later," Rachel said.

JON opened Roy's car door and slammed it shut. Hard shut.

"Hey," Roy said. "Easy on that."

"This better be good," Jon said. "Seriously. It is four in the morning."

"No one made you come down," Roy said. "How's Rachel?"

"Just drive."

"Why are you mad at me?" Roy asked.

"It is four in the morning," Jon said.

"That is a fact. That isn't a reason."

"Where are we going?"

"This guy," Roy said.

"Can you be more specific?"

"Not really," Roy said. "No. Not really."

THE GUY was at a place. The place was outside the city a bit. Roy had to take the highway, then a series of small, back roads. It was five in the morning when they finally got there, this small house with a porch light, slight grass, a dirt drive way and a faded, white picket fence.

"You got cash?" Roy asked. "We'll need cash."

Inside, the house wasn't cluttered, like Jon thought it would be. There was barely anything in it. A few books stacked in the corner, a table with a computer on it. A kitchen. A pot of coffee on the kitchen table. A man sitting at the kitchen table, drinking the coffee, looking up vaguely when Roy and Jon walked in.

"You they guy who called?" The man asked.

"Yeah," Roy Wilson said. "About two hours ago."

"You got cash?"

"Yep," Roy Wilson said, holding up the money Jon had given him.

"Cool," the man said. "You two come on over and have a sit over here."

Jon, for a brief moment, wondered how he got where he was, and if getting out was even an option.

"There's always an option," the man at the table said. Jon stared at him. The man winked at Jon. "My name is Victor. Don't call me Vick."

"Does everyone call you Vick?" Roy asked.

"No one calls me Vick," Victor said. "It sounds like I'm about to walk across the yard and stab Mickey the Mick in the spine with my switchblade or something."

"They call it a shiv," Jon said.

"Who calls it a shiv?" Victor asked.

"They people who walk across yards and stab people with them. They call them shivs."

"You're the reason he called me," Victor said, pointing at Roy Wilson but looking at Jon Filmore. Then he looked back at Roy Wilson. "Is he the reason you called? It is five in the morning."

"Tell him," Roy said, bumping Jon in the arm.

"It isn't anything," Jon said.

"Tell him so we can go get pancakes," Roy said.

"You guys going to get pancakes after this?" Victor asked.

"Maybe," Jon said.

"Can I come?"

"Maybe," Roy Wilson said.

"What seems to be the trouble," Victor asked.

"Who are you again?" Jon asked.

"I'm Victor," Victor said. "Don't call me Vick. And I'm a

Shaman."

Victor got up from the table and put a kettle on the stove, after he had poured water in it, and after he turned the eye on, twisting the knob until he heard a click and the click caught the gas, making a flame. As he did all this, he explained. He said that God sent him here. God sent him here. He was sent to give people clarity. That was his purpose. To give understanding. It seems slight, he said. But when you boil it all down, wash everything to the core.

"That's all that matters," Victor said. "Clarity. Understanding. Who wants some tea?"

Roy Wilson raised his hand. Jon kept his hand down.

"Earl Grey," Victor said. The kittle whistled. It whistled quickly, almost quicker than it should have. Victor just grinned a bit, poured the hot water into the teacups, the tea bags waiting.

"So," Victor said, sitting back down. "What seems to be the trouble?"

Jon leaned back, rubbed his neck with his hands.

"Dreams," Jon said.

"Ah," Victor said. "Finally. Dreams. Describe them."

Jon did.

"Both about that oil spill?"

"I'm telling him that he watches too much T.V.," Roy Wilson said.

"Please be quiet," Victor said. "Not to be rude, but be quiet."

"They are just dreams."

"But you had one when you were awake," Victor said.

"How do you know that?"

"I just know it."

"Crazy," Roy Wilson said.

"Please," Victor said. "Please, be quiet. Here."

Victor extended his hands. Both of them.

"Take my hands," Victor said to Jon.

"No," Jon said.

"When was the last time you got a full night sleep?" Victor asked. "I can help you."

"I just need a full night sleep," Jon said.

"I can help you with that," Victor said. "Just take my hands. Take both of my hands."

"What do you want me to do?" Roy Wilson asked.

"Stepping outside would be nice," Victor said. "He'll be out in a second."

"You cool?" Roy asked Jon. Jon stared at Victor the Shaman.

"Yeah," Jon said. "Go smoke one or something."

Roy laid the money on the table and moved around his friend to the door, walked outside.

"Give me your hands," Victor said. "Close your eyes."

Jon closed them. For a moment, all he saw was the darkness, the back of his eyelids.

"Just breathe," Victor said, his voice like gravel rolling over asphalt. "Just try and breathe."

Jon breathed. Victor squeezed his hands and Jon instinctively tried to pull his hands away, to get his hands away from a man, that odd feeling when someone new is touching you. But then Jon smelled something. Gas.

"Is something burning?" Jon asked, opening his eyes. But he was no longer in Victor's trailer. Jon was in his first house, the house where he grew up, when he was little. He was right there.

"What do you see?" Victor asked. Jon could hear the voice, but he couldn't see it, he couldn't see where the voice was coming from.

"What is this?" Jon asked. "What are you doing?"

"I'm here," Victor said, squeezing his hand, squeezing Jon's hand. "Do you feel that?"

"I feel it," Jon said, looking down at his hands, which were open and free, but he could still feel Victor's hands on them, could still feel Victor holding them. A phantom grip.

"Where are you?" Victor asked. "What do you see?"

"This is where I grew up," Jon said. "This is where I spent my childhood. Can't you see it?"

"I can't see what you see," Victor said. "I can only hear what you say. What do you smell? Did you smell something?"

"Gas," Jon said, walking to the kitchen. His mother was in the kitchen, cutting vegetables, cutting them with the big knife that Jon always liked, but never used. He never used it, even when he was older, he never used it.

"Hey, baby," Jon's mother said. "Do you need anything? I'm getting ready for the cook out."

"No," Jon said. "No, I don't need anything."

"Who are you talking to?" Victor asked.

"My mother," Jon said. "She's...she's so much younger now. She is so pretty. I remember this day."

"What happened this day?" Victor asked. "What is so special about this day?"

"There was a cook out," Jon said. And there he was. At the cook out. It was in their back yard and that is where he was. It was hot, but not too hot. Boys and girls were running around, spraying each other with sprinklers. It was his tenth birthday party. He remembered that day so clearly, with such clarity.

"Do you smell that?" Jon said. One of the fathers was sitting in a chair, drinking a beer. Jon's father wasn't there.

"Where was your father?" Victor asked.

"Gone," Jon said. "There was a funeral in West Virginia, I think. He was gone for the weekend."

"Why was there a cookout?" Victor asked.

"Happy birthday, motherfucker!" A young Roy Wilson said, running up to Jon and punching him in the arm. Jon was the size of Roy Wilson, little ten-year-old boys.

"Shush!" Jon said. "If my mom hears you swearing, we can't hang out!"

"Your mom is a nag," Roy said. "Hey, Dad!"

"Yeah," the man in the chair drinking a beer said, looking over at his son.

"Can Jon and I have a beer?" Roy said, too loudly. So loud that the other mothers and fathers could hear. So that Jon's mother could hear.

"Don't be stupid, Roy," Roy's father said. "Go play in the water or something."

Roy ran to the water hose. Jon was about to follow.

"Hey, Jon," Roy Wilson's father said. "Come here a minute."

Jon walked slowly to him.

"Here," Roy Wilson's father dug into his pocket and pulled out a small, shiny thing.

"A Silver Dollar," Roy Wilson's father said. "They don't make these much anymore. Do you see the year on it?"

"Yeah," Jon said. "That is the year I was born."

"Don't lose it," Roy Wilson's father said. "Take care of it."

"I will," Jon said, taking the coin, looking at Roy Wilson's father's hands. They were black. A worn out black, as if they had been soaked in grease, grease in the creases of his hand.

"These hands," the old man said. "You can scrub and scrub and scrub, but it doesn't come off. Mechanic hands. And you always smell like gas."

Jon Filmore, the ten-year-old on his birthday, looked over at his mother. She was standing there, wrapping herself in her arms. Looking at Roy Wilson's father. Roy Wilson's father looked over at her. Roy Wilson's father got up from his chair, bent down.

"Your mother," Roy Wilson's father said. "She's very beautiful."

"You think so?" Jon asked.

"I think so."

"Word to the wise," the old man said. "Don't become a mechanic."

"Where are you now?" Victor asked.

"I'm back in the house," Jon said. "But it is night time and it's dark."

"What do you smell?" Victor asked.

"Let go of my hands," Jon said. "Please. I want you to let go of my hands."

"What do you smell," Victor asked again. Jon closed his eyes and pulled and pulled and pulled and when he opened his eyes again, Victor was in front of him. Jon jerked both his hands away.

"Fuck this," Jon said. "Fuck you."

"We were close," Victor said. "Whatever is bothering you, we were right there at it."

"Fuck you," Jon said, getting up.

"Jon," Victor said, standing. Jon turned. "You need to deal with it. Whatever it is. You have to."

Jon walked out.

"What happened?"

"Nothing," Jon said. "And fuck you for making me go in there."

"Life's an adventure," Roy said.

"Every time you make me do something crazy, you say that. How much adventure do I need? Really. How much?"

"Your well is dry," Roy said. "Your well is deep and dry."

"What time is it?" Jon asked.

"Around 6."

"Is your Dad's shop open?"

"Dad's up, yeah," Roy said, looking at his friend. "Why?"

"Let's go."

"Dad's shop is an hour away."

"Life's an adventure," Jon said, putting his head back on the headrest. "Let's go."

Jon dozed off. It was just for a few minutes. He was trying not to fall asleep, but he had been sleeping so horribly. He was in the house, the house he was raised in and his mother was there, cutting vegetables, cutting, cutting, cutting. And she was naked, except for all the oil covering her body.

"Do you smell gas?" she asked him, turning to her son. "Do you smell that?"

Then, she opened her mouth and oil began spewing out of it, spewing out in waves. Torrents. Wave upon wave of black filth and it all hit Jon. One wave after another.

"Hey," Roy Wilson said, shaking his friend. Jon woke up. The sun was coming up, that red and purple beauty. The sky was still black, in the places the sun hadn't touched yet. Jon opened the car door and Roy Wilson was out too, walking to his father's garage. The garage wasn't lit very well. The gas pumps had light, but the store part of the garage was still closed. Only the garage door was open, and Mr. Wilson, Roy's father was where he usually was, bending into a car's engine.

"Dad," Roy Wilson said.

Mr. Wilson raised his head up, looked at both the young men.

"Boys," Mr. Wilson said. "It is the butt-crack of dawn."

"Adventures," Roy Wilson said.

"Why can't it be, looking for work?" Mr. Wilson asked. "Why can't that be the excuse?"

"I have a job," Jon Filmore said, walking up with his hands in his pockets.

"You're the good one," Mr. Wilson said, lifting his head from the engine, walking towards both of them, grabbing a rag and wiping his hands. "Since you're here, we might as well get breakfast."

"That egg place open?" Roy asked.

"That egg place is always open," Mr. Wilson said, putting his hands on his son's shoulder, pulling him in close, but not hugging him.

Oil and Water ... and Other Things That Don't Mix

THE EGG PLACE was right down the road, heavily lit, huge like all truck-spots are, right off the interstate and a beacon for everyone who drives ten-hour stretches. The three men sat at a round table, eating and eating and eating, talking only in the sense that they were mentioning things. The weather. The politics. The job market. The oil spill came up.

"Hell of a thing," Mr. Wilson said. "Just an all around shitty shit."

"Whatever," Roy said.

"You don't care about anything," Mr. Wilson said. "That's your mother. That's problem."

"I care about my liver," Roy Wilson said. "Where's the bathroom?"

"If you care about peeing, that's your kidneys, you dummy," Mr. Wilson said. "Back there. To the right."

Roy Wilson got up and headed back. Jon Filmore leaned back in his chair, played with his Juice glass.

"What are you boys really doing out here?" Mr. Wilson asked. "Him I can see. Him I can see roaming out in the middle of nowhere for barely a reason. You've never been that type."

"I haven't been sleeping," Jon said. "I've been having some bad dreams. These weird dreams."

"What about?" Mr. Wilson asked. Jon wanted to tell him. Jon wanted to tell him that it was about oil. About the feel of it. About the smell of it. About how it seems to pervade him, overwhelm him, take him at ever twist and turn. How, in almost all of his dreams, he is drowning in the mess. Then, like someone taking a flashlight and sticking it right in the eyes, the world was something else entirely.

WHEN Jon was five, he was thirsty. He went downstairs to get some water. Boys are light at that age. They don't make the stairs heave. They don't make the stairs squeak. He got to the

90

kitchen, to where the opening to the kitchen was and there was his mother, standing in the kitchen. Just standing. She was wearing a jump suit. Her hair was down. It was early late at night and early in the morning. She was just standing there, in a jump suit, staring at the sink.

"Mama," Jon said. She turned, a bit startled.

"Baby," she said, bending down, taking her little boy in her arms, pulling him close. He smelled it then. Such a strong smell.

"YOU smell like oil," Jon said.

"What?" Mr. Wilson asked, at the egg place.

"That smell," Jon said, leaning it. "Do you always smell like that? Do you get use to it?"

"You get use to it," Mr. Wilson said. "You don't like it. You never like it."

"I bet."

"Some things you just do," Mr. Wilson said. "You know that. You're a man, now. You know that there are some things that people just do. You know? They don't make any sense and they are hard to figure out. But you do them anyway."

"Doesn't make it right," Jon said.

Mr. Wilson stared at Jon Filmore and Jon Filmore stared back. The gap in-between the two of them held many things, most notably the weight of the planet and all the problems associated with it. Roy Wilson came out of the bathroom, clapping his hands.

"Yo," Roy Wilson said.

"Did you wash your hands?" Mr. Wilson asked, still looking at Jon.

"We aren't cavemen," Roy Wilson said. "But that would be nice."

Oil and Water ... and Other Things That Don't Mix

THE DRIVE BACK, Roy Wilson asked two questions.

"What did you and Victor talk about?" Roy Wilson asked.

"Nothing," Jon said.

"What did you and my Dad talk about?" Roy Wilson asked.

"Nothing," Jon said.

"I don't believe you," Roy Wilson said.

"It doesn't much matter," Jon Filmore said.

ROY WILSON dropped Jon off and Jon got off the car and waved. Roy Wilson gave him a slight head nod. It was a head nod of recognition, but Jon could feel that it wasn't the same. Twenty years of friendship ending like burnt toast. Something you didn't mean to happen, but it happened because you weren't watching it. Because you weren't taking care of it. Because you took the whole process for granted. Roy Wilson dropped Jon off. Jon gave him a wave. Roy Wilson gave him a head nod and then Roy Wilson drove off.

It was still early in the morning, close to nine. He could have gone inside, tried to smooth things over. He could have done that. But when Jon looked at the street, the sidewalk was covered with oil. The walls of Rachel's apartment building had oil dripping from it. There was oil pumping out of the grass. The sky was grey. It stank of petrol and rubbing alcohol and jet fuel. He looked over at the steps of the apartment and his mother was sitting there, wearing an oil drenched jump suit, oil all in her beautiful hair.

"I'm sorry," his mother said.

"Don't be sorry," Jon said. "Sorry for what?"

"Just to be sorry," his mother said. "Wasn't she mean to you? When she left?"

"She had a right to be," Jon Filmore said. "She had every right to be."

"Jon?" Someone said. Jon turned. It was Rachel, on the street. She was holding a cup of coffee, a clear plastic bag of bagels.

"Hey," Jon said.

"Who were you talking to?"

"No one," Jon said. "My coffee?"

"Nope," Rachel said. "My coffee."

"You want to take a walk?" Jon asked. "So nice out."

And it was. A blue sky like the sky was painted. Grass a green that shouldn't be green. Jon inhaled and the air tasted. It tasted like salt water.

"The ocean isn't really that far away," Jon said.

"You want to walk to the ocean?" Rachel asked, a bit taken a back. "Are you ok?"

"Fine," Jon said. "Fine. Are you fine?"

"I'm fine," Rachel said. "What made you think of the ocean?"

"I smell salt water," Jon said. "Smell the air. It smells like salt water. Smell it."

"Yeah," Rachel said. "I guess it does."

"You really didn't breathe it in," Jon said.

"Yes, I did."

"No, you didn't."

"Fine," Rachel said, taking in a deep breath, and then exhaling. "Yeah," she said. "It does. It does."

"Come on," Jon said. "Let's walk down the block. Get me a cup of coffee."

"You can have this one," Rachel said.

"Thank you," Jon said, taking the cup.

"It's cold," Rachel said, bumping into his arm, and then taking his arm.

"That's all right with me," Jon said, walking slowly next to her, down the straight, towards that bakery that they both liked. The one that smells like eucalyptus. In the morning.

Tradition
By Cherie Reich

HOW was he going to tell his dad UCLA accepted him on a full soccer scholarship?

Michael Merriweather pondered this question while he felt the shrimping vessel reduce speed as it rumbled through the warm Gulf waters. Waves lapped against the sides of the *Merriweather Delight* and a lone seagull swooped toward them in hopes for a quick and easy dinner. He tossed the hacky sack into the sky. The colorful, knitted ball twirled in the air and struck his right foot. Adjusting his weight, he tapped it with the left foot before catching it behind his neck.

"Michael, quit playing around and prepare the rigging. We'll haul up the trawl shortly," Louis Merriweather called out from the bridge.

"Sure thing, Dad." Michael tucked the hacky sack into his pocket and went over to where his cousins, Charlie and William, watched the trawl. "Did we catch much?" Charlie and he were strikers, but William was his dad's first mate.

"Hard to say," William drawled and spat upon the deck. He raised a hand to shield the blinding sunlight upon the water.

"We haven't been getting anything to speak about lately." Charlie removed his cap and ran his fingers through his curly brown locks. "I'm real glad they're letting us fish again." He sniffed. "It doesn't even smell like oil in these parts."

Michael breathed and detected only salt and fish. "Yeah, smells like normal." His nose wrinkled, though, and he glanced back to his dad at the helm.

"You best be getting to that rigging, boy." William pointed to the cables and ropes.

Michael stiffened at being called "boy." He turned eighteen a couple months ago. In August, he'd be attending UCLA. He hoped. His gaze fell upon his dad once again. His dad didn't even know he applied. Chewing on his lower lip, he checked the rigging while knotting ropes and making certain they could pull up their day's catch. "It's ready."

"Good," Charlie said, jogging over to the levers and preparing to lift the trawl upon the boat.

"Stand back, Michael." William motioned for Charlie to begin as the boat slowed. The trawl crept closer and lifted in the air. Fish flopped and shrimp wiggled in the netting as it lowered upon the boat.

"Not a bad catch." Michael watched the trawl set down upon the deck. The stench of sea life struck him, and he moved toward the bow.

His dad placed a hand upon his shoulder and startled Michael. "No, not a bad catch today. Much better than yesterday." Louis studied his son, causing him to squirm under his parental gaze. "And what's with you, boy? You been quiet since yesterday evening."

Michael swallowed hard and avoided looking at his dad. He didn't want to tell his dad his plans in front of William and Charlie. "It's nothing."

"Hey, you know you can talk to me about anything, right?" He placed his big hand under his son's chin and forced him to meet his eyes. "Is it about a girl?"

"Oh, no." Michael blushed.

"Then, what is it?"

He glanced over to where William and Charlie were. They were busy removing seaweed and other gunk from the shrimp and fish. "I got accepted into a college." His voice was small, hardly heard above the boat's engine.

"College?" His father blew air through his nostrils. "You know we don't have the money for you to go, Michael." He motioned to their catch. "We weren't doing that great before the oil spill, and now..." He shrugged. "I'm sorry."

"I know, Dad, but I got a full scholarship. I'll be playing soccer there." Michael rubbed his shoe against the dampen boards. "UCLA wants me. I'll have room and board paid off too. It's a chance in a lifetime."

"UCLA? That's not in Louisiana."

"No, it's in California."

"What the hell would you do at this school, Michael? Fishing and shrimping is in your blood. We Merriweathers have been patrolling these waters for six generations. I can't afford to train another striker to set up the nets." Louis planted his hands on his hips and loomed over his son. "Are you going to turn your back on all this?"

Michael looked at his feet. The fisherman boots always felt too big and awkward on him. "I want to be a graphic art designer, Dad. I hate fishing." His dad was several inches taller than Michael, who took more after his mother with his blond hair and lean physique. "I'm sorry, Dad. I wanted to tell you before, but I just couldn't."

"You hate fishing?" Louis emphasized each word.

William and Charlie looked over at them. "Everything all right?" Charlie asked.

"No," Louis roared, "My son hates fishing."

Michael pressed his back against the boat's side. He considered jumping overboard, if they didn't toss him first. "I'm sorry." His stomach rolled with the lapping waves and he wanted nothing more than to disappear. The hatred and disappointment in his dad's tone overwhelmed him, but he couldn't back down either. "I'm going to UCLA."

His cousins went back to the seafood. They didn't want to get involved.

Louis's face flushed a deep purple, and he glared at his son while sputtering for speech. "No. No, no, no! You're not going to UCLA, Michael David Merriweather. Don't bother coming back if you do. We need you here, especially since the oil spill. We can't afford to be a man down." He slammed his fist upon the railing. "End of discussion."

"But, Dad—"

"No. That's final."

MICHAEL shoved a handful of boxers underneath his folded shirts when his mom entered his bedroom.

"Michael, honey, don't leave like this." Patricia snatched her son's arm. "Please. Talk to your father again."

"Dad said all he had to say on the boat, Mom." Michael sat upon his overloaded, brown leather suitcase and struggled to snap it shut. "I know he wants me here, but I can't do it anymore. I gave him all my summers since I was fourteen. It's time for me to live my own life."

She sighed and pulled him into a hug. "I know, but he still loves you. You're his son." She laughed and yanked him off the suitcase. "Here, let me do it." She opened it and began to straighten up the clothes and toiletries. "Are you sure you have enough money? It's a long way to drive to California."

"Mom, I'll be fine. I've saved up my money." Michael had close to a thousand dollars with him, and there was a little more in his bank account. He was less certain about the stability of his '97 Buick Skylark, but if the car could get him to California, then it was good enough for him. "Josh is going with me too." His brilliant friend had gotten a full-ride to Stanford.

She tucked his shin guards and cleats into the suitcase and closed it with no trouble. "I'm glad Josh is going with you. I'd hate for you to go alone." Her eyes brightened from unshed tears.

"Mom, it'll be fine." He hugged her while glancing around his room. The white paint was peeling away in places and his walls were bare. His small closet sat open and empty of clothes, and he had stripped the bed down to the mattresses. The room he grew up in seemed naked and vulnerable, and Michael wondered if he was making a mistake.

"Let's get the rest of your things in the car." Her voice grew thick with emotion and nearly broke over the last few words. She grabbed his duffle bag and fled the room.

"I could've gotten that, Mom," he called out after her while he carried his suitcase down the rickety stairs.

She handed him the bag at the foot of the stairs. "Have fun in California. You better call and come back here to visit." She kissed him on the cheek. "I love you."

"I'll call, Mom." Michael didn't know about visiting. His dad made it quite clear to him he wouldn't have a place here if he left. She opened the door for him. "Bye, Mom. I love you too."

"Bye, and don't be mad at me." She gave him a quick squeeze and shut the front door behind him.

His dad sat upon the faded porch swing. "Your mom told me you were leaving."

Michael halted in his place. He was torn between passing his dad and going back inside the house. His tongue felt thick and heavy in his mouth. He licked his lips. "I have to go."

"When my brother died, I was trying to get into the army. They said I had flat feet and wasn't suitable for combat, but it was the only way I could think to afford college." Louis laughed, yet it sounded dry and forlorn. "Your grandpapa told me I had to get back to the boat. We had mouths to feed. William was five at the time, and Charlie was two. Your Aunt Sally didn't know what to do with Jimmy gone, so I went to the *Merriweather Delight* and worked on the family boat."

His dad ran his hand over his chin and inspected the day-old stubble. "You've got your mom's brains, son, and her talent. She

98

always liked doodling, and she was much smarter than this old sea dog. Still is." He sighed. "So, I reckon if this is what you want to do, then you'll have to do it." He finally looked at Michael. "I'd rather you stay here, but William and Charlie talked to me. They know a fellow who can take your place. He's a fine striker and knows some good spots left in the Gulf."

Michael felt relief wash over him like a wave at high tide. "I didn't want to disappoint you, Dad. That's why I didn't say anything for so long." He stepped down the stairs and set his bags on the browned grass. "I was never really good at fishing."

Louis laughed, and the joyous sound rumbled from deep in his belly. "That's the God's honest truth, my boy! You were awful, and you still could never tie a slipknot right. I always had Charlie check your work."

"You did?" Michael laughed along with his dad.

"Yeah."

"Why didn't you tell me? Why did you get so mad?"

"Sit down a moment, son." Louis waited for Michael to join him on the stoop. "I thought you'd pick it up like I did. I wasn't always the fisherman, and even a worse shrimper." He shrugged. "It's what was expected of me, especially when Jimmy died during Hurricane Allen." He shook his head at the memory and placed a hand on his son's shoulder. "I thought you would follow in my footsteps. We've been on the water for six generations. I hated to see the tradition die."

"It's not what I want to do, though," Michael insisted.

"Oh, I know. It took a bit to understand." He laughed. "As I said, your mom is the bright one." He patted Michael's shoulder. "You're the first one of us Merriweathers to make it to college. You'll do us proud, even if you aren't a shrimper." He smiled. "I'm proud of you, son."

Michael's lips twitched into a grin. To hear that his dad was proud of him meant the world to him. His fear and anger disappeared, and his dad's words bolstered his courage to carry on and walk down uncharted territory for the Merriweather men. "Thank you, Dad. I won't let you down."

A Bowl of Red
By Jenne' R. Andrews

TODAY while dusting in my kitchen, I pick up Erna Ferguson's *Mexican Cooking,* inscribed on one page to my mother by my uncle. The words there: "To H. with love from R." were written in 1943; a lifetime ago now, she held this small volume in her hands as she dreamed of her home and children to come. Packed with simple yet elegant recipes acquired from the archives of colonial New Mexico, it has been one of the important texts of our household.

As I read through the foreword, I am spellbound by the picture of daily life in the early days of New Mexico Territory, when the landed and well-married señoras oversaw the grinding of corn in stone *metates*, when fruit was dried and stored in the cellar, when a lamb was butchered, dressed and the flesh cut into strips of jerky, when the great full pods of banana-shaped chili were harvested and made into potent, acrid *ristras* hung at doorways to redden in the sun.

As I read, my father's recipe for chili con carne—chili with meat—falls out of the pages. Suddenly, I want to close the book, but I can't. I read his careful notes, and as I read I am once more taken back many years.

Although he was a classic Yankee, born and bred in New England, and a "Yalie" with a time-worn family clam chowder recipe of his own, my father loved the West and Southwest— most particularly as he found it embodied in my dark-haired, green-eyed New Mexican mother and the culinary rituals and traditions so important to her family.

Oil and Water ... and Other Things That Don't Mix

In the early years of their marriage, after my brother and I were born and before succumbing to depression and addiction, my mother schooled him in the art of "a bowl of red," pungent and wonderfully spicy chili con carne made from quintessential ground New Mexico chili and to which it was heresy to add anything that looked like a pinto bean.

Shortly after our family's move to Colorado from Albuquerque in 1960, my father was diagnosed with emphysema. As a forest pathologist he had been thrilled with his new job as Chief of Disease Research for the Roosevelt National Forest, but soon had to cut back on his research, and then to retire altogether.

Still alert, vital, interested in everything, he busied himself. In becoming our consummate caretaker, he made the perfection of his clam chowder recipe and the family chili an art and a science.

I would return from college, or in the later years, from Minnesota where I taught as a poet in the schools, and he would be standing in the kitchen, breathing through pursed lips, stirring a black Dutch oven full of deep red, aromatic chili. He would turn to me, and although he was running out of oxygen, he would smile, steam fogging his glasses.

In the study off the kitchen, my mother would be dozing in her pale blue robe. She would sometimes wake up and look at us where we stood in the kitchen, steam rising from the redolent pot on the stove. She would smile crookedly, a way she had of beaming in her worst moments.

My father would announce his endeavor to us, and prepare the kitchen for a ritualistic culinary undertaking. He would set out gleaming utensils on the worn counter, sharpening his best kitchen knife. Then he would carefully chop flank steak and slabs of pork into small chunks, and cut an onion into half-moon slices. He would lightly sauté the meat, and then mix chili powder, salt, oregano, flour and masa—fine white cornmeal—in a bowl. He would stir this mixture into the meat and juices, adding one, always one, Number 303 can of tomatoes and two cans of "fresh tap water." He would lean against our butcher-block top dishwasher to take in more air, compensating for the diminishing ability to breathe.

Then he would set a place for me, for my brother, and, after the requisite number of hours had passed for the *sabor*, the flavor, to peak, he would proudly serve us each the steaming "bowl of red" that had its origins right from the secret recipes of the señoras in their haciendas who tended their valorous conquistadores, filling the men's bellies, later giving themselves under the rising New Mexico moon.

One of the recipe cards reads, "A Parable of Talents." At some point my parents had the idea of going into business with his clam chowder, and what had begun as mother's chili. *Que lastima, la enfermedad de mis padres.*

AT NIGHT I would do my homework and drift off to a stack of symphonies on my Sears and Roebuck stereo. I dreamed of what life might be one day, or who might step into it to turn me into a woman. Often, in the middle of the night, her bedroom directly overhead, my mother would wake; afflicted with night terror, she would maraud through our house, cursing, empowering herself with anger. I would get up and argue with her, demanding that she go back to bed. Afterwards I would curl up and cry, or lie face down on the bed in a despair that became an underground river of sorrow and shame.

Finally, I would sink into exhausted sleep and hear my father's voice calling me from a great distance, telling me it was time to get up to catch the bus to go to school. I would curse him but he would keep on, gently, and make eggs and toast for me.

One night, years later, I came home for Christmas, drinking my way from Minnesota across the West. My father struggled to breathe, and the house was in shambles. At the end of the living room, in the window where it always was, stood a perfectly trimmed Christmas tree, and in the refrigerator, a standing rib roast and asparagus, our traditional New England Christmas dinner. His emphysema had taken him down to a shrunken, almost malformed small man, his neck distended from trying to breathe.

He made our Christmas Eve dinner, and we talked over a bottle of wine. I laid into him about the house in disarray, that Mother was nearly comatose in her chair. In a drunken rage I got up and knocked down the Christmas tree, and grabbed my suitcase and hit the road for Cheyenne. I found a cheap motel and tried to drug myself to sleep before attempting to drive on, back to the Midwest.

But I lay in the dark, in anguish. I got up and drove back along the dangerous freeway with snow stinging the windshield of my red Volkswagen. I went home, took my small father into my arms, and straightened up the tree, re-trimmed it, and stayed on into the next day.

In May of that year my father went into his last crisis, and slipped, at last, into the relief and release of stillness. I lay next to my mother in her bed at the nursing home, her back to me, refusing to speak, dry-eyed in her grief.

We put our father's ashes under the Ponderosa pine trees on the place, and held his funeral at St. Paul's Episcopal Church, where we all would go on sparkling Colorado Sunday mornings.

It was a relief to me to feel the powder in my hands, the incredibly fine and delicate dust, to understand that a human being, one's own father, can become something so benign and quiet as ash, a substance signaling an end to incomprehensible and endless suffering that would diffuse and settle with the rains and winter snows to come. There was relief, and incalculable absence and loss.

In that moment as we knelt together, I looked at my brother

and saw my father in him, in his gentleness and implacability. Sometime later our cousin, an Episcopal priest, wrote at the end of a letter, "Remember the good: God has erased the bad."

I PUT the recipes away; it is dusk. The woman writing in the autumn window bound by blood and shared travail to her brother, held fast in unnamed communion with the retired school teacher next door out raking leaves, the squirrel running along the fence, the Golden Retriever, Tess, asleep in her crate, has laid claim to the room where there are ghosts as surely as frost laces the pane.

Forever after, I will think, *Que fuerte, el amor de un Dios que nos ayuda sobrevivir un pasado como este.* How powerful, the love of whatever God that helps us outlive such a past.

So it is that a bowl of chili throws off the light of my father's love and perseverance. As with the pine knot fire laid at the hearth, the polishing of the silver when there was alcoholic disarray everywhere, when he and my mother were free-falling in slow motion down the icy face of a mountain toward the coffin-narrow ravine below in the blatant inevitability of a deterioration no one could stop, such moments—the greater context of the ritual of the chili and the afterglow of the past around us like fading, antique starlight—stitched one moment to another. Now, from my own chasm of depression and anger, I see him on the rim of our family past—his being, his will to keep on shouting that if his love for us kept him alive, so should ours for one another.

Fellowship at Hardee's
By Shonell Bacon

"UH, yeah, I did hear that the Greyhound was a perfect spot to meet your soul mate. Excuse me, please."

Kensington crawled over the man's lap, a man who was all too happy to allow her rump to traipse lightly against him. Twenty people on a bus that sat fifty-six and the stinkiest piece of human flesh had to sit beside her *and* had the audacity to think he could pick her up. On a Greyhound. Kensington wasn't about material things, but she wasn't impressed by the man's lack of a vehicle...and good hygiene.

As she trudged down the aisle, a hand reached out to her.

"Chile, can you see if there are any napkins in there?" a woman asked. Kensington nodded, to which the woman smiled, closed her eyes behind her wire-rimmed glasses and responded with, "God bless you, my chile."

"Help *me*, Lord," Kensington gritted between teeth as she headed to the back of the bus.

"I'M GOING to throw up if that toothless wonder touches my knee one more damn time," Kensington muttered as she stared down at the toilet bowl; a wave of nausea threatened to rise within her. She had promised herself that nothing would make her place *anything* naked of hers on a bus toilet and for three hours since leaving Baltimore for Maine, Kensington had kept with that vow.

She squeezed hand sanitizer into her hands for the fifth time.

She shined the sapphire stone on the gold ring that encircled her left middle finger, a ring she had been given just before her departure, a ring that held the remembrance of a kiss and a declaration of love that spun Kensington's already crazy life into a tailspin. A blush hid behind the brown of her skin.

Kensington looked hard at herself in the mirror. Her fingers snapped to attention and pulled the wisps of hairs that had fallen onto her cheeks back up under her Orioles cap.

She breathed.

"Kensington," she whispered. "This is good for you. Clean air. Water. Lobster. Nature." She stared at herself, unblinkingly, until her eyes began to moisten. "Distance."

The university would be good for her, she told herself. She could write. She could immerse herself in a whole other culture and lifestyle and set of people. She could find herself, whatever the hell *that* meant.

The bus came to a halt and pitched Kensington forward, her forehead smashing against the mirror. She bounced back against the wall and came forward again, this time she threw her hands out to steady her. She fell to her knees, her left hand sliding straight into the toilet. Water swirled around her hand. She screamed.

"What the fuck?" she cried out before wrenching her hand from the toilet and ripping a pile of napkins from their dispenser. She sat on the toilet, drying her arm until her skin grew ashy.

"Are you okay in there?" someone called through the door.

Kensington reached up and unlocked the door. It opened a crack and the woman who had asked for the napkins stuck her head in. "Something's wrong with the bus," she said. She looked at Kensington. "Your head's bleeding, chile. Why are you rubbing your arm and not your head?"

Kensington shrugged.

"This bathroom is too small to do anything in," the woman

said. "But bless the Lord, He provides us with *some* space to take care of our needs. You get up, honey, and I will help clean the cut."

The door closed and Kensington lowered her head and took note of the spots of blood that dotted her white tank top. She shook her head; she knew a bit of pain was going to be involved in this.

THE SUN glowered down onto the parking lot of Hardee's and the strip mall where a broken bus and twenty passengers steamed.

Sweat trickled a line down Kensington's neck to her cleavage. Every few seconds, she had the urge to wipe her forehead and remembered the three Scooby Doo Band-Aids that the woman had placed there.

She sat on a grassy knoll that separated the parking lot from the interstate and listened to her MP3 player while she nibbled on fries and pressed her fountain soda against her neck.

"Why not go inside, sweetheart?" the bus driver asked when he came out to call on the bus coming to pick them all up.

Kensington lifted her eyes and replied, "Too much preaching going on in there."

"People need a good preaching sometimes."

"In a Hardee's? Gives me indigestion."

"Well, you'll burn up out here."

Kensington had already felt flames licking on the back of her neck as she stood in line waiting to order something at Hardee's. She had found out, while being doctored up, that the woman needing napkins was Pastor Michaels, a young woman full of big dreams and sincere hopes; a young woman who was devout in her faith and vocal to those who didn't have some kind of faith. She was on her way to a revival in New York, where she would give her first major sermon to a congregation of well over 1,000 people. She was most definitely in the spirit in the holiest of ways and was burning with the love of God to tell all of the WORD.

"That chile there needs to be saved," Pastor Michaels had said. Kensington froze in her spot and cut her eyes back in the line. She let out her breath when she realized she wasn't the pastor's target. The *victim* was a girl the color of paste, whose short crimson hair made her even more pallid. Her thin eyebrows shined with the silver of studs, her lips were slashed with red, and the electric blue mascara contrasted with the gray of her eyes: the color of rain clouds.

"May I take your order?" the sullen Hardee's worker had asked.

Kensington turned away from pale girl and replied, "Can I get a bit of praise with my Famous Star Burger and a side order of hope with my fries?"

Pale Girl opened her mouth, bubble-gum pink tongue and tongue ring flashing, and howled, causing a giggling rippling effect through the line.

"Young people these days don't understand the Word of God," Pastor Michaels said, loud enough for everyone in the line to hear. "They think it's a joke."

Kensington lowered her eyes and glanced toward Pale Girl. Their eyes connected and each smiled. Kensington saw Pale Girl's hand wrapped around the hand of a thin, evenly tanned girl, a girl who could have passed for a *Teen* magazine cover girl: shoulder length, salon-conditioned brunette hair, big blue eyes, full lips, contoured cheek bones, thin yet shapely figure clad in low-riding jeans, and a red, midriff-baring tank top. Kensington saw something mischievous shimmer in Pale Girl's eyes, and then her mouth dropped when Pale Girl pulled Cover Girl to her and they fell into a lip lock.

"Oh Lord," cried Pastor Michaels, who went limp. Her flunky, a chubby brown sister with a great smile but short, nappy hair, grabbed the pastor under her arms and helped her to her feet.

"They know not what they do," flunky whispered up to the greasy ceiling. "Forgive them for their transgressions."

Kensington looked at pale girl and cover girl, still in their kiss and thought of her sapphire ring and Gail, and the heat that rose in her cheeks. She turned back to the cashier, mumbled her order and hurried out of the restaurant, her nerves trembling.

PALE GIRL dropped down beside Kensington on the knoll and stole a fry.

"Hey," she said. Kensington nodded.

"That was pretty funny back there."

"You weren't that bad yourself."

Pale Girl rubbed her milky arms and laughed. "Yeah, well, I just get pissed off when people try to ram their beliefs down my throat, you know?"

"I do." She twirled the ring around her finger.

"Anyway, my name is Amber," Pale Girl said. She pointed toward Cover Girl, who was walking across the parking lot, toward Dollar General. "That's my girlfriend, Tiffany."

Kensington coughed, and then laughed. "Unh unh," she said. "Amber and Tiffany? They are two of the most un-gay names ever."

Amber giggled. "I think it's a cruel joke, or something."

"I'm Kensington."

Kensington looked at Amber and noticed her delicate features, despite the studded armor and vibrant makeup. She reached out and touched Amber's neck, and then her arm. Amber's eyes widened to two silver disks. Kensington pulled her hand back fast, as if she touched something hot.

"I'm sorry," Kensington said. "Thought you were wearing body makeup. Never seen anyone that pale before."

Amber laughed. "Should see my dad. He's translucent."

Kensington winced and rubbed around her band-aids. Her dad was translucent too. "Do you burn?" she asked.

"Yeah. Stay out here too long, and I'll start peeling and looking blistery red." She ran her fingers over her hairless arm.

"What 'cha listening to?" Amber picked up Kensington's MP3 player and began clicking buttons. "Somebody might think you're old if they see The Four Tops, Temptations, and Marvin Gaye in there. I think the most recent thing I saw was Prince's *The Hits* and that is unbelievably sad."

Kensington chuckled. "Feeling old school lately. This stuff mellows me out."

"So where you headed?" Amber asked.

"Maine. Going to school there. You?"

"Connecticut. Tiff's father lives in Baltimore, so we visited him for a few weeks. Heading back up to the university."

Kensington shook her head and chuckled. "Tiff? Whoa. Tiff and Amber live in Connecticut, practically the white bread state of the country? How could it get better?"

Amber smacked Kensington's bare arm and they settled back on the knoll, eating Kensington's fries and sitting in a silence reserved for people who had been lifelong friends.

They watched people leave Hardee's, immediately recognizing their fellow bus mates. Many of them, young and rebellious, were jumping, bouncing on the balls of their feet, as if caught by the Holy Spirit; some rolled their Rs and spoke in backward English and Pig Latin as if God Himself had possessed them; others had faces lit by the Word—as transmitted through Pastor Michaels. They flocked around her like disciples.

"They mock the Word," Pastor Michaels said, "because they do not understand it."

"Yes they do, Lord," flunky chimed. "They don't know how great You are."

"Thank you, Roberta," Pastor Michaels said. "I'm not great. I just try to do His will."

Amber nudged Kensington. "Just like her to think she was *great* and not God."

Pastor Michaels stopped a good ten feet from the knoll, as if a ring of fire circled the hill, keeping the hellions away from her and her good-doers.

"How's your head, my chile?" she asked Kensington, though she stared at Amber, indignation blazing in her eyes.

"It's okay," Kensington answered. "Stings a little, but pain always has that lasting effect." She took a wad of napkins and mopped at her neck.

Tiffany ambled back across the parking lot, a Dollar General bag in one hand and a half-eaten Twix in the other. The small group parted, and she walked up the knoll and plopped down beside Amber. She was a sinner, so the ring of fire gathered her in with a lover's embrace.

"Do you believe in Satan?" Pastor Michaels asked Amber.

Kensington watched Pastor Michaels gather strength through her small brigade of followers, who nodded and *amen*-ed before she even said anything. She noticed the tightness around the pastor's mouth, the downcast of its corners, the rigidity of her body. *Her righteousness makes her old and mean-looking*, Kensington thought.

"Not really, no," Amber replied. She reached out and threaded her fingers with Tiffany's.

"God?"

"Sometimes."

"So you're not a Christian?"

"How can she be a Christian, Pastor, if she's doing that?" Roberta said, pointing a pudgy finger at the connection of their hands.

Kensington pushed her earphones down around her neck. She began cracking her knuckles, one finger at a time.

"This is a sin, chile," Pastor Michaels said, her voice lulling. "Woman was made from man. You are a part of him. You are to be connected with him, to procreate and raise children who are God-fearing and loving."

Woman was made from man. *Bullshit*, Kensington thought. She was made from a man who never let a day go by without telling her that she wasn't good enough. That she needed to try harder. That her B+ needed to be an A++. That if she smiled more, she could get a man. That a woman needed to have a man to guide her and make her into the woman God intended her to become. That she would burn in Hell if she thought differently.

You are a part of him. Through every vice that God could create, that was true, Kensington admitted. She drank too much. She smoked too much. She hated too much. Just like him. But also like him, she shared a love for Motown, and when things got bad, she hung on to The Four Tops singing *I'll Be There*, and thought that someday, somehow, she would be there to give her father all the love he needed after all his vices had forsaken him.

"How can you tell me that what I do is wrong?" Amber asked. "I love my mother and father, I love people, and I love this girl. Why is that wrong?"

Why was it wrong, Kensington thought. Why did her lips go pliable when they met with Gail's, and yet she felt the urge to throw up, repent, and ask the Father, the Son, and the Holy Spirit for forgiveness?

She took in Amber and Tiffany's hands, tightly intertwined, and then closed her eyes. Flashes of last night, she and Gail on her parents' porch, invaded the nothing behind her eyelids.

"How you gonna just pack up and leave?" Gail had asked. She sat beside Kensington on the porch steps as they watched the souped-up 80s cars with gleaming rims zoom by, slicing up the night.

"I'm going away to school," Kensington replied. "Remember when I applied to all those schools for my MFA?"

"Don't be a smart ass, Ken." Gail kicked Kensington in the foot. "Just last week you were going to stay here in B'more. I was gonna help you pack your things and take you to the campus apartment. Now you're going 500 miles away?"

Kensington dropped her head to her knees. "I changed my mind."

"A week before school starts?" Gail sucked in the moist, night air. "Is it because of what I told you?"

"No."

"Is it because of the..."

"No." Kensington stood and paced out to the sidewalk. "I don't want to talk about it."

"I can take it back."

Kensington turned. Her brown eyes had grown black, like they always did when she was confused and wanted a one-way ticket out of her life and sticky situations.

"You can't take back an *I love you*," Kensington said. "Or the kiss, or this." She stuck out her left hand; the sapphire ring reflected light from the streetlamp overhead. She ran her fingers through her thick, curly hair, and groaned. "I thought this was a friendship ring or something, and then you kissed me. I let you kiss me. I wasn't expecting that."

A siren moaned a few blocks away, its sound languid and mournful.

"I wasn't expecting it either," Gail finally said. "We've been friends how long?"

"Since the crib," Kensington responded, her eyes downcast, watching tiny ants march in single file across the pavement.

"Exactly. We shared horror stories about guys. We even dated the same guys sometimes to compare their techniques."

"I know." Kensington looked up and caught the confused

expression in Gail's sable-colored eyes. She fought the urge to go back to the porch, to put her arms around Gail's wispy body—she knew she would remember how she compared Gail to porcelain the night they kissed: fragile yet beautiful to look at and too irresistible not to touch.

"You're my best friend," Kensington said. "You my *girl*, my ace boon coon. How did *this* happen?"

Gail rose and tentatively stepped toward Kensington. She dropped her hands into the pockets of her jean shorts. When she was a good foot away from Kensington, Gail stared her in the face and said, "I feel comfortable with you, Ken. I don't know how else to describe it. Don't you feel comfortable with me?"

"I do, but..."

"Don't you like me?"

"That's a stupid question to ask, Gail."

"Don't you think about me? Just a little?"

Kensington wanted to take Gail by the hand and kneel upon the pavement and raise their eyes to the dark sky with its chipped stars, and beg for God to cleanse whatever coursed through them. She couldn't remember wanting Gail before the kiss, but as their lips made contact that night, she felt something inside her expand, airy and light, and it scared her shitless.

"I do, but..."

Gail reached out and with slender fingers touched Kensington's cheek.

"Shut up," she said. "I just want to remember the *I do*. Keep the ring. It was meant as a friendship ring because you are my best friend. Will you just do me one favor?"

"Okay."

"Think about this. Play around with it in your head. Write a story about it. See what your alter ego thinks about it."

Despite the thick confusion in her head and the sadness that sat upon her heart, Kensington laughed. "I will."

Gail opened her arms. "Hug?"

Kensington slipped into the circle of Gail's arms. Gingerly, she wrapped Gail into her own. They stayed like that, gently clinging, in the dark. Gail sighed, and Kensington held hers in.

Over Gail's shoulder, Kensington saw the front door slightly ajar and her father's figure in the shadows. She pushed Gail away just as the door banged shut. Gail turned to the door, and then to Kensington, whispering, "I'm sorry."

Kensington's heart thudded in her chest and she realized she was sorry too—for wanting to hold Gail and for pushing her away.

"THIS POOR CHILE," Pastor Michaels preached. She turned slowly, her eyes connecting with every bus passenger that would bore into the eyes of this holified creature. "This poor creature wants to know why what she does is wrong." Pastor shook her head and looked up into the bright, hot sky, as if hoping to receive the definitive answer from God. She swung her head back to them. "Homosexuality is a sin," she stated simply.

"Yes, Lord," Roberta and her brethren echoed in response.

Kensington laughed. She threw her hand up to her mouth to quiet herself, but the laughter escaped.

"You laugh at the word of God, chile?" Pastor Michaels asked. "We must listen to God, read His Word, live by His commandments and the instructions He sets out for us."

For the majority of Kensington's twenty-five years of existence, God had been a steady diet in her life. She reveled in Him. She thought of her earlier years, her mother and father, her grandparents, the whole family going to Grace A.M.E. and living in the Word. She read her favorite Psalms to her father up until she turned 16 and he stopped going to church and stopped believing. His religious instruction for Kensington increased despite his loss of faith. She thought of the nights he sat on the steps that led upstairs, a can of Schlitz in one hand and his fiery red Bible in the other and quoted passages that would singe Kensington's minute belief in herself. She thought all these things, and more, and then laughed.

"It's a wonder we even have people who still believe in God," she said.

"What?" Pastor Michaels stepped closer to the ring of fire, the flames caressing her high yellow cheeks, and then she stepped through, the fire enveloping her.

"You are what makes people give up on God. You spoon-feed scripture down people's throats, but only your interpretation of the scripture. If someone doesn't think just like you, then that person is off to hell."

"There is but one interpretation of His Word and His Will," the pastor added. Her hands balled up into tiny fists and her eyes flashed. Kensington removed her headset completely and stood, staring down the slight hill at the pastor and her flock who stood outside the ring, afraid of entering the heated conversation.

"There isn't just one," Kensington said. "That's what makes God so good. He gives us instruction, but in a way so that we can select our own paths. You're so blinded by the Word you have lost yourself, Pastor. What does God really mean to you?"

Before the pastor could respond, Kensington added: "Take away your flock, your *amens* and *hallelujahs*, your pulpit and congregation, and tell me, what's left for you? I tell you, for me, I love God: the Father, Son, and the Holy Spirit, but sometimes, you can't pay me to believe in it, or to want to believe. That doesn't make me a sinner, Pastor. It makes me human, just like Amber and Tiff, and a lot of other people."

Kensington stole a glance toward Amber and winked.

Roberta waddled up to the pastor's side and handed her the Bible. "Pastor Michaels, teach her the errors of her ways," she said. "Before it's too late."

Twenty-one heads suddenly turned in the direction of the interstate as three strong horn blows sounded. Several people whooped and hollered and parted to get their belongings. Kensington gathered up her MP3 player and trash.

"Thanks for that," Amber said, as she stood up.

"No problem," Kensington replied. "I have no doubt that you could have handled yourself."

"But you handled her for us, and yourself."

Kensington nodded. "I did."

The trio stood on the knoll, watching the bus roar up the interstate and turn into the parking lot. As they walked toward the broken bus, Amber said, "Thank God this bus is finally here. I don't think I could have lasted much longer."

"You and me both," Kensington added. She reached under the bus and pulled her luggage out. Behind her, she could hear Pastor Michaels talking to Roberta.

"See," the pastor said. "I told you that chile believed in God. She gonna tell me *sometimes* she believes, but she just said, *Thank God*. She's gonna be alright if she just follows the right path."

Kensington's smile slid from her face, and she looked toward the pastor, and then Amber and Tiff, all headed to the same destination despite their paths. She sighed—her path uncertain —gripped the handles of her luggage, and followed.

Renegade Vegetarian
By Mollie Cox Bryan

ONE OF THE MANY ways in which I have failed my parents is becoming a vegetarian. Mom took it personally and my Dad still goads me by inviting me to dinner and having a ham. I am an adult and don't see why my dietary choices seem to cause such a calamity when I visit.

Up until about ten years ago, mom still tried to sneak meat into me any way that she could. The last time, I almost threw-up on her couch when I realized what I was eating. It was Christmas and she made my grandmother's baked beans, with brown sugar and pork, it turns out.

She offered me the beans and I took a bite. I noticed something odd and stringy with the texture. The first thing I thought was, "Did the cat get into this?" (She had a longhaired cat that shed incredible amounts of hair.)

"Ma," I said. "Something isn't right with these beans."

She looked at me and I saw deception in her eyes. "What do you mean?" Her face held all of this tension. In the way she was holding her mouth, with clenched jaws, I knew she was either trying not to laugh or trying not to cry.

My eyes met hers. She knew I was on to her.

"I-I'm sorry," she stammered. "I thought I picked all the meat out." She held out her hand for my plate.

Even my childhood neighbors were in on the anti-vegetarian crusade. Once they were trying to feed me and I passed on the meat. "Oh," said Carrie, the oldest daughter, "That's right, you are vegetarian. You just *have* to be different, don't you?"

I've thought about that statement for a long time and the adolescent cruelty of it. But in truth, I still have to defend my dietary choices, even with grown-ups who should certainly know better.

I became a vegetarian, early on, simply because I didn't like meat. Somewhere along the line, I also made a clear connection between my love of animals and not eating meat, to wanting to live my life lightly on this planet, and not wanting to support the cruelty of factory farming. I was not recruited in any movement. I was all this before I even knew there was a term for it.

Ironically, it was my mother who taught me to be kind to animals and even to plants. Once, I pulled the arms off of a cactus and it bled thick white stuff—I was punished because I hurt the plant, which, after all was a "feeling being."

And to this day, when I tell Mom that I am sick with a cold, or the flu, or whatever, the first thing she says is. "You just need a hamburger."

Baked Beans with Pork

THIS is my mom's grandmother's recipe. Her grandmother, Annie Snowwhite, always used baby lima beans, which call for soaking over night. Mom used to soak those beans and make everything from scratch. After she started working, she discovered canned beans. "They are still good, though not quite as delicious as those baby lima beans." Any kind of beans good for baking will do. These beans are also delicious without the meat.

4 pork chops
1 large onion
2 bell peppers
4 strips of bacon

Renegade Vegetarian – Mollie Cox Bryan

1/4 cup molasses
1/2 cup brown sugar
1/2 cup ketchup
2 cans of baked beans, drained

Brown pork chops in the skillet with the onion and green pepper. Place drained beans in roasting pan. Add pork, onions, and green peppers to the beans and place in the oven. Place cut bacon strips on the top. Bake at 375°F for 45 minutes, or until bacon is done.

"No Thank You"

By Carl Palmer

I don't remember who I was talking to
or what I was talking about,
but it was my voice I heard
and I remember saying it.
That's what woke me up.
"No thank you."

Had I said it on the telephone
to a telephone sales person
persistently selling telephones or
a cellular telephone service plan,
that kind of "No thank you!!"?
A dismissive, condescending, agitated,
"No thank you"
voiced toward the slamming hand set?

Or was it said to a person or persons in mass,
handing out blue and pink flyers at the fair
almost blocking pedestrian passage,
thrusting their advertised wares
as I verbally elbow past
avoiding eye contact?
"No Thank You"
barely slowing down.

Or to the red-headed waitress
as she asks on the brink of pouring,
if I need a warm-up just after
I've added the right amounts
of milk for color and sugar for taste.

"No Thank You" – Carl Palmer

"No thank you"
with a smiling shake of my head
and a blocking hand over the cup.

Or maybe a singing retort
at the sticky-faced toddler
in the waiting room, ripe diaper,
crawling toward my seat,
offering gooey green gummie bears
from his fuzzy little open hands.
"No thank you,"
quite loud, backing into my chair
trying to get the parents' attention
to keep their odorous brat at bay.

Perhaps a polite refusal,
though, to an offer
of something I actually desire,
like another slice of hot blueberry pie
or more peaches with vanilla ice cream,
the unconvincing sort,
that if asked again,
may not be that vague, unmeant
"No thank you"
that was automatically voiced.
whereas, if offered again,
"Are you sure?"
just surely might be accepted.

My pondering now abruptly curtailed
by yet another question
from the other side of my bed.
"Still wanna get up early?"

"No thank you."

Now I'm asking myself..."Who was that?"

Loving Lola
By Dania Rajendra

WHEN I WAS first getting to know the man who would become my ex-fiancé, I visited his office, one floor down from mine in the Minneapolis Labor building. "Ohhhh," I had said, spying the framed photo on his desk. "You have a dog," I cooed, as if I were a pet person, a dog lover. I was not, but I wanted to be his lover, and I was already doing that stupid thing of morphing myself into my sense of what he wanted.

It wasn't long after that early summer day that I got what I wanted and he wanted, too. I spent the night at his house and met Mandy. For fourteen years, Mandy had been Clarke's most stalwart friend. He told me that she had loved him when not even his own father would talk to him. Always a good dog, Mandy had given him a reason to get out of bed and get a modicum of exercise through his worst depressions. They were long in the past, he assured me, as we built our romance. I assured him the same of mine. As summer waned, we were a serious item. I stayed at his house more than my apartment, enjoying an easy weekend morning domesticity: coffee and his homemade scones, or maybe poached eggs, consumed on the deck while leafing through the paper, Mandy under the table, panting happily. We'd walk Mandy slowly through East St. Paul, chatting about our week and our plans and our love. In the evenings, in his living room, he'd sing that David Gray song, "This Year's Love," to me, strumming his guitar. Then I got fired, and he held me in his strong arms as I sobbed, fed me while I was broke. With those strong arms he helped me pack my belongings into his basement for safekeeping. At Thanksgiving I met his dad and stepmom. For Christmas, I knit him socks. In January, I had moved into his cozy house, just big enough for a grown man, a medium-sized dog, and a small woman.

But now it was February, only a month in, and she was dying in front of us. A black-lab-pit-bull mix, Mandy had been visibly aging—graying, walking ever more slowly—over the few months I had known them both, but when we woke up one February morning to find her back legs paralyzed and saw some first convulsions, it was clear that day was her last.

As the morning progressed, Clarke went wild with grief and panic. He called two ex-girlfriends, one a vet tech who confirmed there was nothing we could do for her, and the other, his former live-in girlfriend, Jules. She was The One, the first The One, the former The One. She had shared a home and a bed and years with Clarke and Mandy, and he knew she would want to say goodbye. "Come now!" he wailed into the phone, before beeping it off and returning to the hard blond wood floor where Mandy lay in her bed, shaking. He wrapped his arms around her and held her while she shuddered.

I was hungover from a party the night before, and quietly sipped seltzer in the background while Clarke made his panicked calls. It was clear to me there was nothing we could do for Mandy, and I was pretty sure there was nothing I could do for Clarke. Though I was fond of her, I also resented the way her doggy needs interfered with my previously free lifestyle, my ability to go from work to happy hour with a big group of friends. I was, perhaps, a little jealous of his attachment. Of their history.

My curiosity took over too, and I watched her. I had never seen another mammal die before. I swallowed seltzer and talked, silently, to my queasy insides: *This morning is a particularly terrible time to be sick, so please don't.* It worked.

The adrenaline swamped the hangover.

By the time Jules pulled up in her little Jeep, Mandy was dead and Clarke was wailing like an Arab mourner, pulling at his thick dark hair and pacing the floor. I opened the door for Jules. She swept in and sank down next to Mandy's body, her coat still on. She reached for her stiff paws, and sniffed. "Her feet still smell like popcorn!" She looked up at Clarke. She started to cry, and murmured to Mandy, or was it to Clarke? "I came as soon as I could."

I could see, in that moment, the life they had had before me. They matched better than Clarke and I did, I thought sourly. Jules is tall, fit, with long dark hair. Minnesotan. Clarke is tall and fit, with dark hair. Minnesotan. I'm short, at the time I was rounder than I prefer, a New York fish out of water in St. Paul. While I was busy being self-absorbed, the two decided that Clarke would take Mandy to the vet's office in his truck, to be alone with her body before turning it over for cremation. Mandy was a big dog—we couldn't bury her in the back yard even if it wasn't frozen solid.

With Jules in my car, I followed Clarke's Ford Ranger onto Interstate 35E, and then south onto Route 52. We passed a filling station and pulled into the vet's office, in a small strip mall in a corner of Minnesota I had never before visited.

After depositing Mandy's stiff doggy corpse at the vet's for cremation, Jules and I both tried to convince Clarke to ride back with us. I don't remember discussing it, but we had the same, simultaneous worry about him driving so upset, or through tears, and plowing into someone or something. We lost the argument, of course. We watched as his truck pulled away, gave him a few minutes of head start, and immediately agreed that arguing with him was the best way to make him dig in his heels. I pulled into the driveway and looked at Jules, a Minneapolis-area native. "Which way?"

"I don't know."

And we were lost. Between the two of us, we had not the slightest sense of direction. We agreed Clarke would laugh at us—and not nicely. We also agreed that we would deserve it. As we laughed at ourselves, and at our agreement on Clarke's reaction, I softened to this person who had loved my boyfriend and loved him still.

As I drove the small Toyota towards a gas station to ask for directions, I tried to sort out my jealousy. I wasn't quite sure what of, exactly. Even in that moment I was shallow and insecure enough to remind myself that I was more beautiful, and, ten years her junior, already more successful profess-sionally. (It seems only fair to note I also had many more advantages.) I think I was jealous of the Clarke she had known, the "unspoiled" one; the one who hadn't yet had Jules cheat on him and break his heart. I was also jealous of how well she had known him. I thought that I, at all of twenty-four, was a seasoned a veteran of heartbreak, and I knew that my Clarke, while he loved and trusted me, couldn't possibly allow me into himself in the same way he had invited Jules. After all, it's how I felt about him.

The directions we procured were faulty but they did get us back to the roads we knew, and after a tour of too many Minnesota highway interchanges, we were on our way back to the small house with the blond wood floors that would be empty without Mandy's toenails clicking on them.

Jules must have felt a similar bonding in our self-deprecating laughter and shared lack of direction because once we started to recognize the highway exits she began to talk in what turned out to be an extended monologue. She mentioned the only other time we had met, about four months previous. She had dog-sat Mandy while Clarke had come to collect me from New York, surprising me with a ticket "home." That cold morning, on the way to her house from the airport, I sat uncomfortably in the passenger seat of his pickup as Clarke crowed about how he had overrode her objections and insisted that we pick Mandy up on our way back from the airport so she could meet me. Jules had wanted him to wait until later in the day, because she was cleaning her house and didn't want visitors. "She's your *ex-girlfriend*?" I remembered asking, pulling down the visor mirror to check my frizzy hair, examine my un-made-up face. "You did *what*? You didn't ask me!"

Clarke smirked, and then stopped when he realized I was upset. He looked contrite. "I know. I'm sorry," he said. I believed him.

When we pulled up, Jules was waiting outside in the chilly fall air with Mandy. "I told Clarke he should be more considerate of both of our feelings," she told me. I looked over at Clarke and raised my eyebrows. But Jules had moved on to other topics. She fluffed my long dark curls with her hand and offered chipper compliments. I remained acutely uncomfortable.

Now Jules was in my car, babbling on about herself and the end of her romance with Clarke five years previous. Each of her pronouncements began with the phrase "When I left Clarke..." I was struck by how insistent she was with the phrase, considering what little I knew about their drawn-out end. Though admittedly my source was a bit one-sided, it had sounded like Clarke had hung on long after things were over, but she hadn't made a clean break, either. Lost in my thoughts, I let her blather on.

She told me about how she had loved him, but it wasn't the right thing. That she had loved him, but wanted more for herself. I understood that she had left him and moved to New York, maybe to make it as an actress? Or to follow a new guy? I couldn't quite remember what he had told me. Whatever it was she had wanted to do she hadn't succeeded at, and now she was back in Minneapolis, cleaning houses and doing a lot of Iyengar yoga. "Her tail between her legs," Clarke told me once, a little too triumphantly. "When I left Clarke, I…" she said, over and over again. She ended with, "I know I can always count on him, and he can always count on me. I just want him to be happy, and he's happy with you, and that's what matters."

I had nothing to say back, because I was still in my head, stuck in my feelings of superiority, jealousy, and fierce protectiveness. Even though she was saying nice and mature things, I—a little bit—wanted to gouge her eyes out. Clarke was so vulnerable at that moment, alone in his truck or alone in his house without his dog, and Jules's bringing up his previous hurts almost hurt me.

And then there was the part of her that had loved Mandy. "She was my dog too…" Jules had said in her soliloquy. But I didn't love the dog, which had been a source of guilt and conflict. Now that she was dead, I felt even guiltier. But despite my cooing early on, I had never had a pet before, and I resented Mandy's normal doggy needs. I was upset that I needed to come home after work to let her out when Clarke wasn't able. Picking up her steaming shit made me late to dinner dates with friends. I thought that if we didn't have a dog, Clarke might be more social, come out more. I was lonely, two months into my life with Clarke in Minnesota, and I blamed Mandy. And now she had died, and Clarke was distraught.

But Jules loved the dog, and it made me insecure about what I didn't offer Clarke. Could we really have a happy life together if I wasn't a dog person?

There was only one way to find out. Everyone told me the only way to get over the death of a beloved dog was a puppy, but Clarke swore he didn't want one. Until he sent me a petfinder.com link to a brown lab-pit bull mix named Karma. She came over, the petfinder people looked us over, and, after our trial period, they posted an update: KARMA WAS ADOPTED BY A VERY NICE COUPLE IN ST. PAUL.

We had to rename her, and the Internet reading I did said to pick something that rhymed, so we went with my suggestion, Lola. Lola is, like Mandy, a half lab, half pit bull mix, but brown instead of black. Lola is a beautiful dog, chocolate brown with white on her paws, and down her nose. She's a dog-shaped vanilla ice cream sundae drenched in milk chocolate syrup. She's got a pit bull face and maybe a little whippet in her, because she never filled out like a lab. From the beginning, she was all over the place, always wanting to play, always needing more attention but so, so eager to please. All sugar.

I had never owned a puppy before, and she had all the hyper, out-of-control, normal puppy character, which drove me over the edge. I cried when we walked her; I cried when she bit me; I cried when she wiggled through the fence. Clarke bought a choke chain and tried to teach me to yank on it to deliver corrections. I cried then, too. Even though she didn't seem hurt when I jerked, I felt awful. He told me I needed to master a "stern voice" to communicate that I meant business. I tried, but it didn't come naturally. I cried some more.

Then, soon after our year anniversary, we moved in New York. It took Lola just a week to learn to pee on pavement instead of our old lawn, but Clarke's transition to big city life was much tougher. He hated everything. He hated our apartment with its old, chipped, repainted-too-many-times, cracked plaster walls. He even hated the parks where we walked Lola, the dog run where we could remove her leash and let her run free after other dogs' tennis balls. In his misery, he mastered the use of the "stern voice" on me. I cried a lot. I sank into a pit of my own depression. And I tried, desperately, to morph myself and our reality into what he wanted.

We were terrible to one another in our own ways, but I'm the one doing the telling here, and my position is that Clarke just got bleaker and meaner, and his meanness became more insidious. I was struggling to get better, but Clarke's misery was holding me down. In an attempt to fix our relationship, we took on more and more projects—renovating our apartment, hiring a dog trainer, planning our overseas wedding. Weekly therapy sessions and endless Big Talks and even Bigger Fights did not offer help. Things continued to spiral. I thought if we just kept busy, made more progress, things between us would improve.

"It isn't that bad," Clarke kept telling me. "It isn't that bad," I repeated that mantra to myself, my increasingly worried friends, my therapist, our therapist, my boss, his parents, my parents, anyone who asked how I was doing. Having a dog and a fiancé meant lots of compromises for me—heading straight home after work instead of meeting friends at happy hour; spending lots of money on a dog walker instead of cocktails; vacuuming up Lola's fur on the weekends; yanking on the leash when we disagreed about which direction to go. Sometimes, more often than I wanted to admit, I was resentful and scared.

But then the third trainer we hired taught us an important dog secret: Lola would do anything, anything at all, for American cheese. Tiny bits of "cheese product" convinced Lola to sit on command, walk without pulling, and even stop barking. Thanks to that neat trick, my relationship with her improved markedly.

Too bad the same couldn't be said for my relationship with Clarke. I could see him struggling, and I felt bad for him. I empathized with his struggle, even when my dad, exasperated, said, "I moved to Alabama from India in 1970 and was better adjusted!" But it isn't easy to upend your life and reconfigure your dreams at thirty-six. We forged ahead, installing new kitchen cabinets, addressing our wedding invitations. By January, we had sent out 250 of them to our nearest and dearest, and picked out the Cuisinart that would define our love and commitment for the decades to come.

The last Wednesday of January, I came home still a little amped from the too much coffee that had fuelled my thirteen-hour work day. It was just before ten, but when I unlocked the door, our apartment was dark. Clarke was already in bed—a bad sign—but out came Lola, barking hello and wagging her tail. Still wearing my coat, I squatted down on the floor to hug her solid doggy body in the unlit hallway.

When I got to the bedroom, I turned on the little bedside light, and Clarke exploded. "Do you have to draw so much attention to yourself when you come home?"

"I can't find my pajamas in the dark," I replied, trying to remain rational and keep my voice calm, the way I had learned in therapy. I shed my coat and my clothes, pulled on my pajamas, and turned the light back off. I climbed into bed to sit there, twisting my engagement ring, furious, hurt, weary from my long day and our fights that never seemed to end. Lola jumped into bed between us, snuggling her dense body into my outstretched leg. Clarke turned away from us. Obviously, he was not sleeping.

I twisted my ring some more, listening to Lola's quick breaths in the dark silence, breathing deeply, trying to smother the panic and rage coursing my body before they exploded. I waited, wishing I could do the same for Clarke's rage. Thirty seconds, passed, then forty-five, and from the other side of our dog, the love of my life hurled his verbal grenades. The screaming accusations were barely coherent: I had undermined him with an email to his friends about the wedding! I didn't do my share of the dog walking! I was inconsiderate of his sleep! Half-listening to a familiar litany of my failures, I felt Lola scramble off the bed, and watched her shape in the dark bedroom. She had flattened herself against the wall, as far from us as she could get.

The spot where she had occupied in our bed turned icy but I continued to sit next to it, still and silent, twisting my ring.

I tuned out Clarke's shouting and stared at the shadowy shape of our dog. She had never bounded off the bed quite like that before. I sat in the cold dark, letting the realization in. If the dog can't take it, it is, in fact, that bad.

It's an ongoing mystery of human existence how any two people go from risking everything on a sexy connection that makes them croon love songs in the living room to tending simmering resentments that flare into screaming fights, slammed doors, and nights on the couch. I had tried so hard not to notice as all the affection drained from our home, our conversation, even our sex. I had tried to hang on to what we had had in brief moments during those the spring and summer nights when Lola was a tiny puppy, when she was not biting or yanking or escaping but chasing her ball or snuggling up close as we, drunk on red wine, did the same on our Minnesota deck, hands clasped, dreams half-articulated to murmured assent.

Against all obvious data, I willed myself into believing we'd "get back" to that connection. Now, in that January night, the winter dark of our bedroom dimly lit by the yellow light hanging on the building next door, my life in its actuality came into focus: a series of logistical arrangements about our wedding, our apartment, and mostly, our dog. In the shape of cowering Lola, I saw my own desperate and overriding emotion, a hope that it just wouldn't get any worse. My family hated him, my friends no longer wanted to be around us, now the dog was taking cover.

Even Lola didn't want to be the glue that held us together.

WHEN I LEFT CLARKE the next month, it was almost two years to the day after Mandy died. When I left Clarke, I fled to Boston to stay with friends for a week. We negotiated the end of our life together—emotional, financial, and canine—long distance, mostly over e-mail. I avoided phone contact because the calls left me doubled over in hysterics. He wrote me about Lola: "You are an important part of her life, so I hope you will find a way to honor that." The line brought back, in full-flashback-mode, the day that Mandy died and how Jules had rushed over to say goodbye. I remembered that just before she arrived, Clarke was sitting on the floor with Mandy's body and I was standing, silently, a pace away, alternating between looking down at them and at the cool glass of gently bubbling seltzer in my hand. Clarke had looked up at me, his arms still around her dead doggy body, and said, "I think Mandy left me because she knew I'd have you to take care of me."

Remembering that moment was a low point in a crater of week. I was heartsick all over again at the loss of our imagined future. Lola had represented our best hopes for a long and happy togetherness. I had thought we would help each other through her inevitable death, our two-person family cemented by having had her, raised her, loved her. I wrote back, "Once we figure out the people relationship and the people logistics, I'm sure we can figure out the Dania-Lola relationship. Of course, I love her very much." I was shocked at how true it was, after so many months of fighting her and her doggyness. Picking up her steaming shit, walking her, feeding her, sweeping up her hair...none of it bothered me anymore, and in fact, I missed it all already. But I had to give her up.

When I left Clarke, I insisted he keep Lola, for motivations both altruistic and not. I was desperately worried about him, and figured he could use a four-legged reason to get out of bed in the morning. I had my friends, lots of them, while he was going to be lonely in New York without me. I also couldn't afford Lola—the walking, the training, the food and toys. Moreover, as much as I loved her, I still knew her doggy schedule would prevent me from meeting my friends for happy hour. And I was going to need a lot of happy hours, a lot of human contact, to emerge intact.

When I left Clarke, I left him in Lola's care. I hoped his family or his friends—maybe even Jules—would step in and help keep him afloat the way I had been, until he was able to take care of himself.

When I left Clarke, he moved barely three blocks away and I would often run into him and Lola on their morning walk. But after he saw me with my new guy, the man I eventually married, I never bumped into them in front of my building again. It took me a while to realize, belatedly, that he had been parading Lola past my door to remind me, or perhaps himself, of all that we had lost. All that I had left. I'm not sure of much about Clarke, but I'm sure he will not call me when she dies. By then, it's my honest hope that he won't have my phone number or my e-mail address. By then, I hope, he'll have stopped Googling me. Unlike Jules, I've allowed no continuing attachments. He can't count on me the way he can still, I hope, count on her. And I can't count on him—but, as I told him over e-mail sometime during that terrible week in Boston, I hadn't been able to count on him long before that day. When I left Clarke.

SOMETIMES, when I talk about Clarke, I catch myself in a monologue that begins that way. I hear myself say, "When I left Clarke..." and I think of Jules. I think, now, I might understand her monologue better. I did know from heartbreak then, but ditching a live-in lover and a dog is a whole other deal. It was watershed moment, a radical reconfiguration of my sense of home. It's a definite before-and-after, a line that divides my life into discrete segments. Now when I think of that time she and I spent in the car, I wonder how long it took Jules to get used to living without a dog, an adjustment that was harder for me than learning to live without Clarke. I wonder how long it will take me. When it's winter, I still miss Lola's hot doggie body in my bed, her paws pushing against my legs, her rapid breathing pacing my knitting. I don't have a new puppy because my husband is not a dog person. This fact does not prevent us from having a happy life.

Oil and Water ... and Other Things That Don't Mix

Even now, years later and happily married, I still sometimes long for Lola, my first dog, my first canine love. I wonder whether she's mellowed now that she's fully grown. I sometimes daydream about seeing her. When I do, it's always the same fantasy, one I dreamt up after I moved out of my and Clarke's Manhattan neighborhood and foreclosed the possibility of ever again randomly or "randomly" running into my dog and my ex. In my fantasy, I'm at a dog park—a specific one, Baltimore's Patterson Park, a place I was with Clarke and Lola once when we were happier, or at least still trying hard to be happy.

In my fantasy, I live in Baltimore with my actual husband and my imaginary toddler. My toddler and I are out for a walk, heading across the park to buy me a coffee and her a juice. Lola recognizes me and comes bounding over. She gives me a friendly whack of her tail, the tail I used to call a weapon of mass destruction, because she would sweep it across the coffee table and send everything skittering to the floor. Clarke is there, in the background, out of focus, calling her. He doesn't recognize me, because, in my fantasy, I'm hugely pregnant. My toddler is fascinated by the dog. Lola runs in circles and barks happily. My muscle memory intact, I perform the hand signal for "sit" that the trainer taught us, and I say it, "Sit!" firmly but not in the "stern voice" I never mastered. Uncharacteristically (hey, it's my fantasy), she sits, she stays. She was always gentle with children and so I show my daughter to how to pet Lola's head, gently. My toddler smiles up at me, trusting me to guide her palm to contact with the dog's head, and giggles at the hairy texture of Lola's milk-chocolate-brown fur. Lola licks her, and my toddler squeals. Clarke calls her, and Lola turns and runs.

A Litany of Bruises
By Dallas Woodburn

MY MOTHER used to tell me that if ever a man hit me, I should end it right away. "Those kind of men have a way about them, Sarah," she would say. "They'll try to worm their way back into your life. Don't you let them. If a man ever hits you, you run away and don't glance back even once."

But somehow, despite my mother's warnings, I ended up with Mark.

When I was a girl, I wondered why women ever stayed with men who beat them. But Mark never beat me—"beat" is too strong a word. He'd hit me a couple times, in a way almost bordering on affection, and he only did it when he came home drunk. To make him stop, I'd unbutton his pants and we'd have at it. The next morning, he'd bring me flowers and hot coffee with hazelnut syrup, my favorite, from the corner café. And that made it all right. I could withstand a few slaps or sloppy, drunken punches for a Mark who would sweetly bring me flowers and coffee in bed.

Lately, though, it's gotten worse. We've only been married two years, and he's already grown tired of me. I think he's seeing someone else. Four or five weeks ago, as he leaned in to kiss my forehead when he came home from the office, I thought I smelled a musky perfume on his sport coat. I was feeling brave that day, so I had asked him about it. I can still hear the petulance in my voice, the shrill, naked fear, the way the question didn't sound at all casual and offhand as it had in my head. Mark didn't say anything at first, just laughed. And then, suddenly, he slapped my cheek. I was surprised how much it stung.

"Why would you say something like that?" he asked, eyes flashing. "Why don't you trust me? I hate that you don't trust me."

The next time he came home smelling of musky perfume, I didn't say anything.

Even so, even when I'm silent, he still finds reasons. Actually, he no longer needs a reason. Which I guess is proof that things have gotten worse. I wake up in the morning with bruises blooming up and down my arms like tea bags slowly soaking their color into water. And I can't stop him anymore by unbuttoning his pants. He must have someone else, or he simply no longer wants me. We haven't had at it in months.

He hits me and I curl into myself, sweeping my mind blank with a chalkboard eraser, waiting numbly for it to end. When I wake up now, there is no coffee and no flowers waiting in apology, just his bulky form snoring on the couch, mouth open, bits of food stuck to his shirt. Each time I tell him, "That happens again, I'm calling the police." I make my voice firm. I remember what my mother told me. Each time Mark nods and looks down at his untied shoes.

But then he comes home drunk again, and it happens again, and I do not call the police. I never do. Mark and I both know this.

AND THEN, on a warm, bruiseless April afternoon, the phone rings. The woman on the other end tells me, in a very calm and measured voice, that my mother has died. She was shopping for groceries at the supermarket and collapsed in the cereal aisle. I am suddenly very conscious of my unsteady knees and the weight of the bulky cordless phone in my hand. The calm voice struggles to tether me to the earth with concrete statements and medical terms: massive myocardial infarction, external defibrillator, nothing we could do, I am so sorry for your loss...

"Mrs. Benson? Are you still there?"

My mouth is dry. "What? Yes–yes."

"I am so sorry for your loss."

"Thank you." I arrange to pick up my mother's things from the hospital the next day. The calm voice says there will be someone on hand to help me with the funeral arrangements.

IT'S NO SURPRISE when Mark comes home drunk, nor is it unexpected when he grabs me roughly by the arm and slaps my face because I didn't have dinner waiting for him. The difference is that this night, tears spring to my darkened eyes and slide down my swollen cheeks. "Stop crying!" he shouts. "Stop it!" And he hits me again, harder.

But I don't stop crying. I can't. I'm still crying two hours later when, eying Mark's passed-out form on the couch, I creep out to the garage, phone in hand, and do what I promised my mother I would do the first time it happened.

"I have an incident to report," I tell the police. "My husband is beating me."

MARK is still drunk when the police arrive. He shouts and curses and even tries to punch one of them—the tall one with ginger hair—who in the end manages to click the handcuffs around my husband's wrists.

I thought I would feel relieved, liberated, safe. Instead, I feel hollow and afraid, removed from myself. I am a child, on ballet-slippered tip-toes, peeking through the crack of a door, watching the climax of my life unfold—not really understanding what is happening or why, but instinctively knowing it is important.

Oil and Water ... and Other Things That Don't Mix

I am strangely sad to see Mark being taken away like a criminal. He's not always this way, I want to tell someone. Yesterday, he sat right there at the kitchen table and did the crossword. It had been a pleasant morning. He asked me for a four-letter word for "finished with" and I, for once, knew the answer: USED. "It fits!" he'd exclaimed, filling in the missing letters with his felt-tip pen, smiling at me like a schoolboy who's gotten a spelling test back with a perfect grade.

Now, I watch from the doorway as Mark is shoved into the back of the police car. He looks up at me, just before the door is closed, and in his eyes flash the same accusation of betrayal I find in my own eyes when I gaze into the mirror.

KNOWING Mark, I don't think it was an accident. I'm not sure exactly how he did it. Maybe he brought his handcuffs down on the police officer's head. Maybe he covered the driver's eyes and refused to let go. I don't think he would have been able to break free of the handcuffs, but perhaps he did—perhaps they never fully clicked into place, he was thrashing around so much when they arrested him—and maybe he reached up front and grabbed the wheel, purposefully steering the car off the road into the ditch.

I don't think Mark was trying to kill himself. I don't think he wanted to kill anyone else, either. It wasn't an accident, but I don't think he meant to do any lasting harm. Mark wasn't one for permanent damage; he inflicted bruises that healed, at least outwardly. I don't think he expected the car to flip over three times and ram into a tree.

I keep thinking of the tall, ginger-haired police officer, the way he didn't seem like a police officer. He was too gentle. I keep remembering the way he dodged Mark's drunken blows and managed to slip the handcuffs around my husband's wrists without needing to hit him, not once. The way he didn't force

Mark to bend over but let him walk out of the house, straight-backed and dignified. Not that Mark possessed any dignity, but the ginger-haired police officer let him pretend. "I'm sorry about this, ma'am," the officer had told me as they escorted Mark out our front door.

I'm the sorry one, I had want to tell him. I am so sorry for your loss. I never expected that calling the police to report my litany of bruises would turn my abusive husband into a murderer. Much less, the murderer of a ginger-haired gentleman with a loving wife and three adorable, freckle-faced children.

But it did.

I CONSIDER getting dressed, but instead spend fifteen minutes making tea and another half an hour watching it turn cold in my mug, steam rising in lazy wisps, and then dissipating altogether. I end up leaving the house in my shabby housecoat and sweatpants, hair still mussed in its ponytail from sleeping. Though I hadn't slept at all. I had slumped onto my side of the bed, face pressed against the pillow and legs pulled up to my chest in the fetal position and watched the minutes pass on Mark's digital clock. When the phone rang, at 2:13 a.m., I wasn't surprised. I was relieved, almost as if I had been waiting for it without knowing.

Driving into the morning mist, I don't think about what I'll say to Mark when I see him, stretched out in a hospital bed with a brace on his neck and an IV needle in his arm. I don't think about the Grief Counselor waiting to help plan my mother's funeral. I don't think about the ginger-haired police officer, whose last act had been my doing.

What I think about is how I finally did it, but I didn't actually do it for me at all. I couldn't do it for me, and I couldn't do it for my mother, my brave, little, furious mother who told me to run and run and not look back.

But I could do it for this pinprick inside me, for the blue cross on the pregnancy test in a drugstore's toilet stall yesterday afternoon. No longer was Mark hitting me and me alone. My mother forgot to tell me the most important part: running away never really fits until you have something to run towards.

Daylight cracks open the sky. I pass the turn-off to the hospital and keep driving.

Excerpts from *Bastard Husband: A Love Story*

By Linda Lou

TODAY I put my bastard husband on a plane to the other side of the world. He wasn't always a bastard. He was perfect and I loved everything about him. Well, almost everything. I may never see him again.

There were no last hugs, not even a half-hearted effort to put a few words together. I could have easily come to a rolling stop at the airport and pushed his ass into the passenger drop-off lane; instead, I parked in the short-term lot and stayed with him throughout the check-in process, hoping, I suppose, to see some flicker of caring on his part. But we plodded through the terminal in silence, and when we reached the security checkpoint where I could go no further, he looked in my direction and said, "See ya."

See ya?

As he walked away and found his place in line, I gave him the finger, right there in the crowded airport. I do that a lot in public places, usually while trying to coax him off a barstool and away from a new-found friend with tavern wisdom far more compelling than anything I have to offer. Hell, I gave him the finger two nights ago in the Green Valley Ranch Casino when I couldn't pry him from the poker table before he marched off on his own because "the dealer gypped him." He is never aware of my gesture, and although it's not my most mature practice, I do enjoy an adolescent satisfaction in my passive-aggressive

143

retaliation. It's just that it wouldn't have killed him to give me a proper good-bye.

See ya?

Now home from the airport, I furiously snatch random items—his *Far Side* coffee cup, shaving apparatus left in the bathtub, nice LL Bean slippers I'd given him one Christmas—and stuff them into an old duffel bag. He shipped out twenty-five boxes of his crap before we moved here, so there aren't too many reminders left. I don't want to see any evidence of his existence; my raging blood pressure is proof enough.

I toss the bag into the front closet and stand in the middle of the living room, chest heaving. The apartment looks nice. You'd never know we've been here only six days—pictures on the wall and everything. This was our third move in less than two years; we've gotten good at it. We've had a fair division of labor—each time he's set up the computer, TV, and anything involving wires or assembly of any kind while I put together the kitchen and bathroom. We had fun determining the best arrangement for the furniture and in no time the place looked like we'd lived in it forever.

I like it here. The vibe is comfortable and funky, with our Native American sand paintings, statues, candles, and rocks we've collected from our road trips throughout the West. From both the kitchen and the spare bedroom I can see the entire Las Vegas valley—Sunrise Mountain about ten miles straight ahead, the Strip thirteen miles to the northwest. Palm trees, sunshine...I feel like I'm on vacation, or on a business trip, living in a Marriott Residence Inn. At night there's an explosion of lights.

Glancing around the room, I enjoy a momentary sense of contentment. My eyes rest on a panoramic photo of the two of us on top of Medicine Bow Mountain outside Laramie, Wyoming. We stand smiling, arm in arm. I look thin and tan, which no doubt is why I display the picture, and he has a cute and happy expression. I've always loved his looks.

Not now, though. I scowl at his image, give him the finger, and return to my anger.

These past few days have sucked. I know he's been deliberately trying to piss me off, probably hoping he might press me to the point where I'd scream, *"Don't come back!"* Though the sentiment certainly bubbled—nearly erupted—no way would I give him such an easy out. He will never be able to say, "This is what you wanted. You told me not to come back."

I think of last Wednesday night when he left the apartment at about 11:30 to go out for cigarettes, and then called at 9:30 the next morning from the Fiesta, a casino less than a mile up the road. He'd been playing poker all night.

"So how much did you win?" I asked, pretending to ignore the overwhelming odds that he didn't.

"About $200." So proud, he was. I later found ATM receipts revealing just how much it took to win that $200.

I said I'd come get him, and for a moment he seemed to consider my offer since the late May sun can be brutal here, especially, I imagine, if you've been up all night and are hung over as hell. He said he would walk home. Of course, he didn't say *when*.

At about 8:30 that evening, I went to see if I could collect him. I walked through the casino, under the strings of multicolored lights, through the rows of ding-ding-dinging Lucky Sevens and Deuces Wild machines, and approached a lady in a purple vest behind one of the poker tables.

"By any chance, have you seen a chubby guy with an accent lately?" I asked.

Her sympathetic smile and the wisdom under her beehive hairdo said, *Let me guess: he was only running down to the Speedy Mart for cigarettes.*

"I know who you mean," she replied. Sure she does—bartenders and poker dealers always know who I mean. "I saw him not too long ago. He's probably still around somewhere."

Within minutes I found him at one of the bars, appearing surprisingly sober. His eyes looked tired, like my father's in the weeks before he died.

I couldn't get him to budge. Though his bar buddy was clearly full of shit, evidently the thought of going home was less appealing than listening to some drunken blowhard. I left alone, in familiar defeat.

A few hours later he finally trudged in, with that "I'm a grown man; I can stay out all night if I want" defiance that made me want to slap his face. He has yet to grasp the concept that when you're married there is another person in the equation.

I may never see him again. I am too angry to be sad.

I WAKE UP on my side of the bed. My first day alone in Las Vegas. No job, no friends, no bastard husband. I don't know exactly what to do today, but whatever it is, I don't feel like doing it. I'll lie here awhile longer. Whatever.

After a day of serious moping around and watching my entire daytime television line-up, I force myself to go pick up one of those arts and entertainment magazines you see in convenience stores. I need to find out what's going on around here; I have to do something.

Wow—does it really take only 15 minutes to walk to the Speedy Mart and back?

Scanning through the listings in the "Meetings" section, I decide to check out a divorce support group, listed between "Cross-Dressers of Las Vegas" and "Friends and Family of Incarcerated People." And I think *I* have problems.

The meeting is held in a preschool room of a Methodist church on West Flamingo and I am relieved to get there without a problem. I love to explore a new city, but hate trying to find everything. Typically I overshoot my destination, and then have to make a U-turn, which usually prompts someone to lean on the horn or give me the finger. What goes around, comes around, right?

I take a seat in the circle and think I cannot believe I am sitting in a divorce support group.

I am sitting in a divorce support group.

Sometimes you catch yourself at different points in life and think, "I am doing *what*?" and you wonder how you got there, but when you piece it all together you realize there are simply no mysteries. And sometimes, like when you're in a plane 30,000 feet above the earth, it's best not to put too much thought into exactly where you are. This is one of those times.

The facilitator is a kind looking man named Chuck. Tattoos adorn each arm, not the intricate artwork I've seen on Harley riders, more like blurred reminders of bygone wartime service. He goes over the rules for the new people. That would be me.

"This meeting is a forum for sharing your emotions about the loss of a relationship," Chuck begins. "Everything you say is confidential, and we ask you don't repeat anything you hear outside this room. We rent the space here—we are not affiliated with the church."

Thank God.

Chuck continues, "This Tuesday night group is for people going through a divorce or separation from a significant relationship. The widowed group meets on Thursday nights."

Those lucky widows. Sorry, but I believe every woman who's unwillingly blown out the last candle of her marriage has wondered, "Wouldn't it be easier if he simply dropped dead?" Yes, anyone who says she'd rather explain the details of yet another failed marriage than bask in the sympathy of widowhood is a goddamn liar. Especially if you wanted to kill the bastard anyway, and believe me, I've been tempted.

I remember one night in Laramie, in our first house out

West. He was stinkin' drunk and acting like such an asshole; the open door to the basement stairs downright teased me. All it would have taken was one good shove to send him flying into a heap on the concrete floor below.

That's not the kindest thought I've ever had. Especially about someone I love.

Chuck starts the meeting by asking each of us to rate our "emotional barometer" on a scale of one to ten, with one meaning you're in the shitter, and if you're a ten, you're on Cloud Nine (my words, not his). I say I am a five. Next, he calls on us randomly to "share."

A perfectly coiffed woman tells us her name is Mona and that she is newly separated after twenty-seven years of marriage. Her expression curdles at the mention of her husband's name. Another lady, also named Linda and who also has crappy hair, was married over thirty years to someone I don't think she liked too much, either. Still, this must suck for them to have their lives change so drastically after such a long time. It sucks for me and it's been only two and a half years. Most everyone here seems to be reacting to someone else's decision to leave the relationship; they're the ones who've been dumped, to put it less sensitively. I guess the ones who did the dumping are happily out there on their own, maybe with their new playmates. Or maybe they're on the other side of the world drinking themselves to death.

I half listen as each broken heart exposes itself; the other half of me prepares the monologue for when it's my turn. I should at least try to make it interesting. A petite woman with what looks to be a Toni home perm currently has the floor.

"Then the washing machine broke... I think it needed a new belt...or maybe it was the motor... and I had to call Tommy to come look at it...I didn't want to see him... but I had to wash my clothes..."

Time goes in reverse as she drones away, and I am convinced

she belongs in the Thursday night widows' group, for surely her husband died of boredom.

Chuck calls on me next. I notice the "Absolutely No Swearing" sign hanging from the ceiling. This will be a challenge.

I open with, "I'm Linda. I just moved to Las Vegas one week ago. I have no husband, no job, and you people are my only friends."

Everybody laughs at my pathetic truth.

"Yesterday my husband left for New Zealand, where he's from. Sorry, I still call him my husband, but we actually got divorced before we left Utah, where we lived for the past year. He still has his job there at the university; he's off for the summer. He doesn't know if he's coming back to the States or not. The only reason we got divorced was in case he doesn't.

"He's my second husband," I continue, "and...he's a drinker. I guess he's what you'd call a 'functioning alcoholic,' but he could be lured into any addictive behavior—gambling, cigarettes, eating. He's a 'fill-in-the-blank-aholic.'"

A few people laugh, some nod.

"Not a workaholic, though," I continue, with my own stupid chuckle. "What I mean is he doesn't have to try. He's brilliant, really." *On paper*, I want to add—as the word "brilliant" leaves my lips I remember the day he thought he was going blind in one eye. Yeah, the guy with the Ph.D. had lost a lens in his glasses. The thought makes me smile. "I still love him very much," I add.

That's enough for now.

The people in this circle are the only ones who know we're divorced; I haven't yet told my family and friends back home. I dread the task, though certainly I've let some details slip that would indicate things are not quite as rosy as I'd like them to believe. It's best to keep this to myself; the concern in their eyes would be unbearable, even over the telephone. No one wants to hear you've slept in a closet to hide from your husband's return from the pub, though sometimes that's the only way to get a good night's sleep.

My story to the outside world is that we moved to Las Vegas because the job opportunities would be better for me here. He'll continue to teach during the week in Utah, driving up on Monday mornings and staying in a cheap motel during the week. And in real life, that is our plan, if he does come back. It's probably not a good plan, since I can already tell Las Vegas is not the best place for a guy who can spend twenty-three straight hours in a casino. Or maybe it's the perfect place for someone like that, just lousy for his wife.

YOU HAVE *a big ass and your kids are brats*. That's what I wanted to say to the woman in front of me at Walgreen's this morning.

He's been gone two weeks. I'm so depressed and miserable, even Jesus would cross the street if he saw me coming. So in a perverse attempt to see just how far I can press the despondency, I'm heading to the mall to shop for a bathing suit.

After sifting through the racks, I enter the dressing room with eight options in hand, holding particular hope for a cute little number with diamond-shaped cutouts strategically running down the sides. Between the hanger and my body, however, something goes horribly wrong and the thought that security personnel might be watching through a one-way mirror sends me into a panic. Not that I'm concerned about modesty; I would just hate to gross anyone out.

I decide on a simple black two-piece (not a bikini, for God's sake) that actually doesn't look too bad. I haven't worn anything but a maillot for the past 25 years, but I've seen what other women wear poolside at my apartment complex and I think I can get away with this.

Excerpts from *Bastard Husband: A Love Story* - Linda Lou

The minute I get home, I try on my purchase again to make sure I didn't gain weight in transit and that the mirrors in the store didn't make me look dubiously thinner. I think sometimes they do, so you'll buy stuff.

I'm still safe. The bottom is cut high enough to hide most of the stretch marks on my stomach and the bra top makes my boobs look a little bigger than they actually are. I don't look bad. Hell, I look pretty good.

There's still about an hour until *Guiding Light* comes on, so I have time for a swim. This is my life: get up, meditate, do some yoga, read the paper and do both crosswords, give his picture the finger every time I walk by it, go to the pool, and then at two o'clock I watch my soap while eating two bowls of mocha almond fudge ice cream. I kind of like this routine, especially since at some point I'm going to have to get a job.

I wrap a mini-sarong around my waist, tighten my abs and strut myself down to the pool. As I approach the gate, I pass a woman about my mother's age and a little blond girl in a frilly pink bathing suit with matching flip-flops. I smile at them with the confidence that comes when you know you're looking good.

The woman smiles back and points to me. "Look, Emily!" she singsongs. "That lady looks like your other grandmother!"

Did she say I look like somebody's grandmother?

Well, I am, in fact, a grandmother, but I do NOT look like one. In good lighting, I can pass for 39, which is much too young to be a grandmother, even in Las Vegas.

Jesus Christ, lady, do you have any idea how fragile my self-esteem is? My dipsomaniac husband left ME because he needs to "return to his homeland" and I don't know if he's coming back or not, and if he doesn't, I'll have to start dating again and break in a new guy, in which case, the situation will eventually lead to nudity—maybe with the lights on—which quite honestly I wouldn't have worried about until you had to make that stupid fucking comment.

Glaring at the bitch, I say to little Emily, "Your other grand-mother must be hot."

THOUGH SHE WASN'T particularly religious, when I was growing up, my mother for some reason started nearly every sentence with *"JESUS CHRIST!"* And, like all mothers, when she was really mad she would yell his full name as listed on his birth certificate, which evidently is *"JESUS CHRIST ALL-GODDAMN MIGHTY!"* So in our house there was no associating Jesus with the all-loving, all-forgiving being worshipped around the world. No, the sound of his name was generally a prelude to an ass kicking.

It's a miracle I can even think about walking into a church since the words "Jesus Christ" should trigger some type of post-traumatic stress reaction, but it's Sunday morning and I'm trying out a "holistic" place I saw advertised in yesterday's newspaper.

Like many people, I end up in church only when someone gets married or dies and that's where they're holding the festivities. This is the first time I'm attending on a Sunday morning without being forced, which surely is a reflection of my current depressed mental state. Plus, I might meet some cool people at a metaphysical-type of church, so what the hell.

I turn off East Sahara into a strip mall housing a bizarre collection of storefronts. There's the Japanese Community Church, some crazy-looking type of Super-Jesus church, the Wig Outlet, and a nightclub offering Korean karaoke. I spot my destination—the University Church Institute.

I am going to a church next door to the Firearms Training Academy.

I'm a little early; I have to allow plenty of driving time in case I get lost. The man at the door smiles and hands me a program. I'm relieved no other church people rush over to welcome me. I

Excerpts from *Bastard Husband: A Love Story* - Linda Lou

take a seat in the back and think how I hated going to church as a kid. Every Sunday, my sister Lori and I were sentenced to the 10 a.m. service at Calvary Methodist Church with our father's parents, Nana and Papa.

No doubt my mother was psyched to get rid of us for a couple of hours, leaving her home with the younger kids, who were pretty much under control. She didn't have to go to church with us because she's Catholic, which I later understood was a major upset in the family since my grandparents were Nixon lovers who had no use for anyone the same religion as JFK.

Not that Mom was a good Catholic—she never went to Mass or anything, which was fine with me because frankly the last thing I needed was another church to be dragged to. And of course, my father conveniently worked on Sunday mornings, which not only excused him from church, but got him away from all the kids and the Jesus-screaming wife.

Nana and Papa were awesome grandparents, the kind who'd cut the crust off our bread and let us stay up as late as we wanted when we slept at their house. They were in with the Methodist "in crowd." Nana was active in the women's craft group that made stuff out of egg cartons and plastic Clorox bottles to sell at the monthly rummage sale. Papa was an usher and they let him collect money when it was that time in the service.

I felt a little guilty about hating church, since they were so into it, but even as a 10-year-old, I felt terribly phony sitting there and found the worshipping concept a bit eerie. All the hymns and the stained glass images of Jesus and his friends kind of freaked me out. To this day, I'm uncomfortable with religious music and pictures of religious figures, although I'm sure they'd be very nice if you knew them.

How I fought with my mother every Sunday morning. In retrospect, I realize she was just trying to satisfy the in-laws, since she was only marginally on their good side anyway for being Catholic and all. But church was not for me. Sometimes to fight my boredom, I'd fill in my name and address on the little cards on the back of the pew, not realizing I was requesting home visits from the minister. After my mother figured out why he kept showing up at the house unexpectedly—and calling her "Linda"—I didn't have to go to church anymore.

And now here I am, sitting in church of my own free will. This place isn't too scary. This strip mall church has chairs instead of pews, and instead of stained glass windows, there are framed pictures on the wall, which my eyes avoid. I hope there's no music.

The service begins and a distinguished looking gray-haired man starts speaking. He's an eloquent communicator and hardly ever mentions Jesus. I'm pleased to be here even though the air is stale.

The topic of today's sermon is "How to Be a Compatible Person." Although I fancy myself as already quite compatible—*I'm* not the one with the problems—I'm open to suggestions. Pastor Man directs us to a list of affirmations in our program, which he encourages us to recite during our personal meditation time at home.

"I radiate peace, love, and healing to others." Closing my eyes I imagine Bastard Husband in New Zealand, happy to be in his homeland. I cannot bring myself to radiate peace and love. No, he's the one who should be sitting here learning how to be a more compatible person.

"I am able to sense another person's needs." That's easy—obviously he needs help. But my sense of superiority ends with the next thought that jumps into my brain from nowhere: he needs love. The truth I feel in that sobers me. I offer a defensive response to my own revelation: No one loves him like I do, and that hasn't been enough.

"I am compassionate when someone is truly suffering." I

154

Excerpts from *Bastard Husband: A Love Story* - Linda Lou

think of the mornings I'd find him asleep at the kitchen table slumped over the incriminations of the night before: a 12-pack of empties he'd knocked over, perhaps a half-eaten chicken carcass, a crushed pack of cigarettes beside a full ashtray, some heavy metal CDs, and scribbles of philosophical insights he could conjure up only while under the charm of alcohol. I'd turn off the light above the sink and steer him to the bedroom, where he'd snore for another hour or two before emerging with the look that acknowledged another broken promise. No one would choose a life of perpetual guilt, the result of one's own collapsed willpower. I know he suffers.

I put on my sunglasses to hide my eyes. I wish I had a Kleenex.

The ushers pass the collection plates, and I'm happy to give. Then things take a dreadful turn as we are asked to hold the hands of the persons on either side of us. I reluctantly link with two complete strangers, imagining the transfer of germs. And, *shit*, they want us to sing.

"Let there be peace on earth and let it begin with me," everyone starts in. Everyone but me. Note to self: if I ever come back, sneak out before the singing starts. I'm not one for audience participation. Why can't I just sit here?

After the service some of us check out the New Age bookstore set up in a room off the sanctuary. I scan the titles, many of which I already own—*Embracing the Beloved, Personal Power Through Awareness, Divine Guidance*—and wish they carried the book I'd really like to read: *Smack Some Sense into that Bastard Husband.*

A pleasant man strikes up a conversation. His name is Danny, he's from Springfield, Missouri, and is considering moving to Vegas. He's a healer, he tells me.

"I'm going to stay for the singles group at 1:00," he says. "How about you? Are you single?"

Am I single? I respond with a vacuous look. On paper, I am.

But no, I'm still attached. I love him, I want him to stop drinking, and I want him to come back to me. Although maybe I'd have better luck meeting someone in church instead of a bar.

"No, I'm married," I tell him, presenting my wedding ring as proof. "My husband's visiting his family in New Zealand."

Small talk ensues. *Oh, yes, I've been there. It's very nice. He's a professor; he has the summer off. He'll be back in August.* How accomplished and exotic sounding, and no one has to know the unpleasant details.

After all these years, I'm still a phony in church.

I DECIDE to call him after dinner—which is a bowl of cereal—and early into the conversation I know I've made a mistake. His polite but distant tone annoys me.

"I have a friend who's looking for a housemate, so I'll be moving out of Mum's," he says, as if he's reporting the weather. I interpret that arrangement to mean he won't be returning to the northern hemisphere. *Did you quit your job in Utah?* I want to ask, but respond with a deep breath and a simple, "Oh."

Goddamn him. I try to keep it under the surface, but as we speak I can hear the bitchiness seep into my voice, and when you hear it yourself, you know the other person does too. To think that today in church I actually tried to be loving and compassionate. Now I couldn't care less about his stupid healing. *Fine, stay out of my life, you fucking drunk.*

Jack Black Flag
By John Klawitter

"WOMEN are trouble, anyway," Harvey reflected with that familiar, knowing hint of old Jewish wisdom rising in his voice. "But when they're already crying before you meet them—that's *real* trouble."

Goldfine and I had been walking along the tarmac at the side of the Tan Son Nhut Airport runway. Harvey was a Spec 4, and I was a newly minted Spec 5; having just been awarded the first curved stripe over the golden eagle on my upper sleeve. We were walking from Davis Station to the White Shack, a stout cinderblock building where I ran a small section that decrypted and translated covert Viet Cong radio intercept. "Small section" summed it up. At the time, I had Goldfine and Raymer, and that was about it.

This was in February of 1965, the "dry time," and so the weather was actually pleasant, not too tepid, and sometimes even sporting a little breeze that blew most of the smog haze from a million Saigon charcoal burners out over the South China Sea. It was late morning and the flapping Hueys were long gone. Air traffic was light, just an occasional war bird lifting off for a carrier somewhere out on the South China Sea, or to drop a little napalm somewhere in the jungle highlands.

Harvey and I were on the noon-to-eight shift, "the swing," as they call it in the army. Having a little time to kill, we had stopped off at a "Westernized" fast food joint that featured milk shakes and massive air conditioning. The weeping woman was young, maybe twenty years old. She sobbed softly to herself while she took our order, and then stood over the shake blenders, her shoulders slumped in grief.

"On the other hand," Harvey observed, "A set of knockers the size of hers I haven't seen this side of Honolulu."

There was no question about the knockers. She was built mighty fine for a Vietnamese woman, who tended on the slight and willowy side. Chinese, maybe, I was thinking to myself. But Harvey was already in action.

"*Co...,*" he said, raising his voice, "*Co manh gioi, khong?*" Harvey never lacked for balls, but his Vietnamese wasn't all that great. Like me, he was better pouring through Hoa's Viet-English dictionary than actually talking to the natives. I knew that, in saying hello, he'd just about maxed out his linguistic skills. But it didn't matter. The girl wailed and rushed into a back room, leaving the blenders unattended. A glum, middle-aged *ba* finally had to take over and bring us our soupy milkshakes.

"She's all yours, *Ong Kha.*" Harvey shrugged. "Meet you at the Shack." With that, he set down his warm shake, put on his olive stovepipe hat and gave me a little farewell finger roll. In another moment he was out the door. This was going to be an epic day; one to go down in military history—Goldfine was actually going to get in to work before I did.

I sat down with my shake and brought out my twin books. I was in the heart of my Francophile phase, and I was slowly churning my way through Camus's *La Peste* with paperback copies in both English and French. I sat at one of the Formica tables and slowly moved my six inch ruler down the page. It was the season of the wet in Oran, a city in Algeria; rats lay bleeding in the streets and things in general were going sour.

After a while, the girl returned from the back room, daubing at her eyes with a tissue. They were large and soft eyes, and I thought her extraordinarily lovely, even in this city of beautiful women. She moved out from behind the counter and for a moment it seemed like she was going to come over to my table. She hesitated, and I smiled, hoping I was displaying friendly encouragement rather than admiration for her breasts.

The old *ba* behind her gave a sharp, hawking sound, something like a throat clearing warning, but the girl ignored her. She came closer and sat daintily across the table from me.

"I did not mean to scorn your friend."

"It's alright," I said. "He's used to it."

Her tears started again, and it was a moment before she could continue.

"Forgive it to me. I am in bad luck," she said. "Bad things have come."

Her hand moved across the table and brushed against mine. That touch reminded me of the soft feathers of a small bird's wing. I wished she'd touch me like that again. Or perhaps her hand might even linger, pausing in some existentially satisfactory way with a light, stroking movement against my own. Camus has that effect on youthful naiveté.

I came back to reality with a start. The old *ba* talked to someone in the back room. She sounded angry. After a moment, an ARVN air force lieutenant appeared in the doorway. He was a lightweight, probably topping the scale at 110, but his moustache, worn dapper in the Nguyen Cao Ky style, was bristling. He crossed his arms, and twisted his lip in our direction in the Vietnamese way of showing scornful disapproval.

The girl jumped up from the table as if to run away. But then, wonder of wonders, that soft touch again on my arm, this time a light caress.

"We meet here tomorrow morning at this time," she whispered.

"What's your name?"

"N-Nhut," she said. "Co Nhut. And you name?"

"Jack."

"Jack," she repeated with a wan smile. She pronounced it *Zac*. *"Giac co den,"* she added. And then she gave the old *ba* and the *zip* lieutenant a dirty look and retreated behind the counter.

I practically sprinted to my gunmetal gray desk at the White Shack, where I dove into Hoa's. *Giac co den* meant "Jack Black Flag," the Vietnamese expression for "pirate." I smiled, thinking that was nice, in a quaint way.

I sighed and set aside thoughts of her sugarplum breasts. There was a war to be won. The normally challenging work seemed dull and boring, somehow remote from my new reality. I translated: SAW TWO INVADER GANGSTERS YESTERDAY. And then I broke a nasty little code and translated: BONG NEED MORE RICE. And another that unraveled into: SEND MORE BULLETS RIGHT AWAY. But, the truth was, my mind wasn't really on the work. My imagination was running with the Co Nhut thing. I was Jack the Pirate Lover, swooping down from my brigantine frigate to carry the pretty and vulnerable Nhut away to my love nest and shower her with doubloons, ruby necklaces, and fancy silks. The low end of the spy business can get pretty dull, even in a place like Saigon.

The next morning I showed up a half hour early for my milkshake, and that pleased her. The old *ba* and the little ARVN flyboy were nowhere around. I told myself the zip flyboy didn't worry me. Americans pretty much looked down on all ARVN officers. The Army of the Republic of South Vietnam, *Arvins* (as they were commonly called), worked for the Americans. I tried to be polite, but I had the same common perception as most other soldiers. We figured a G.I.'s stripes were worth more than any ARVN officer in the whole damn country.

Co Nhut didn't have any problems with the flyboy not being there, either. She came over to my table and sat down. Her eyes were puffy and she looked like she'd been crying again.

"You education man." She indicated my twin editions of *La Peste*. "This very good. I need education man help very bad."

"Anything. How can I help you?"

Unfortunately, at that moment a group of four Vietnamese air force officers burst in the door, glared at our little tête à tête, and headed angrily for the back room. Now we had three zip lieutenants and a captain. The captain called angrily to Nhut, nodding his head, she was to follow them. She looked angry, but she stood up all the same. She hissed at me, a low whisper I barely heard. "Tomorrow. Here. But even more early."

"Of course. I'll be here."

Again, that hand gently brushing my arm. And then, one quick kiss on my cheek and she was gone.

That night and the night that followed were filled with lusty pirate dreams. The next morning I ran naked from my barracks to the shower and back again. I dressed like I was on automatic pilot, enduring a few jeering mutters from Harvey, "...the things a guy will do for a piece of ass." Having dispensed that bit of wisdom, he squirmed around under his triple mosquito netting and put his extra pillow over his head.

It was still half-light and, as I hurried along the tarmac, a pair of SuperSabers thundered down the runway. Their tails glowed as they followed one another into the low fog, off somewhere to do the war. Swarms of olive-colored choppers rose, circled overhead, and flapped away, mostly heading north and west. An occasional dragon ship drifted in like a weary bee, returning from a night of dropping flares and spraying bullets around the perimeter of distant hamlets.

True to her word, Nhut was waiting inside the restaurant with a steaming cup of café au lait. We sat at a table and she began to pour out her heart.

It was about her brother, she said. She slowed her Vietnamese down so I could catch the general drift, and repeated in halting English when she saw I wasn't following. A few years ago, the unfortunate brother had died in an unlucky airplane crash. Now the United States wanted to dig up his body. But such a desecration of a grave violated all the laws of Buddha. The ghost, or *ma,* of the brother had to rest in peace. It was an outrage, a religious desecration. What sort of barbarians would violate the sacred rights of the dead?

"My English no so good," she said. "You can come to talk to them?"

"Where?" I asked, startled back to reality by her question. Nhut was wearing a red blouse of thin and clingy silk, and I'd been wondering if she was wearing a bra. I didn't think so.

"Downtown," she said simply.

I tried to get my brain in gear. I worked the noon-to-eight detail so it was do-able. Why not? We agreed to meet at the main gate.

This would be something new for me. I'd learned my little decoding games at the Puzzle Palace in Maryland, and I had a green Top Secret badge with my picture on one side and thumb print on the other, but in truth, I had a lot to learn about the rest of the war. I could tell you roughly where the Viet Cong cells were nestled like cancer in this or that province in South Vietnam, but I wouldn't know an actual VC unless he stuck a gun in my face.

Co Nhut showed up at the main gate wearing the innocent, white *ao dai* and black pants of a schoolgirl. The only thing missing was the conical straw hat. If it wasn't for the knowing look in her eyes and that great body, she looked like she might throw one leg over a bike and pedal off to the girl school academy.

"We go to my apartment first," she said. Hot damn! I thought. We jumped in a cab and rode off towards Cho Lon.

The apartment was clean and bright. But when I entered, a wrinkled old woman fixed me with a silent stare. All these old *ba* ladies hanging around! Nhut let out a string of sing-song. Not Vietnamese. I thought it had to be Chinese. Whatever it was, the old woman understood she'd better get out. A healthy two-year-old girl remained, staring up at us from a seat on the sofa.

"The bedroom is there," Nhut said pointing as she looked at me.

But for me, the bloom was off the rose. I couldn't see doing it—not even with *gorgeous her*—with a little kid a few feet away.

"Let's talk about what we have to do."

Nhut looked relieved, and that, in turn, took the pressure off of me. I was thinking: You never know how a woman is going to react when you turn down a roll in the hay. Looking back, I am amused how little I knew! We sat at a small kitchen table. I had brought my briefcase and took out a ballpoint pen and some paper.

"There is now one evil woman of America," she said.

This was a new complexity, an evil American woman. I wasn't sure why yet, but I felt like I was walking ankle-deep in warm and slippery butter.

"Hmmm. What did this evil woman do?"

"I already tell you," Nhut said. She sounded nettled, sorry she had confided in someone so stupid. A Vietnamese woman can cut you with a glance. *Su tu Hao Gam*, the legendary tiger ladies of Hao Gam.

"Bad Evil Lady want to disturb the *ma* of my brother."

My loose plan of action had been a roll in the hay, hear out her story, and then go to the American authorities, but here I was getting puzzling little scraps of story that didn't seem to connect.

"Why don't we just go over there and talk to them now?"

That was a mistake. Her face brightened instantly. "You do this for me?"

"Sure. Where we going?"

"I show you."

She took my arm and hustled me out the door.

JAG-MACV was the legal arm of the U.S. military in Vietnam. It was on the second floor of an ordinary-looking building on Le Loi Street. A pimply clerk-type E-3 gave me a sour look as he shoved a sign-in clipboard at us. "What are you doing here?"

"I'm with her."

"Oh, *her*. You have an appointment?"

"We no need no appointment!" Co Nhut's voice went up a notch. The E-3 eyed her warily, and then retreated to an office behind his desk. After a moment, he returned with a U.S. Army colonel in tow.

"Hello, I'm Colonel Greene." He was about 55, a tall, professional-looking fellow with curly gray hair.

I was in civvies and unsure of the protocol, but I decided to salute, anyway. The colonel waved off my gesture. "At ease, son. How'd you get involved in this?"

My heart sank. *Involved.* I wasn't just helping a native girl, I was *involved in something*. "Well, sir, I'm stationed at Tan Son Nhut, and—"

"Unit?"

"3rd RRU, sir. Army Security Agency."

"Clearance?"

"Top Secret Codeword."

"Badge?"

The colonel held out his hand and I reluctantly passed my badge across. We were never supposed to wear our badges downtown, and never *ever* supposed to hand them over to *anybody*. The colonel gave the plastic square to the E-3, who immediately got on the phone, presumably to call my CO. The colonel pointed to a chair. "Sit over there. I'll talk to her first, and then to you."

"No," Co Nhut protested. "He come with me!"

"I didn't ask you, Ba Minh." The colonel's voice took on a flinty quality.

He took her arm and led her into his office. My thoughts rattled around inside my head. The colonel had called her *Ba Minh*! *Ba* meant she was married! *What was going on?*

"Sit over there," the E-3 said disdainfully, confident I was going to catch a pile of *merde*.

I sat down in the chair and picked up a *Newsweek*. The kids at Michigan State were staging a protest against the war. That seemed oddly unpatriotic. I couldn't concentrate on the details. I flipped through the pages. Ford had a new sportster called the Mustang. Lucky Strikes meant fine tobacco. Canadian Club was smooth as velvet. From behind the paneled wood walls, Co Nhut—*Ba Minh's*—voice was shrill. I couldn't make out the words, but the colonel's solid bass was right in there, counter-punching and undercutting her blow for blow.

After ten minutes, the door opened and Nhut marched out, a study in red-faced defiance. The colonel's cheeks were also flushed, an unhealthy crimson contrast to his gray locks. He nodded with a weary gesture.

"Okay, Spec 5. Your turn."

His office had dark, mahogany-paneled walls, and there were volumes of maroon and green law books behind glass-paneled sliding doors. I stood at ease, shifting my weight from one foot to the other. The colonel sat on the edge of his big wooden desk, fiddling with the chain on my TOP SECRET badge.

"Ordinarily, I wouldn't say two hoots to you," the colonel said. "But we checked out the clearance. As a top secret guy, I don't expect any of this will be news to you."

I felt a little shiver of anticipation. The colonel was making the mistake people who weren't deep in the spy biz often made; that clearances were broad, when actually, by their very nature, they were narrow as possible, defined only by the phrase "need to know."

"I'm going to fill you in," he continued in his weary tone. "In return, I hope you can talk some sense into your lady friend, who is nothing but trouble."

Okay..." I nodded my head slowly. "I'll do my best. But what is this stuff about her dead brother and the grave and everything?"

"Husband. It's her *husband*. There is no brother."

I blew out a deep breath. I'd just met her a few days before, and it wasn't that I loved her or anything like that. I just felt like a sucker. "Well then, what about the evil lady from America?"

The colonel gave me a clipped little laugh. "That's what she's calling her now? That would be Mrs. Harris, the wife of Captain Harris, U.S. Army, now officially deceased." He saw my puzzled look. "Look, let me start further back, and then it might make some sense. Let's just say there's an unofficial program, a sort-of joint venture between the U.S. Rangers and the CIA and ARVN Special Forces."

"A training program?"

"Something like that." He gave me an approving nod. I was ASA. I knew about these things. "What we are—what we *were*— doing was training special teams of expatriate North Vietnamese to go back into the North to stir things up. Blow up bridges and dams. Stir up trouble."

"Right," I said and nodded confidently back at him. I was ASA. Of course I knew about it.

"Our good-but-now-dead Captain Harris was a gung-ho type. Probably too old to be out in the field, but that's what he wanted, and he was good at it, so they let him, and that's what he did."

"He trained groups of sappers."

"Yes. And his little teams of black-pajama devils were *his boys*. Problem was, though it was strictly against regulations, this one time he went along with them."

"Into North Vietnam?" I exclaimed.

The colonel held up a placating hand. "Well, not exactly. They always have to be—*had* to be—strictly ARVN missions.

You know, international propaganda, world opinion, the whole mess. No U.S. involvement whatsoever. Harris knew all this, but he was so damn proud of his boys, you see. He wanted to go along in the flying boxcar, pat 'em on the ass as they jumped into the dark over the Red River Delta or wherever."

"And *did* he go?"

"Damn straight. That's what all this is about." The colonel swung a thumb towards the door and Co Nhut behind it. "This happened around Christmas, 1961. The Da Nang airport. Night. Bad weather, lots of rain. Harris finagles his way on the plane that's supposed to wing eight of his finest north past the DMZ and drop them with their black parachutes like little poison seeds on enemy soil."

"Are they effective?" I asked, the words blurting out.

The colonel fixed me with a bleak look. "Not to my knowledge. Are they?"

"Not that we've heard," I said, thinking quickly. "You ever hear any of them come back?"

"Nope. But I'm saying more than I should about that." The colonel stood and began to pace in front of me. "Anyway, none of that matters, because Harris and his merry band never got to North Vietnam. They never got anywhere. Boxcars aren't all that great in bad weather, and the damn thing slammed into an isolated hilltop a few miles north of Da Nang. Killed everybody on board."

"God! Harris too?"

The colonel nodded. He took off his wire-rimmed glasses and rubbed his eyes. "Harris too. Trouble is, the plane went down in a bad area. Hard to get to, and the terrible weather...We put some heat on, you know, to get troopers to go out there and get the bodies, but it had to be ARVN personnel, and they're not too keen on the brush war, if you've noticed."

I gave him a knowing nod. Our allies in Army of the Republic of South Vietnam had pacifist Buddhists who shot over the enemy's head, and Saigon Cowboys who hunkered down in their positions and never shot at anybody at all.

"Not that there was much left out there, anyway. The Boxcar flew smack into the rocky side of a hill, and there was nothing but charred bits and smears of bodies scattered everywhere. Nothing big enough to be identifiable. We finally brought the bits down in body bags and gave every coffin something, though they all were a little light. The way it goes, you throw in a brick or something and they don't open it up and nobody ever says anything. We buried the locals here, shipped something of Harris back, and that was that."

"Sad...but I don't get the problem."

"Well, like I said, Captain Harris had this wife. And Mrs. Harris couldn't understand how her husband died when he had a safe and cushy administrative desk job. The coffin shows up back in Kansas or wherever and somebody notices it's light and there's no way to truly identify the remains. We can't tell her the actual nature of his mission. We say something vague and unsatisfactory about a training flight, but that can't be true because he's in the friggin' Army, not the Air Force. So suddenly she's not sure he's even dead. In fact, she's more and more convinced that he's not. And we can't prove he is. So she wants *all* the coffins opened."

Here the colonel threw his hands up. "Everybody else cooperates, but your little princess out there sniffs blood."

"It's only natural," I said. "She has strong Buddhist feelings against—"

"Buddhist, my ass. She's a goddamn, money-grubbing, little bitch!" The colonel's face flushed again. "See, Ba Minh's husband was the pilot on that flight. His remains are spread in all those boxes, just like the rest of them. Only difference is, she won't let us dig him up."

"What are you going to do?"

"It beats the hell out of me, Spec 5. I've got to open that

coffin, but I don't know how to get it done. My hands are tied. I don't have the kind of money she's talking about. And if you start paying one widow, you have to pay them all."

"This is all about money?"

The colonel nodded and handed back my Top Secret badge. "Yes, it is. I'm going to have to pay her something, but I've got people leaning on me. I just hope whatever I can scrape up is enough. Look, talk some sense into her. Tell her maybe a few thousand. You'll look like the hero, because right now, she's getting burial expenses and that's it."

And then the colonel had his arm around my shoulder and was guiding me to the door. He nodded curtly to Ba Minh. In another minute we were down the stairs and out on the busy street. It was late morning and the air was already stale and hot.

She shrieked angrily for a *xe hoi* taxi and a little blue-and-cream Renault scuttled right over. Another second and we were rocketing back towards Cho Lon.

"I've got to get back to the base..."

She reached for my arm, leaning close so that the nearest of her fantastic breasts brushed against me. "No, no, no. You not leave me. I need you help *now*!"

"Look, Co—or *Ba*, I should say..."

She burst into tears. "I had to tell you that little lie. Yes, he was my husband. All people say if you know I marry, you not help me!"

"Never mind about that. Look, the colonel said he will give you some money. But he has to see that body."

"How much money?" Her eyes glittered bright and dark through her tears.

"Some thousands, even. Maybe two or three thousand."

"Three thousand, *my kim*?" *My kim* was Vietnamese for "American money."

"Yes, *my kim*."

Her face went dark and she spat on the back of the seat in

front of her, an involuntary, ugly gesture.

"It not enough!" she shouted. The cabby in the front seat cringed like he'd been shot. She grabbed the front of my striped polo shirt and started shaking me.

"You know how much wife of dead National China airman get? $25,000 *my kim*! $25,000!"

"So this isn't really about the Buddhist problems with disturbing the dead?"

"I am too a Buddhist," she shot back angrily, as if I was pond scum to suggest otherwise. "I also a business woman. America come over here, take advantage of Vietnam person. Take my husband, give a few hundred *my kim* a month to live on. How I to live on that? How I to buy clothes and raise my daughter?" she shrieked.

By now the cab had reached her address. The cabby sat hunched over his wheel.

"I don't know! Why are you asking me?" I was surprised to hear myself shouting back at her.

"You must help me."

"I've already helped you! They will give you $3,000 *my kim*!"

"*Khong phai*," she wailed. "No! You help me more!"

"What do you want me to do?"

"Come to apartment. We alone now. We be together. Then you write me letter to Mister President Johnson. He will give $25,000 *my kim*. Who know? Maybe more!"

Before meeting her, I had always thought of myself as somewhat a fool for love. I was the kind of guy who would stand on a doorstep for hours with a bouquet of wilted daisies just to make a point about romance. I was a *guitar, jug of red wine, and thou* type of fellow, motivated to go to great lengths to get it off and get it on. The quest was as important as the conquest, and I didn't go much deeper than that in my relationships with women. But in that moment, I saw something so corrupt and vile that I was overwhelmed with anger.

"You're nothing but a money-grubbing bitch!" I yelled at her in Vietnamese.

"*Sao lam*," the cabby agreed, joining the conversation. He leaned over the back of the front seat and nodded at me. "*Sao nhut!*" *The ugliest!*

She looked from one of us to the other, and for a moment I thought she would scratch us both to death with her long red fingernails. And then she opened the door and stalked away.

I never saw her again. Nor did I find out if Mrs. Harris actually identified for certain whether any of the remains belonged to her husband. I was sure Harris wasn't her real name. Whether or not I was a Top Secret guy, Colonel Greene was no fool.

The weeks passed and I moved on. I finished *La Peste* and began my slow way through the pages of *L' Homme Revolté*. I spent the rest of my tour decoding and translating covert radio messages, and finally the glorious day came when I caught the big Pan Am jet back to "the world." The war continued its slow slide into inevitable chaos and ultimate loss.

It was almost thirty years later when Jack Black Flag heard again about the exploits of the ARVN black-pajama troopers who'd been inspired to fly North and take up the uncertain life of terrorists. Some brief newspaper article, buried on page two or three of the *L.A. Times*, caught my eye. There was no real news; officially, even that long after they had been kicked out of Vietnam, the U.S. was still denying these guys existed or that such adventuring had ever place. That was the current problem; the newspaper article was about the few aging Vietnamese lucky enough to have lived through their terrorist days. These poor guys thought maybe the people who'd trained and flown them on their missions owed them some small pension, something more than "the thanks of a grateful nation."

I thought about the tantalizing lilt of Co Nhut's full breasts, with a dim reverberation of that faded and forgotten old lust, and felt a twinge of nostalgia even as I remembered once again Harvey's cynical wisdom: Women are trouble. Of course I should have known better. But it was my first experience with that sort of thing, my waking realization of how different and yet how inextricably mixed together—like oil and water—the twin concepts of love and money could be.

Lost Bay
By Nicky Wheeler-Nicholson

IN AUGUST, when the deep red of the bee balm gives way to the pale lilac and creamy ivory of the phlox in my civilized New England garden, I become obsessed with the Weather Channel. When I hear the words—"Alabama Gulf Coast" or "Florida" panhandle—it usually means a hurricane is brewing and headed towards the place I call home. I was born in Mobile, Alabama over 60 years ago. When I was a teenager, my family moved to the Eastern Shore of Mobile Bay but I spent all my summers on Perdido Bay off the Gulf of Mexico on the Alabama/Florida line. "Perdido" is Spanish for "lost" or "hidden" and from the Gulf, the bay appears to be a small inlet. Once you come through the Perdido Pass and into the bay, it opens up into a large expanse of water that is fed by smaller bays, bayous, creeks and rivers. Only a short boat ride away from all the overdeveloped condos on the Gulf, it's still pretty wild with marshy grasses, palmettos, and live oaks dripping Spanish moss from their branches hanging out over the smaller waterways. The wildlife ranges from alligators to porpoises and water birds of all sorts as well as cardinals, mocking birds, and tiny humming birds in the spring and summer. Deer saunter along the edge of the woods, as do raccoons and the armadillos that appear like small rodent crusaders about to face the infidels. Sometimes at night, in the winter, when all the summer people are gone, I've heard the almost-human screams of what can only be a Florida panther. I've watched the baby kits of foxes tumble and roll down my long drive and resisted the urge to go near them. Besides all the wildlife, Perdido Bay is also the territory of lurking tales of pirates who used the bay as a perfect hideout during the early years of Spanish, French, and English explorations along the Gulf Coast. Pirates Cove across from Orange Beach is still a good hangout for unruly buccaneers.

In later years, when our grandparents retired to the little cottage on the high pink-and-red clay bluff with the piney woods behind and the bay below, it truly became the center of our family. Granddaddy called it Siesta Bluff, establishing the guidelines for any and all activities to be commenced. It is now my Siesta Bluff. The house has been through a lot of hurricanes since it was built in the early '50's, but Hurricane Ivan the Terrible was the worst. In 2004 from our home in Massachusetts, my husband and I watched the television in horror as the graphic of the spinning wheel moved inland from the Gulf right across Perdido Key into Perdido Bay and the eye of the hurricane almost literally passed over our house. I got down there as soon as I could. My friends in Montgomery warned me not to go by myself but to stay with them so that we could all drive down and face the destruction together the following morning.

I had gotten reports from neighbors of the damage, and as far as anyone could tell, the house was okay, but no one was absolutely certain as there were several huge pines up against it and the barn-like garage appeared to be split in two. It was much worse than anything I could ever have imagined. The trees were down everywhere—as far north almost to Montgomery and all the way from there to the coast. Huge live oaks and tall pines with trunks that were three to four feet across had fallen like matchsticks and it took a lot of people with chainsaws to cut through the roads, and then cut through the mass of trees on the long drives to get to the houses on the bay. The fallen trees lined the roads were stacked like dead bodies. There was no power, no water, no cash available, no gas and few stores open anywhere for miles and miles of coastline. It was one of the worst disasters to hit our area. It took years to clean and restore and repair. I was luckier than some because Granddaddy was an engineer and he built the little house to last. I had to replace the shingles on the roof and the ceilings inside, but structurally it was sound. It may not meet *Southern Living's* standards, but it's solid and as one contractor told me, "Nicky, this house isn't going anywhere."

There was no hue and cry from the media after it was over, and it was a month or more before we ever saw FEMA. This was the year before Katrina. Six years later, I'm still cleaning fallen debris in the woods between the house and the road. We're used to being ignored by the outside world.

I thought I had weathered the worst. The storm literally changed the landscape of our lives. The thick forest of pines and live oaks, magnolias and wax myrtle all along the bluff was mostly gone, but as everyone kept saying, the bay is still there and in the best of Southern traditions, people got outside of their small social encumbrances, banded together, and helped one another out. At night, after working in the heat and humidity, we would all gather on the bluff and the breeze would come in from the Gulf, the wine uncorked and bottles of beer opened with the celebratory pops and hisses. Libations were poured all around and the stories of our childhood would begin—stories of hiking to the "sand pit" where we gathered clay and returned to fashion the inevitable ashtrays that disintegrated in the sudden sub-tropical rainstorms leaving pink stains on screen porch sills; stories of heroic exploits, "Remember the time the storm came up, and the line to the mainsail broke?" Using just the jib we had managed to make it to shore at Innerarity Point on the Florida side with the oldest among us twelve and at least seven smaller children on board. And then would come the stories of the characters long gone—Clara Ida and her antics, among them always showing up at cocktail time and staying for dinner, testing our grandfather's constant good humor and patience; going to the Dutchman, Buehday's farm to buy vegetables, who was noted for building his barn before he built his house; hanging out at Paul Shreck's, the sail maker whose exploits informed us of seas and oceans beyond our small shores—all these stories related to our lives upon the bay. And as we worked and talked, we slowly began to accept the changed landscape; we began to live with it. Some things will not come back in my lifetime, but other things survived.

Granddaddy's camellias, or *japonicas* as he called them, made it through, one of them had to be cut back a little, but the rest with trunks as big as small trees and as tall as the house were fine. The jasmine and *rosa rugosa* survived the salt burn and slowly recovered, the coral vine came back, the gardenias, and the electric neon blue French hydrangeas bloomed profusely the next year. I began to research plants that could tolerate salt and harsh winds and everyone along the bluff built a seawall to protect the eroding 30-40 foot high bluff. Since I'm not one of the ladies who lunch, it was a big expense for me. But it was well worth the sacrifice because it stabilized the bluff and I slowly began to feel that all was right with this world.

I have no business owning a second home. I don't have the discretionary income for it since I practice the trade of my father's side of the family: writer and frequent bohemian. Siesta Bluff is a huge sacrifice for me and I often do without things I need to keep the place up. I have to travel 1600 miles to get to it and take care of it so other people can rent it and enjoy it. I spend most of my time there working to keep it in good shape. My friends often tell me I need to sell it, that it's not a smart financial decision to hang on to and it adds a lot of stress to my life. Sometimes, when I'm there and have to listen to people that I otherwise truly, dearly love, go off on their rants slightly to the right of Attila the Hun, I think, "Okay, this is it. I can't take this." Then there are the few descendents of pseudo plantation owners who are living in some fantasy of a hoop skirt wearing world, at the beach, no less. When they occasionally band together over some petty issue and exclude someone for some unknown, disdainful reason, it's enough to make me want to catch the next plane for the south of France where at least— *ma cher*—people speak French. I feel sorry for them, these inlanders (bless their hearts) because apparently they lack the true Gulf Coast gene of irony streaming through their DNA. We know how to laugh at ourselves down here on the coast. Mardi Gras is our sacred ritual and it separates the riff from the raff.

So why? Why do I do it? My reasons, up until the Great Oil Spill, were somewhat vaguely articulated by my ancestry, as I'm a seventh generation Gulf coastal inhabitant. My mother's people came to Pensacola from New Orleans in the early 1820's and settled on Escambia Bay so I'm very much at home on this coast. Our grandparents, two of the kindest, most generous souls who ever lived, found this particular bit of coast around 1950 when they were looking to build a vacation home for themselves and our large extended family and friends. And they found it from the water. It never occurred to them to *drive* to look for waterfront property. Both of the Grands could tell a joke and a tall tale with equal ability, and both were fantastic cooks, though not necessarily in the same way. There was always a house full of people drinking and eating and cooking and talking and laughing, children running in and out slamming screen doors and dogs underfoot looking for stray scraps that fell off the plates onto the floor with someone's inevitable grand gesticulation. Our grandparents were everything that is good about being Southern. Grandmother's admonition to me upon any concern I ever had over social situations was simple—"Nicky, the essence of good mannahs is puttin' other peepul at ease." The stories about the two of them are legend. So I would explain to my jaundiced eyed friends, most of whom had never been below the Mason Dixon line, that it was a cultural thing and a family root kind of thing why I hung on. But now I know for sure that it is much, much more than that.

THE HORRORS began with the videos of the spewing well seen every day in the news and long past the days of a silent spring it is now the surreal landscape of a silent summer—almost no animal life—no birds, no porpoises—where are they? Very few people on the beach, houses empty—it's like the dead of winter only it's the deadly summer. No boats in the water other than the Coast Guard boats checking booms. Signs in restaurants— "raw oysters as long as they last." And everywhere, underneath the "normal" flow of life, the worry that once the oil well is capped, the questions remain—where did the oil and dispersants go? And what's in the toxic soup of the water that will end up in the food chain? The unthinkable that has happened, the loss of human life, of animal life, the loss of a way of life, a culture, the loss of the life of the water itself has made me realize that I have hung on because what I feel is as deep as the cells in my body. It is the salt water that flows through me.

I am now aware of the little rituals I have enacted each time I go home—the unconscious urge to go to the Gulf, even when I am pushed for time. I make a quick trip in between the errands to Foley for the inevitable paint, plumbing supplies, and lumber, taking the long way back to Gulf Shores, Orange Beach, Perdido Key. I trudge through sand white as snow and stand in water, the color of a perfect lime margarita with waves rushing in, swirling around my feet, staring out at the horizon, and for just a moment, there is no thought, nothing, just being there, in it. I reach in and scoop the salty water and taste it on my tongue. I do the same thing on the bay in front of the house the

Lost Bay – Nicky Wheeler-Nicholson

day I leave to go back "up north." I go down the 50 steps from the bluff to the beach and often find my eyes welling with tears in some human grief, but it is just the water that I'm leaving, the salt water of the bay.

I have been in this water, drunk it, snorted it through my nose, spit mouthfuls of it at my siblings and cousins in mock battles, tasted it as I have moved through it my entire life. From the time we have been too small to swim and our parents held us in their arms and let us float in it to our grandparents wrinkled bodies in their faded, saggy bathing suits, floating in that salty tang of water, we are always in it. Swimming in it, floating in it, turning over and staring straight down to the sandy bottom watching the crabs scuttle along and the minnows silvery flash as they move in schools. Kayaking across it in the early morning stillness when the bay is like a sheet of shimmering glass with schools of stingrays flying underneath the boat and below the surface of the water like strange silent birds. Sailing on it, skiing on it, flying across it at top speed with motors roaring, walking through it at night, speaking in hushed tones, looking for flounder to gig and watching the gars with their needle noses moving in and out of the light shining down into the darkness of the water.

When I was a child, we slept in the heat of the afternoon with the breezes from the Gulf singing through the tall pines causing the curtains to billow out like white clouds and bringing a tantalizing smell of the not-so-far-away Caribbean. The porpoises would come into the bay, spouting water from the tops of their heads, their smooth bodies undulating through the waves. They followed our small boats as we dragged for shrimp, throwing them the trash fish caught in the nets. Nothing is ever wasted here. Everybody gets something to eat. You can hear the porpoises chattering to one another in the late afternoon and watch them circle the schools of mullet as they feed. They are another race of beings, supernatural creatures, travelers to our shores, bringers of omens, and they share the water with us. The gulls and brown pelicans float along the top of the bluff and osprey dive straight down from far above to snatch an unwary fish. A lone heron stands in the dusky light of evening like a statue on the pier, waiting for supper to glide by. Like these animals, we too have eaten from the waters—oysters, shrimp, crabs, mullet, flounder. We are what we eat. When the moon rises, it streams across the bay toward us. Everything in this world is a part of who we are.

I wake in the half-light of dawn and the word "threnody" floats through my jumbled mind. I long to tear my hair, beat my breasts, and wail at the top of my lungs like some ancient Greek woman, but there is no forum for such a ritual. This is the truest of tragedies. Unlike hurricanes, I'm not sure we can bounce back from this horrific gushing of oil from the body of the earth that arrives like red blood on the shore. I don't know that we will eventually see things differently, adjust, accept the change. I'm not sure what will be left, will survive, will come back to our Perdido.

Once, when I was a child, Granddaddy and I sat on the bluff in the swing as everyone else got out of bathing suits and into Sunday clothes for church. Someone yelled out the porch door, "Are you going to church, Granddaddy?" And he took his cane and waved it across the view before him—of the bay, the shore beyond and the huge blue sky filled with cotton white clouds and said, "This is all the church I need."

Amen, Granddaddy, Amen.

BoP This

By Tynia Thomassie

Billowing auburn geysers of hubris vomit ton by ton from the
gulf floor,
Spewing titanic promises and top-kill assurances,
slick globs in glare on pelicans' backs.
Frantic eyeballs of smeared gulls, gloved hands scouring
greased plumes,
dabbing at the collateral damage
of two dollar-and-change gas.
Outside it's America.

Befuddled suits propound lofty strategies—
a concrete chapeau for Hydra's many heads,
pumping mud in tubes within pipes at
never-tried-before-never-tried-before depths.
This, as huddled terns
and towns of twice-hit fishing folk
squint at the darkening hues of the marsh,
scrape rust tar balls amassing in the reeds.
Outside it's America.

Armchair activists defend the drill, baby; click "don't whine
when you get five-dollar gas."
Yachtsmen massage their crude: "...wouldn't say it failed..."
rather,
"...what we attempted to do last night didn't work."
And as steepled fingers point at, or up, or away, never toward
the chest,

Oil and Water ... and Other Things That Don't Mix

the 3-state-and-widening tongue laps at the lip of Louisiana, where
true oysters hatch little more than black swirls.
Outside it's America.

In the Forest of My Dream

By L B Gschwandtner

IN THE FOREST of my dream grows a little evergreen, whose tiny spikes of needle hair reach out to grasp the new spring air. My dream takes shapes that grow and shift and all at once my form appears as if by magic old in years, trodding on the leaf strewn path, my arms outreaching toward the light that showers down upon us all, creatures living by our wits.

In the forest of my dream, fearsome demons lurk and wait, tall as oaks and fast as snakes, they hiss and spit and bare their fangs. I am anxious, I admit, afraid of what they'll do to me, afraid of what they'll say of me, afraid of being overwhelmed, I scream to no one in my dream. When I wake in my own bed, damp and nervous, out of breath, I find it's true, the scream I hear, it is my voice that fills the room. Where is the forest of my dream? Not here at least, not in this space.

In the forest of my dream, as real as any wooded glade, palpable and full of fright, at times a truly blessed realm of refuge taken from the storm, I walk through life so delicate, unfolding in the dappled light, with ferns and Mayapple, and over the hill, Dutchman's britches I see them still, in the forest of my dream, where time stands still and rushes round, making sleep a busy zone, where rest eludes me for one night, while dreaming takes me far afield.

In the forest of my dream, when I again return to sleep, a cat appears in silent stalk. A tiny baby bird it seems, has fallen from a nest on high, and helpless on a little knoll, wobbles and chirps for me to hear. I want to lift it from this floor, but when I try my feet are stuck like two great boulders on a cliff, and while I pull and twist about, the cat slinks forward toward her prey. And then from up above the trees a bird appears, with wings unfurled, and razor beak about to strike, talons open for a fight, in the forest of my dream, where creatures never play for real but where they tell me what I feel.

In the forest of my dream, the bird is gone and so the cat, curls up against my leg and sleeps, purring like a rumbling truck, as if she never left my side, nor looked upon a baby chick as if it were a bowl of cream, in the forest of my dream.

When morning comes and I arise, my cat is really by my side, and out the window I can see, a forest where the rain has come, and sprinkled dewdrops one by one, so all that slumbered these past months, can now begin to bloom anew. And what dreams do they have this spring? I wonder if, as they grow old, eternity will treat them well, if in the forest of my dream, as I begin to say goodbye to all the creatures of the earth, as seasons pass and come again, the forest dream will live again, or will there come a day too soon, when all the forests big and small shall melt away and finally fall.

Butterfly
By Mylène Dressler

"I DON'T KNOW who broke our butterfly," Brandy tells us, "but when they find him, hand him over to me and I'll break his legs."

We're 150 feet underground. The air is close, eighty-five degrees. The light is artificial. Brandy's cheeks are warm and flushed.

Sometimes, you need to go down to go up. I'd visited the Caverns of Sonora, Texas when I was twelve, but hardly remembered them. As a college student hitchhiking to California, my husband had once gotten as far as the cavern entrance, but didn't have enough money to go inside. In those days, the cave was a small, family-run affair. It's still a family affair, and the same family still owns the place, but now there is a gleaming Visitors Center and a campground with RV hook ups and a parking lot big enough to attract tour buses.

Yet on this quiet day, we were the only ones in line.

Before we were able to go down, our guide Brandy had to take a call from her daughter's elementary school.

"So sorry," she blushed afterward. "Your child starts coughing, and right away they want to send her home with swine flu. I really apologize you had to wait, but once we're down in the cave, we're completely cut off from everything." She smiles. She's a tiny thing, not much bigger than a child herself, her long blond lashes like wings.

She's sealed the air-tight door behind us, and we're heading down towards the two miles of open cavern network. In less than a minute we're in another world, squeezed into a plane of jewels. The Caverns of Sonora make Carlsbad look like an abandoned strip mine. Here, everything is so close and so beautiful, it takes all you have not to touch it to make sure it— and you—are real.

Brandy begins teaching us the names of the formations we're seeing: popcorn stone, flowstone, cave coral, cave drapery, columns, dogtooth spar, quartzes, soda straws, stalactites, stalagmites, helactites. Geodes "bake" in the damp air, like crystal-packed muffins on the walls.

"Now, all of this grows at a rate of one centimeter per 10,000 years," she says as we pass a huge column growing out of the floor, achingly close to touching its twin spire descending from the ceiling. Called the "Kissing Column," the two formations are—ah!—a mere centimeter apart.

My husband, who loves to talk to people and ask questions, asks:

"So...do you like doing this for your job, Brandy?"

"I love it. Well, I love both things I do. I guide in the morning, and then I go to nursing school in San Angelo at night. And then I practice my anatomy down here." She points out metacarpals of flowstone, brachial tubes of coral, helactites in the shape of mandibles. She also directs our attention to formations that look like bacon and pork chops. She savors her work.

My husband, ever interested in the consequences of actions over time, now asks: "But if you like guiding so much, what will you do when you're all done with nursing school?"

"I don't know," Brandy grimaces, and switches off the lights. All through the cavern, she's been turning the lights on and off as we go, so that what lies in front of us always remains in darkness, and what lies behind us is in darkness, and the only place illuminated is the place where we stand. "I don't want to think about that right now. Ask me later."

We pass signs of damage, places where tourists, unable to keep from reaching, have blackened the calcium walls with human oil. We pass through chambers of pure, undamaged white to reach Horseshoe Pond, an emerald lake surrounded by a halo of pearls. The water is so clear it almost hurts to look at it.

"This is my favorite room," Brandy says.

"Mine too," my husband exhales.

At the deepest point in the cavern, Brandy turns off all the lights so we can appreciate the total blackness of its true state. She informs us that if we stayed down like this for two weeks, we would start to go blind. "The retina starts to decay," she says matter-of-factly. "This isn't a place made for humans." Then she puts the lights on again. "Okay, so now I'm going to take you to see our butterfly—sad as that is."

The butterfly was once the glory, the pride and the emblem of the Caverns of Sonora. I remembered seeing it when I was twelve, a thing deliciously small and amber-colored and perfect, a marvel of accident and time. But a vandal had since come and broken off one of its translucent wings, while trying to steal it. It was a two-man operation, Brandy explains: during a tour of more than thirty people, a "plant" at the head of the tour distracted the guide, while a man at the back hopped the railing, attacked, and stuck the piece in his pocket. The damage wasn't discovered until the next tour came through.

"And then we cried." Brandy lowers her gaze. "All of us who work here cried and cried and cried and cried. It was horrible. They did end up figuring out who it was. From his credit card. He has a history of doing things like this, if you can imagine. The Texas Rangers are still after him. But so far no luck. Anyway we don't do big tours anymore. No more."

The mood turns somber for a moment—but no sooner has Brandy turned the lights behind us off and the ones in front of us on than she beats her long lashes and goes back to teaching and pointing. There is so much to see down here, after all, she says. Maybe we would discover something else just as beautiful. Maybe she would. There were seven miles of cave, in total. She was always looking, among the thousands of formations, for the next butterfly.

As we begin to emerge from the depths, my husband asks Brandy what kind of nurse she would like to be.

"Life-flight," she answers.

The Grass is Greener

By Zetta Brown

> *Pictures of Crippen, lipstick smeared.*
> *Torn wallpaper...have the walls got ears here?*
> *—Kate Bush, "Coffee Homeground"*

"GO ON! Get outta here!"

The stone bounced off the cat's rump making it run faster. Della Chapin didn't like strays wandering onto her property. She couldn't afford to have a cat or a dog digging up her yard or eating the plants. She lived off the profits of her garden. At first, she used to shoo them away, next she built a fence. Now, her measures were more extreme, and she was beginning to think that it was her special compost that made her crops grow so well.

A tall woman in peach-colored shorts and matching thong sandals shuffled along the sidewalk carrying a Power Ranger lunch pail.

"Afternoon, Miss Gwen," Della called out. "I see your boy done forgot his lunch again."

"Yep. He ran off before I could stop him. You feelin' all right, Miss Della?"

"Can't complain."

Gwen came into the yard and leaned on the old-fashioned lamp post. With one of her long feet, she made the pinwheel of leaves turn on one of the six giant, plastic sunflowers Della had in her yard.

"I swear that boy would leave his head behind and not know it until suppertime." Gwen sighed, and then looked at what her neighbor was doing. "Are those peas for the meeting tomorrow?"

Della nodded. "I heard that Bishop Grimes liked my pea salad. Since he's this Sunday's guest, I thought I'd give him a treat."

"Well, that's all right then, Miss Chapin. We know that when you cook, you get down and put your foot in it!" They laughed and Gwen left the yard.

As her neighbor sauntered down the street, Della continued to shell peas on her front porch. A breeze rustled through the clothesline, and she thought the sun was slowly turning the sheets whiter. She tried everything to get out the stains and figured a good airing would help. She could hear her mama lamenting about getting blood and shit off her apron after slaughtering a chicken. Those birds were nothing compared to what Della dealt with, but blood was blood.

The last few peas dropped into the giant blue bowl she balanced on her lap. One pound of peas. She could tell by how full the bowl looked.

Wiping the sweat off her brow, she stood to put the peas into the kitchen.

"Miz Chapin!"

A little boy about ten-years-old walked up to her porch. His denim shorts were dusty with dried red mud the color of his skin as if he had been crawling around under fences.

"What can I do for you, Peter?" She grinned.

The little boy looked around her yard, his lips curved downward and his expression mixed with concern and agitation.

"Have you seen a black and brown dog with big floppy ears and a long tail? He's been gone for about three days."

"Oh, was that *your* dog?" Della came down the steps before him. "I saw that dog wandering around my clothesline a few days ago."

"Have you seen him since?" Peter whined. "Please, Miz Chapin, you gotta help me. I've been looking for him everywhere!"

Della put a reassuring hand on his shoulder. "Was he on a leash?"

"No, ma'am. He must've jumped the fence after a rabbit or something. He does that a lot."

"Well, young mister, I hope you find him. Mind you." She leaned closer. "If you do, you make sure you keep hold of him, you hear? You never know what folks'll do to some animal they don't know."

The boy nodded and skulked out of the yard continuing with his search, whistling and calling, "Buddy! C'mon, boy, whereyouat?"

Della entered her home and was greeted by the cool, humid air from the swamp cooler. The constant gurgling of water running through the works was the only sound. She entered the kitchen and set the bowl of peas on the spotless, shining counter top and commenced to make her famous pea salad.

She kept a neat, tidy house despite running her cottage industry—her garden.

Sometime later, she looked up. The black cat clock on the yellow kitchen wall twitched its tail; its eyes shifting from side to side. The clock hands on its white belly indicated three o'clock.

"Damn." She yawned. "I better take my nap."

Shuffling into her bedroom and scratching her hip, Della's knees felt stiff as did her ankles. Her 60th birthday was the last one she acknowledged, and although she looked years younger, she didn't kid herself about the changes in her body. The aches and pains she could stand, but the dryness...

Della enjoyed a sex life to rival those half her age, but sometimes the discomfort that came with pleasure made her think about forgoing sex altogether.

Her four-poster mahogany bed draped in a white chenille blanket had several feather pillows on it, making it look soft and inviting.

"Mercy." She sighed and sat on the edge of the bed. Maybe she would take her vacation in New Orleans early this year. She could use the break and a change of scenery.

Putting on her satin eye mask and pushing her "Sunset Autumn"-tinted curls into her hair net, Della stretched out across the bed and fell asleep.

SHE AWOKE out of habit. Removing her eye mask, Della could see the pink and amber glow of the sunset coming through her window. She rushed outside to get her laundry off the line. It was six o'clock when she returned indoors, dragging her green plastic laundry basket. She set it inside the kitchen door. She'd have to fold the clothes later. She was running late.

Back in her bedroom, she opened her wardrobe to decide what to wear.

It was Friday night and time to get paid so she chose a money-green jersey jumpsuit that complimented her ebony skin. She admired the result and the way the deep neckline enhanced her bosom.

"Wonderbra, my ass." She smirked.

She began to apply her makeup; drawing in eyebrows, coloring her lips, mortaring her crow's feet. Looking out of the window again, the sun was over the horizon and in a few minutes it would be dark.

Going out the back door, Della hopped onto her little blue Moped to ride to the other side of her property. She followed a path that wended between cottonwood and poplar trees and past the greenhouse where she made her special compost until she reached a large barn.

She always arrived before the Jaguars and BMWs to get

ready for business.

People came from all over the county to buy her marijuana and hash from sunset to sunrise every Friday and Saturday. Her reputation for selling quality product and for keeping trouble away meant no one ever messed with Della Chapin—twice.

She expected to be busy. She had three employees: Oakley, Casey, and Howard who helped with the harvesting and kept the peace as she did her thing. She sat at her highly polished cherry wood desk set in the middle of the barn with the effects of business neatly arranged on top. To the right of that was a console on wheels with an elegant, silver libation service on top making it a portable wet bar. Della opened a black leather book with the word DIARY embossed in gold on the front and scanned the page.

"Oakley," she called. "It's nearly 7:30. Look out and see if you spy Pinky's Lexus coming."

A bronze giant of a man complied and opened the barn door to take a peek.

"Yes 'm. He's driving up, now."

"Okay—places everybody." She looked into the small mirror on her desk and pushed a few hairs into place.

The barn door slid open, scraping hay across the ground and kicking up pollen to reveal a tall, thin man in a brown leather jacket, a white silk shirt, and brown leather pants. He wore a dark grey fedora tilted over his left eye.

Pinky LeBeau got his name, his grey eyes, and his fair complexion from his white father and got his kinky hair from his black mother. Della grinned.

"Right on time, Pinky. Have a seat."

"Evenin' Miss C. What 'cha know good?" The man sat in the low-backed chair directly in front of her desk.

"Guess what I have, Pinky." She smiled when the thin man shrugged his shoulders. She leaned over and got something that was out of view. It was flat and covered with a blue and white checked linen napkin. "It's your favorite."

Pinky's eyes sparkled out of pleasure. "Don't tell me—"

"Yep! Oatmeal chocolate chip." Della whisked off the napkin to reveal a platter full of giant, soft cookies still warm with the cinnamon and chocolate giving off a pleasant aroma in the damp and dusty barn.

"Help yourself, baby. I remember how your mama always tried to get my special recipe. But I knew that if she did, you'd never come around to see me."

Pinky shook his head and laughed. "I'd always want to see you, Miss Chapin. You always fixing up something good in the oven...or in the garden."

Della's thick lips turned up in a seductive, but kind, gentle smile. "You want some milk, baby?" She purred. "Or would you prefer whiskey?"

Pinky indicated the latter so Della motioned for Oakley to fix the drink.

"Just place it on the coaster, Oakley, thank you." She leaned back in her chair, her fingers touching and making a pyramid. Her hazel eyes never left her client's face.

"I'm glad you were so prompt tonight. It'll give us some time to discuss your account."

"My account, Miss Chapin?"

She nodded, opening a big, black leather book that matched her diary, but this one had the word FINANCES embossed in gold on the front.

"What's wrong with my account?"

"Well, baby, it seems that for several weeks, there has been a downward spiral in your collections while your orders are increasing. I'm showing you were short $300 a few weeks ago, and $350 a few weeks before that."

"I must've miscounted." Pinky shrugged.

"No... no, honey, you didn't miscount because I have a double-entry system. Nope. You short. Only thing is...this has been going on for some time and I want to know why. No, help yourself, darling. Them cookies are for you. We're just visiting. I want to help you out."

Pinky's chewing slowed and he took a swallow of whiskey.

"Have your boys been short changing you?" she asked.

He hesitated a moment. "It's...it's possible. It's easy to lose track on the volume we handle. See, I got boys over near Baton Rouge and—"

"But, baby, I can do it," Della interrupted. "And I definitely have more volume than you. You want me to send Oakley, Harold, and Casey to lend you a hand?"

This suggestion made Pinky look over his shoulder to see the men in question. There they were, all of them, sitting on bales of hay like three prize fighters, staring at the two of them sitting at the desk. Pinky touched the crescent-shaped weal across his throat; a souvenir from the last time the boys "helped" him.

"Need another drink, sugar?"

"No. No, I'm fine, Miss Chapin."

"Good. Because I'm beginning to wonder if you're trying to drum up some action at my expense." Della's smile disappeared and the warmth she exuded minutes ago evaporated between heartbeats. "I can't allow that. Because, you know what? You have nickel and dimed your way to a debt of $6500."

Pinky shook his head. His lips set in a thin, straight line of defiance. "Now, I have paid for my shit, Miss Chapin."

"Shh, baby. Don't get excited. It's not that you haven't paid, Pinky, it's that you haven't paid enough."

The skinny man pushed his hat high on his forehead and Della saw the anger flash sparks from his pale, grey eyes. Little beads of sweat formed on his pasty face.

"Pinky, if you had been paying me consistently—in full—there would be no call for you to be nervous."

"Nervous? Why should I be—"

Della cut him off by raising her right hand and her

employees made their presence known by approaching the desk.

"Let's cut the crap, sugar. You owe me." Della's tone was harder than diamonds and her message just as clear.

"Don't threaten me, Della," Pinky ground out from behind clenched teeth. "You and your boys don't know who you messing with."

"Now hold up there, Pinky." She arched her eyebrow at him and her icy gaze froze him in place. "Since when did we get to be on first names? Contrary to what you think, I know exactly whom I'm dealing with. Pinky, you mistake yourself to be one of my good customers. Actually, I've been doing some figuring...and it turns out I can do much better without you."

Della poured herself a bit of Hennessy. "I'm a business-woman. I have my overheads to consider." She looked pointedly at the ceiling and Pinky did the same. That's when he saw it.

A rope hanging from a beam with a noose.

"Aw, c'mon, Miss C! You can't be serious!" He put his hands on the edge of her desk. "We've been friends a long time!"

"Time's up, sugar."

Pinky withdrew his hands as if he'd touched a hot stove. Della could see the condensation his sweaty palms left behind.

"I can make it up to you next week." He smiled. "I promise."

Della shook her head.

"But-but, Miss C...you sponsored my niece at her baptism!"

Before Pinky could blink twice, Della's boys had the skinny man in their grip. She watched, impassively, as they subdued him and dragged his unconscious body up to the loft.

"Casey!" She hollered. "Go get his car out of the way and high tail it over to Musky Ben's."

Musky Ben was Della's nephew who owned a chop shop. She got a hefty commission for any cars she sent his way.

Meanwhile, Oakley and Harold got Pinky bound, gagged, and the noose slipped around his neck.

"You boys have him ready yet?" she barked.

"Yes'm!"

"Well let's go! Mrs. Hancock'll be here in thirty minutes to pick up her order."

Della turned her attention back to her desk to prepare for her next appointment. She didn't even look up when she heard the ropes being thrown across the beam and the sound of Pinky LeBeau being pushed into oblivion. But she did hear a loud snap followed by a squelching noise of a body hitting the ground. She swivelled her chair around to see something roll a few feet in her direction.

"God—*damn it!*"

The deep roar of Oakley's voice drew Della's attention up to see the big man covered with blood. She threw down her pen.

"Aw, hell, boys! How many times do I have to tell you to shorten the rope?" She nudged Pinky's severed head out of the way with her foot. She wanted to kick the thing. "Stupid little—" she muttered. "Always making things difficult. Can't even die simple."

"We sorry, Miss C," said Harold as he began sweeping up the bloody hay.

Della walked past the blood oozing from the corpse and examined the rope.

"What is this?" she cried. "What the hell you mean by hanging a man with a nylon rope? *Use hemp!* How hard is it to get? We grow it for Christ's sakes!"

Mumbling more embarrassed apologies, Oakley took Pinky's head and placed it in the dead man's fedora leaving Harold to scamper off with the offending carcass.

"It's lucky for y'all that I'm making a new compost heap out of that mutt of Peter's or I'd be using *you* to get me started!" Della shook her head. It didn't matter how many times she tried to tell them, you just couldn't teach the congenitally stupid.

DELLA watched the taillights of her last appointment fade into the predawn. The red lights twisted and bounced down the dirt path between the trees like a pair of fireflies. She inhaled, taking in the smell of the wet grass and earth.

"Well, well...what do we have here?"

An orange truck with its headlights off cruised down the path towards the barn. The truck stopped about twenty-five yards away, and then turned its lights on and off twice.

Della gave a short, high whistle.

"Yes, Miss Chapin?" Casey answered.

"You and the others can leave. Mr. Carl's here now."

Della watched her three goons get their things and walk towards the door.

"'Night, Miss C," they said as they filed out. She handed each an envelope with $200 for the night's work. Compared to the amount she took in, they were cheap, but worth it.

"You boys done good tonight. Get some rest and come back here tomorrow in time for dinner."

That perked them up, and Della thought that if she had had any children, she would've wanted boys like them; strong, but clinging enough to where a home-cooked meal was reward in itself.

She waved in the direction of the truck and stepped back inside the barn. For the thirtieth time that night, she checked her appearance in the mirror. This time, she took out a perfume atomizer from her desk drawer and spritzed her neck, her wrists, and then placed a few sprays on her crotch.

Mr. Carl was no ordinary customer. He had certain privileges. Carl tested all the "herbal blends" she developed before passing them along to her customers to keep them coming back.

And as long as he could make the fillings in her back teeth rattle like the headboard of her bed, Mr. Carl would continue to get 40% off his purchase.

She sat on the corner of her desk with her legs crossed waiting for Carl to appear dressed in his signature faded blue jeans, which he filled out quite well for a man several years her junior.

Yes. It had been a long, hard week, and she couldn't wait to experience something else that was long and hard. So when a tall, willowy girl dressed in black appeared instead, Della's shock made her lose composure.

"What are you doing here? I don't know you! Get off my property!" Della hopped off the desk to rush the intruder. She tried to lay a hand on the woman's shoulder, but the woman shrugged out of the way.

"How's business, Miss Chapin? You looking well."

Della froze. She took a closer look at the young woman: skin the color of tanned leather, long black hair with honey-blonde highlights, but it was the face. Della had never seen the girl before but there was something about that face.

"I'm Carl's baby girl, Rosie."

"Rosie?" Della repeated, trying to sound calm. Now she remembered. Carl rarely mentioned his daughter except to say how disappointed he had been with her.

Rosie who had ran with a gang.

Rosie who had ran away from home.

Rosie who had joined the police academy.

Della put on her neighborly persona and the transition from angry to cordial was seamless. "Well! I guess you better come on in."

Rosie, her hands deep in her pockets, glided past Della and looked around the barn. When her eyes came to the damp puddle of earth, the puddle that, if examined closely, would reveal the events from earlier that evening, made Della speak up.

"Have a seat over here. Can I get you some tea? Cognac?"

Rosie shook her head. Della sat in her chair and took a few deep breaths as if getting comfortable. Actually, she was cursing for not smoking a blunt before opening shop like she usually did.

"I was expecting your daddy."

"Yes, I know. Daddy can't make it tonight."

"Oh? Not feeling well, is he?"

"He's dead."

Della's stomach suddenly got a chill. Here she was, a drug dealer, sitting with the cop daughter of her now-late lover.

"How did he...?" Della cleared her throat. She needed a drink.

"Seems as if Daddy took one toke too many on some pretty potent hash," Rosie said casually.

Della nodded. She couldn't cry. People died every day. If anything, she was going to miss her handyman's weekly service-ing.

"I'm sorry to hear that, dear." Della sighed, trying to inflect some emotion. "Really, I am." She lifted her right hand as if to wave off an invisible fly, but it was actually her covert signal for the boys to prepare for some trouble. But she froze mid-gesture. Her signal would be ignored.

Her goons had gone home.

"It's a shame that Daddy should pass away tonight," Rosie said, walking away from the earlier crime scene and towards Della's desk. "I had some news that would've finally made him happy."

"Oh, really?" Della smiled as she turned and reached for the bottle of whiskey and a glass from the libation tray. "What news is that?"

Della heard the unmistakable sound of a gun being cocked. She turned around to see a gun pointing at her forehead. Rosie's lips twisted into a lopsided smile.

"I've dropped out of the police academy."

The Maslins
By Ginger McKnight-Chavers

A WEEK shy of Halloween, and we're still in short sleeves. Synthetic matching cardigans, the color of overripe tomatoes, cinch our waists rather than cover our nine-year-old arms. We ditched the sweaters as soon as we escaped carpool this morning, accessorizing our red and navy pleated plaid skirts with dangling belts of cherry acrylic fuzz. Now that we're back in carpool and out of Sister Mary Catherine's sight, Lou and I have shoved our thin white knee socks down our ankles, baring our ashy calves to the world. The nuns may have been open-minded enough to welcome Negro girls like us into their school long before the public schools in this part of town were forced to, but they cannot seem to tolerate bare legs. Paula's socks still grip the base of her knees, her gams swinging and slapping the hard rubber heels of her saddle oxfords against the concrete retainer wall we're sitting on, *bump bump bump*, as we wait on my mother to pay for our ice cream.

We have weird weather down here. Or at least that's what Mommy's college friends tell us when they come down to visit from places like D.C. and Chicago and San Francisco. One Thanksgiving we'll be watching the Cowboys in T-shirts, and the next year we'll be swaddled in stadium blankets and stocking caps. We're used to the day-to-day being random and a bit fickle, but other folks seem to find Texas too irregular.

Bump bump bump. I wish she would stop that. I give Paula a stare, like the one Sister Mary Catherine would give me if she caught sight of my dark legs baking in the Southwestern sun.

But Paula's focused on the triple tower of lemon custard that's streaming down the sides of her sugar cone and coating the tips of her fingers, not me. *Bump bump bump.* I swirl my tongue around my one scoop of Rocky Road, catching every hint of drip in a single, neat swipe. If Paula keeps slurping down ice cream like that, she'll be as big as Mommy's second cousin Maudie Bee. Maudie Bee is an extraordinarily sweet older lady, who happens to be extraordinarily obese. It's weird because nobody else in Mommy's family is fat. But that's Texans for you. Random.

Bump bump bump. I cross my legs to mimic Lou, who always sits proper. Lou and I both have bird legs the color of my Daddy's morning coffee; chicory with a healthy splash of real milk, not the Cremora everybody uses these days. Paula's legs are fleshy and tan like the salted caramels Uncle Buddy makes me for Christmas. She continues to thud those stockinged caramel legs against the wall and suck on her sugar cone, ignoring how perfect Lou and I look in comparison. It's probably not a fair contrast because Lou's not into sweets, and she can sit like this for hours. That's why she's the only popular Black girl in the fourth grade. She sat like Jackie Kennedy all the way through *Fist of Fury* last weekend, even the scary fight parts, whilst I had to curl my legs under me and cower in the crook of her brother Darryl's arm. I won't hand myself a foul on that one, however, because Darryl was supposed to have taken us to see *Sounder*. The grown-ups had bribed him to take us to a nice, G-rated movie so they could play cards and drink Old Fashioneds in peace, but he used the ticket money to expose us to kung fu battles instead. I almost peed my pants at first, but I eventually adjusted to the violence and was sittin' pretty just like Lou in no time.

Paula needs to see how cool girls act so that maybe she'll stop embarrassing herself. And embarrassing me, since I'm forced to carpool with her every day. Like today, when Lori and Katie finally talked to me after school. I sit next to them on the broad brick steps in front of the school's white-columned entrance every day while we wait for our rides. I watch the swing of their grosgrain-beribboned ponytails and the bob of the backs of their heads, as they only focus on each other. They aren't mean, they just never seem to notice me. So I'm never included in their conversations about horses and Schwinn bikes and what happened at the lake last weekend. Only white girls have horses and weekend houses at the lake. But I finally persuaded Mommy to throw out my fat, synthetic yarns and instead secure my long braids with stiff, flat cloth ribbons like theirs. And I started carrying my older sister's crocheted bag with the wooden beads to school, after she decided to start dressing like Texas' Miss America, Phyllis George, instead of Peggy Lipton. Lori and Katie noticed my new bag and were right in the middle of telling me how "cu-u-ute" it was when Paula walked up, with fat yarn ribbons tied around her short, fat Afro puffs and a trail of toilet paper on her shoe. Not even Lou could save me in that situation. If I didn't have to carpool with Paula, they might have invited me to the lake one weekend, or to that new roller skating rink near them, which is probably better than the one near me. The teenagers keep taking over the kids' time at the rink near us, and they keep knocking me down when they try to do *Soul Train* moves on skates.

"Let's go ladies," Mommy chimes as she breezes past us with my older sister Ann Marie in tow. Ann Marie doesn't grace us with even a glance as she sips a chocolate malt from a tall waxed cup. She finishes it before she reaches the front door of Mommy's Eldorado, tossing it into a tin trash drum and taking a thick cylinder of lip gloss out of her faux leather bag before seating herself beside Mommy in the front seat. Lou and Paula and I slide into the wide back seat, with me in the middle and Lou and Paula at my flanks.

"I need to make a relish tray," Mommy murmurs. Ann Marie

doesn't respond, as she is fixated on her watermelon-flavored Bonnie Bell Lipsmackers and the *Right On!* magazine she just retrieved from her book bag. Mommy wasn't talking to her anyway. Mommy is so engrossed in thoughts of the bridge club meeting she is hosting this Saturday, that she doesn't even notice the verboten lip grease Ann Marie is repeatedly slathering onto her perfect, petal-shaped lips every 30 seconds. She must think the gloss evaporates the minute it touches her lips, like alcohol exposed to air. As Mommy steers the car back onto the freeway, both she and my sister are too absorbed in their respective obsessions to notice what we're doing in the back seat.

We're playing the Maslins. The Maslins are an imaginary family Lou and I dreamed up to pass the time during the long drive back to the neighborhood across town where we all live. They are a dysfunctional brood of what we, in our narrow nine-year-old minds, deem to be the extremities of beauty and ugliness, though Mommy repeatedly forbids me to call anyone or any living thing ugly. Only actions can be ugly, not appearances. It's easy for Mommy to say things like this, because she has always been pretty. Mommy went to Spelman College, which has the "prettiest coloured girls on the planet," according to Daddy, and she was on the homecoming court at Morehouse. But the nuns agree with her: "*Do not let your adorning be external,' girls...the Lord says to 'let your adorning be the hidden person of the heart with the imperishable beauty of a gentle and quiet spirit.'*" Only within the confines of our Maslins car game am I permitted to perceive things as ugly, so long as I don't talk loud enough for Mommy to hear. Not only can I call things ugly–in the car, I am actually the grand arbiter of all that is ugly or pretty in the world, unlike at school, where I really don't have a say in such matters.

Lou and I are the beautiful Maslin daughters, Kayla and Sue. Lou plays Sue, a splendid ballerina and the youngest of the

Maslin clan. I am Kayla, the equestrienne, who travels around the world competing in horse shows. Not the dusty, redneck rodeos of our hometown, mind you, but elegant spectacles of black velvet hardhats, stiff tan breeches and tall, shiny boots, like the ones in *National Velvet*. Kayla walks straight and tall and typically wears a fitted black blazer and her breeches to school, as she often has to head to the stables immediately after the closing bell. Kayla and Sue have frilly, pastel bedrooms, each larger than our real-life living rooms, with wrought-iron balconies and wood-burning fireplaces. They have gold-framed cork boards that are festooned with brilliant blue ribbons and family photos taken in places like Paris and Acapulco and Waikiki Beach. Their bureaus are coated with tall, gleaming trophies.

Then there are the Maslin twins, Noodle and Punk. Paula, poor clueless Paula, plays the twins. Paula's unfortunate circumstance is due to the fact that she's a newcomer to the school and our game. She just joined our carpool this year when her family moved here from Beaumont. Though Paula's addition to the carpool has not helped my social standing at school in the least, I have to admit that it hasn't been an entire loss. It has helped us endure our cross-town commute a bit better, because Lou and I have been playing the Maslins for over three years now, and we were running out of interesting new scenarios, since neither one of us is willing to play a villain or, God forbid, someone UGLY!

The game hums along in the usual way. "Noodle and Punk, they smell like skunks...," sing Kayla and Sue.

"I just wanna eat my chips," Paula rasps as she pulls a bag of barbecue potato chips out of the navy canvas satchel resting on her lap. "I don't like this game."

"We're not eating with y'all. Y'all eat raw onions with booger sauce, and then you fart onions," Kayla taunts.

"Eew! Gross!" says Sue, holding her nose.

"Come on, y'all. I don't wanna play," Paula grumbles as her chubby fingers grip the sides of the cellophane bag and pull it open.

"Your daddy barbecued a pig last night, and y'all ate the whole thing by yourselves. That's why you're FAT!" Kayla grabs her throat and sticks out her tongue in a gagging effect.

"Shut up!" Paula's voice trembles.

"We just can't take y'all anywhere," Kayla continues. "Do y'all always have to wear flood pants with your long underwear showing?"

"Especially in this heat?" Sue adds. "Y'all are just too MUSTY! Haven't y'all ever tried deodorant?"

Paula's eyes glower at us, at me particularly, but Kayla is on too much of a roll to stop now. "You two need to get the gaps in your teeth fixed," Kayla says.

"I would take you to my dentist just so I don't have to look at your mouth anymore, but I have a performance." Sue sniffs. She folds her hands, one atop the other, and lays them gently on her crossed knees.

"And I have to groom my ponies, so I don't have time to take you," Kayla adds. "But those yellow stains on your teeth, and your nasty breath...and those naps in your head, y'all are just...just UGLY!"

I didn't intend to scream the word UGLY at the top of my lungs, but I don't have time to dwell on it. Paula grits her teeth and growls like a mad dog. Before I know it, she is lunging straight at me, her short, wide hands heading straight for my throat. Lou cowers against the car door, legs still crossed as she raises her knees and rolls into a ball. I have nowhere to run and nothing to do but allow Paula to choke me and shake me like a rag doll while my terrified expression turns, well, just plain ugly!

"WHAT DID YOU SAY, YOUNG LADY! YOU APOLOGIZE RIGHT NOW THIS MINUTE BEFORE I HAVE TO GET OUT

OF THIS CAR AND WRING YOUR NECK!"

Paula beat Mommy to it and is already wringing my neck. At the sound of Mommy's voice, however, Paula freezes and quickly drops her hands. I don't know when or how Mommy pulled into the breakdown lane and stopped the car on the side of the highway, but the car is silent, and Mommy's eyes are on me, not the road. She has swiveled her torso around in her seat and is staring straight at me, her expression meaner and madder 'n a pack of hornets. Her lips are squashed together in a taut, tense line, and her eyes are shootin' lead bullets. Mommy's outburst has stopped all of us in our tracks like the bark of a drill sergeant. Ann Marie has even raised her eyes from her magazine and ceased her lip glossing. The Maslins shut their dangling mouths and slink their small bodies into the seats in order to disappear.

The world is still and eerily motionless, like the prelude to a tornado. No one moves or speaks. Life as we know it stops and is suspended in dread, except for the *whizzz* of the pick-ups and Peterbilts that pass us in a blur. I wait for the twister to touch ground. A pinch of the ear? A sharp slap on the shin, since the car seat is shielding my bottom? No *Brady Bunch* for a month?

"Sorry," I whisper.

My feeble apology has no effect. I start wishing for the tornado. Just knock me down and release me from the grips of Mommy's awful stare, and all this awful waiting in a fear far more terrible than any Fist of Fury.

After what feels like centuries, Mommy turns around and starts the car. I feel small relief. Like Medusa, Mommy has the power to turn people to stone just by looking at them. Lou remains curled in the corner of the back seat, moaning to herself, her forehead pressed against the ridge of the door below the window. She knows Mommy's gonna tell her parents. I slant my eyes to glance at Paula, who's wearing a small, shy smile like a badge of honor.

Oil and Water ... and Other Things That Don't Mix

Years from now, I will remember this day as the moment in time that I began to recognize beauty in things other than grosgrain ribbons and riding boots, albeit by force of sheer terror, not divine revelation or *"the imperishable beauty of a gentle and quiet spirit."* And it will forever be marked as the day that Paula was transformed from Noodle and Punk, booger-eaters, to the new persona of Carrie Maslin, supermodel.

Tomboys and Peach Chiffon
By Kimeko Farrar

I COULD feel my systolic level rising as I sat at the kitchen table clutching the permission slip my daughter handed me. It wasn't my normal nature to be so negative and dramatic, but the words on the sheet of paper stirred up memories I thought I had forgotten, or at least had gotten over. Judging from the bulging blue veins that stretched from my knuckles to my wrist, it was obvious that I had not.

For a moment, I starred at my only child and studied her features. From the sliver of sunlight showing through the window blinds, she glowed with caramel-colored skin, long and skinny legs and raven-colored hair pulled into two side ponytails. Gapped tooth and carefree, she was the spitting image of me. Practically a mini version of who I was at that time, at that moment, in that kitchen, many years after I had grown up. Only her views weren't tainted by the world yet. The image of her made my stomach do a million flip-flops and I felt a little woozy. I looked down at my sweaty palms, still squeezing the ink from the maroon-and-white permission slip, and I thought about shredding it or accidentally stuffing it down the garbage disposal when Zion wasn't paying attention. I knew that sounded a little crazy, okay maybe cuckoo crazy, but the sight of the permission slip took me back to the boondocks of Alabama, and that's not where I wanted to be. I wasn't convinced that *things* had not changed enough, and to protect Zion, I would throw a mean shoe if I had to, the pointier the Jimmy Choo heel the better.

Almost thirty years had come and gone, and a childhood memory was embedded so deep into my psyche that will, might, and major achievements couldn't get rid of it. I was a successful business owner, and I had a shoe collection to die for. I owned enough tailored clothes to wear once, and then give to charity. I had a standing appointment every Thursday at the House of Claire because looking my best requires professional maintenance. I owned a beautiful home on a cul-de-sac in an ethnically diverse and gated community. So what was the problem? The problem was that my life wasn't always that way and the past clings like a leech.

On the opposite side of the kitchen Zion was stretched up on the tips of her toes, searching for an after school snack with the stainless steel refrigerator door wide open. I seized the opportunity to stuff the slightly damp permission slip inside my Wonderbra and pretend it had disappeared. My brown almond-shaped eyes danced with evil excitement, and my size 10 foot tapped swiftly against a leg of the table at the thought of the slip vanishing into the land of extreme cleavage and excessive padding. I practiced a stunned and confused expression to make sure I could pull off my plan. One fold...Two folds...Three folds...I examined the size of the slip between my index finger and thumb. It was almost small enough to fit. Just one last fold and the permission slip would be buried in my cleavage forever, out of sight and out of mind. Surely, a seven-year-old wouldn't think to look there. I wasn't sure she knew what cleavage was. At seven, I knew I didn't.

"Did you say something, Mama?" Zion swirled around in my direction, slurping a juice box.

"Huh, oh no, I didn't say anything."

My eyes stopped doing the tango and my leg, the one that had been doing acrobatic stunts moments earlier, went limp. Feeling defeated because my plan was busted, I banged the folded permission slip against the kitchen table, and then flicked it hard, pretending to play paper football. It landed right on the edge of the table. Geez! So far, the slip was kicking my butt and starting to work my nerves.

"So can I Mama? It has to be signed and turned in by tomorrow. Can I be in the beauty walk? *PLEASE*?"

Ugh! The horrid words were released in the air. During Saturday morning cleaning I would have to fumigate the room. Zion was doing her *Mama-can-I* dance and waiting for my reply. I knew she was excited about being in the pageant, even after I tried to deter her. I paused and bit my lip before I spoke my mind out loud. I wanted to avoid being negative again and crushing her spirits. The words *ignorant beauty competition* coming from my mouth earlier had left a bad taste. The air was already polluted with words I didn't want to hear. It made no sense to clog my throat with words I shouldn't say.

"Sweetie, let Mama think about it for a while okay?"

"Okay, Mama. We can shop for dresses and shiny high heeled shoes. I can get my hair and nails done like you, but I think I want French tips. Can I wear your diamond earrings? Or maybe your diamond necklace? Oooh, I can't wait!" she shrieked.

Wow, who did this kid belong to? She went on and on. She looked like I did as a kid but our personalities were like night and day. I forced a smile and retreated to the living room, ready to TiVo and mocha latte my stress away.

LATER THAT NIGHT I showered, and I thought about the permission slip. I brushed my teeth, massaged my legs with Nivea, and I thought about the permission slip. I turned on my bedside lamp, and there it was, the permission slip, neatly unfolded. How lucky for me that kids never forgot what parents' promised. I told Zion I would make a decision that night. Placing the permission slip where I could see it was her way of not letting me forget without actually saying anything. She had used that tactic before with Christmas lists, lunch money reminders, and dance class schedules. I picked up the creased piece of paper and starred at the words "Annual Beauty Walk." There was no logical way to explain my doubts to Zion. She was just a child, younger than I was the year I participated in my first beauty walk. I leaned back against my leather headboard and let the memories of 1981 race through my head.

FROM THE MIDDLE of first grade to the twelfth grade, I had attended Morris Palmer School, a predominately White school in Alabama located just north of Birmingham. I lived in a predominately Black neighborhood with my mother, father, brother, and grandmother. It was hardly middle class, but at least it was a few pegs higher than the projects. For us, that was reason to be proud. At school I knew I was different and kind of the outsider, but in my neighborhood, whatever I was—was fine, for a while anyway. I struggled to make sense of it all and fit into both worlds at the same time. I was horrible at playing the fence, even in softball, which I loved.

My mother was quite different from me. She fit in every-where and everybody knew Mona. She was always impeccably dressed with manicured nails, a freshly powdered face, and she wore 4-inch heels to football games. I, on the other hand, didn't give a flying flip about formal dresses, fancy hair, or lip gloss. I was a certified, card-carrying member of the tomboy club, so torn clothes, sweaty armpits, and nappy hair didn't bother me at all. My mother, who had her own idea of how I and everyone else should act, was a seamstress at the local coat factory during the week, but was a kitchen beautician on the weekends. Our house was filled with ladies and men getting their hair fried, dyed, and laid to the side every Saturday. Jheri curls, perms, pineapple waves, finger waves, asymmetrical cuts, and press-n-curls. If you could describe it, my mother could do it. When I wasn't vandalizing anything, I hung out with Grammy, Mama's mother, and listened to the latest gossip.

"Child, you and me are cut from the same cloth," Grammy said as she shucked corn or picked beans. "I always did my own thing too. These old bones don't understand folks trying to keep up with the Joneses or whoever. You know your mama is the ring leader too." Grammy nudged her head in the direction of the kitchen. "Look at Josephine over there. Her head looks like two wild birds have been fighting over a worm in a nest, but because Patti LaBelle wore that style on *Soul Train* last week, she loves it. I wouldn't be surprised if Jesse attacked her with a fly swatter as soon as she walks in their door. She's gonna scare that poor man to death."

Grammy winked at me and I rolled around the floor in laughter. I almost forgot that it was my turn to sit in the broken-down brown styling chair. I was in the second grade, and my mother had signed me up to be in the Morris Palmer beauty walk. In her words, I had to be "pageant ready." Of course Mama could have made it easy on herself and finished my hair on Friday night instead of working me in with her regular clients on Saturday. She said she didn't want my hair to snap back during the night. Plus, I was a rough sleeper and would wake up looking like Pippi Longstocking. Now, I know better. She wanted to show me off to everybody that day and prove that she actually had a girl and not two boys. I don't remember how I felt about all the fru-fru stuff before the beauty walk, but I do remember the events of that day like it happened only hours ago. Like any other Saturday morning, I had climbed the tree in the front yard, chased the neighborhood mutt around our house, and wrestled my little brother in the grass. I didn't give a second thought to chiggers and ticks. My rear end paid a dear price, though, and after I got fussed at and cussed out for being such a boy, I took a bath, got my hair washed, and then waited quietly in our living room and tried not to get dirty again.

"Shila, come here so I can press your hair while Ms. Janice is under the dryer."

I had dreaded those words all day. I walked out the living room and down the short hallway to the kitchen. I dragged my hand along the wall paneling, letting my fingers feel the edges of each piece of wood and deliberately tried to stretch out the walk as long as possible.

"Come on, girl. We don't have all day." Mama pointed at the worn out chair and motioned for me to sit. I plopped down and winced when I felt the heat from the stove near my face. I was not amused! My bottom lip hung so low, I could have scooped ice cream with it. Ms. Janice giggled and shifted her head from under the dryer so she could run her mouth as usual. Mama always told her that her hair would dry a lot faster if she wasn't so dang nosey.

"Mona, honey, I don't see how you do it. That girl hates to get her hair combed, and she has so much of it too. She must be extremely tender-headed."

Mama heated the straightening comb on the stove and loosened the cap on the Blue Magic.

"No, my baby's not tender-headed," Mama said while combing the tangles from my hair. "She just doesn't understand the importance of being well dressed and pretty, yet. She'll catch on soon enough."

Mama spent the rest of the afternoon running the pressing comb through my hair so I could wear curls that night. To her, the pageant was something special, probably ranking just as high as Christmas and Easter. Ms. Janice stayed around and looked me over as Mama blushed my cheeks and put pink gloss on my lips. I could tell that she approved because she was quiet. When Mama was finished, I stood in front of the mirror and admired my peach chiffon dress, white lace socks, and new patent leather shoes. For just a moment, I didn't mind the itchy material or all the fuss. I even stood still for pictures. I was finally mommy's little girl.

WHEN WE ARRIVED at the gym, my father kissed my forehead and went to find seats while my mother took me backstage. A short and round woman, who looked a little too homely to be directing pageants, went over a few last minute details before sending everyone except volunteers to their seats. As long as Mama was standing there smiling, with her manicured hand on my shoulder, I was fine. As soon as she left, I felt sick as a dog. I couldn't remember how to walk, stand, turn—nothing. My mind was blank. My patent leather shoes clicked clacked across the room as I moved to a far away corner to seek refuge from my surroundings. From there I could see that no one else looked like me. None of the other girls had spent hours getting their hair pressed straight with a hot comb and hair grease just so it could be curled. I desperately tried to appear invisible, which wasn't hard because no one took an interest in me anyway. I slid tighter and tighter into the cool corner. I felt like I was being punished. With my back pressed against the gray concrete walls, I said nothing, but my eyes surveyed the room. There were young boys goofing off, women talking and attempting to get everyone in line, and little girls twirling around in their new dresses. I stood all alone, scratching at the fabric grazing my knee. The thumping in my chest eased slightly when I finally saw someone I recognized, Janica, the sweet, but pudgy, Amish-looking girl I had sat with on my first day of school. She waved at me, but I don't remember waving back. I kept my eyes locked on her until she disappeared from the room and down the hallway.

When I made it to the front of the line, the boys were joking around and giving me *that look*. They changed positions in line and argued over who would escort me to the gym floor. They were supposed to wait against the wall near the stairs, grab the next girl's hand and escort her to mark one. The announcer called my name, Shila Martin, and I took off as fast as I could, practically jumping down the steps all at once. I was on auto-pageant contestant. Even at eight years old I wasn't going to beg anyone to walk with me anywhere. The peach chiffon swayed and my patent leather shoes stomped against the hardwood of the gym floor like I was killing roaches. I wasn't graceful but I was focused. I hit my first mark, and then turned to the right like a robot. I hit my second mark and struck a pose before walking over to stand next to Janica, the girl I barely knew. I went to the most comforting place, but it was the exact wrong spot! Who knew pageants could be so complicated? Oh well, I didn't dare move. I stood there like I was totally right and everyone else was totally wrong.

After fifteen minutes of fidgeting and watching my mother gesture for me to smile, I didn't win and I didn't care. I was glad it was over. We didn't go away completely empty handed either. For participating, each contestant was presented with a pink carnation and a miniature baby doll. Now what was I going to do with that?

Swinging the doll by her neck, I ran to find my family in the audience after the pageant was over. They laughed and teased me about leaving my escort behind when I walked out, unlike the other girls. My eyes filled with tears and the drops fell to form polka dot stains on the peach chiffon. I told my parents that I walked out alone because the boys wouldn't hold my hand and walk with me. Maybe it was because I was Black, maybe it was because I looked poor and out of place, or maybe it was because I wasn't all that pretty. Maybe, just maybe, they were acting like most immature little boys do. I guess I'll never know why, but I knew my mother would be disappointed if I didn't walk down those steps with my lips pursed and my chin held high after all the effort she put into it, so I strutted what little stuff I had by myself. I may have looked like a newborn giraffe walking for the first time, but I did it. We drove home and my pageant days were over. We never discussed the ordeal again. The only reminder was a few pictures and a doll head in the bottom of the toy box.

NEATLY TUCKED under silk sheets, I lifted my coffee mug to my lips and drank the last warm sip of my latte. As I thought about being rejected, something occurred to me. I had reminisced about that beauty walk story at least fifty times over the years and had probably told it just as many times, but I never really thought about it from beginning to end. Sure, I thought about the details but not the lessons.

I rubbed the handle of the mug against my forehead in an effort to focus so my mind wouldn't stray back to rejection. The experience wasn't really about if I was treated poorly, if I lost a contest, or if I wasn't a blond-hair-blue-eyed beauty queen accepted by Morris Palmer. It was about the hysterical and unconditional love of my Grammy on that day and the strong support of my Mama. Both of them did things the best way they knew how as women and as mothers, but most importantly, it was about my own courage. I had found the guts to stand tall, suck it up, and push through my insecurities on the day of the beauty walk. Well, that's what I decided I would take from it.

I realized that Mama was trying hard, too hard, to give me something that she never had as a child, which was approval from others. In my own time, not hers, I grew from being a wild and ashy tomboy to being a confident woman. I did take some cues from her guidance so I guess it all worked out for the best, but I planned to do things differently with Zion so she wouldn't have to undo any damage I started. I can guide, but ultimately, her experiences are hers to have. Even after my newly found positive attitude, I knew I couldn't save her from a big bad wolf that hadn't shown its head yet. And if the truth must be told, I'd still rather sleep with a pack of snoring grandmas than be in a beauty pageant, but that was me.

I glanced at the alarm clock, and at 10:12 p.m., I knew it was time to let go of it all. I reached for the permission slip, smoothed it out, and signed my name. And then I wrote: *I have pageant experience and would love to volunteer.*

Civil Rights in Black and White:

Searching for Viola / Willie Nell Avery's Advice
By Melanie Eversley

Searching for Viola

SHE FASCINATES ME.

I can't remember when or where I first heard of Viola Liuzzo, but once I knew about her, I couldn't stop trying to figure her out. She was water. She didn't care who knew about her disdain for oil even though Donna Reed trappings grounded her life.

A few years ago, I was taking a bus tour to civil rights sites in Alabama. The bus pulled up onto a grassy hill on the side of a quiet highway and we all piled out, climbing to a marker on top of the hill. Congressman John Lewis of Georgia was leading the tour. It was sunny and we squinted our eyes as we listened to him. He told us in a solemn voice that this was the spot where Viola Liuzzo died. She was shot and killed March 25, 1965, by members of the Ku Klux Klan. She was a 39-year-old white housewife from Detroit who dropped everything to volunteer in the voting rights marches.

I locked onto the fact about Detroit. I'd lived in the Motor City for two years and knew how segregated it was. A lot of people compared it to a donut, with the black people on the inside in the city of Detroit, and the white people on the outside in the suburbs. The differences were stark, economically and socially. A lot of people in the area often noted how you could drive along East Jefferson Avenue in Detroit, with your car bouncing up and down from the potholes, and you'd know the second you'd crossed the line into the suburbs because your car would stop bouncing. That's because the roads were smoother and that's because the residents were more affluent, less brown, and could afford well-paved streets. In fact, Detroit and Chicago often tied or vied for the top spot of the country's most segregated metro area.

I lived there in the 1990s, so I imagined the segregation was even more pronounced when Liuzzo was running her household in the 1960s. A lot of friends have questioned why I, as an African-American woman, would latch onto trying to figure out the motivations of a white woman when there have been so many African Americans who made similar (the same or even more) sacrifices. The best way I can answer it is I know and can feel the motivations of those African Americans who marched in Selma, sat in Greensboro, and decided they weren't going to and couldn't live with oil. But I also felt that I could understand where this white woman was coming from, and that I could relate to her, and that was a feeling that fascinated me. It was different. After my experience of living in Detroit, I could not imagine someone from white Detroit picking up and volunteering in the Selma-to-Montgomery marches. I was curious. The more I learned about her, the more I liked her.

Congressman Lewis grew up in Alabama. He often tells audiences when he speaks that when he was growing up in poverty in segregated Troy, he felt out of place. Segregation, and having to put up with segregation, bothered him. The way African Americans were treated bothered him. It wasn't until he began listening to Dr. King on the radio that he found ideas he could latch onto. He found an acknowledgment of the oil and a method for responding to it that fit with his religious beliefs as a budding ministerial student. He found validation for his desire to "get in the way," something he advises today in his speeches.

The object of Congressman Lewis' admiration, Dr. King,

borrowed from the Bible in his "I Have a Dream" speech when he compared justice and freedom to water. In a nod to Amos 5:24, King said African Americans would not be satisfied "until justice rolls down like waters and righteousness like a mighty stream."

Viola Liuzzo was a force of water that drew me in. Whenever I traveled through the South on trips related to the civil rights movement, I would see a particular photo that was usually attached to literature about her. It was taken before the times of sophisticated lighting and photographers who knew how to draw out their subjects. But whenever I see this image, I feel as if I am with Liuzzo in person, talking with her. Her compassion and even her sense of fun seem to radiate in this picture. She looks innocent and kind, and unaware of or even uncaring about her beauty. Her eyes are gentle. Her face is soft.

VIOLA LIUZZO remained a curious mystery to me until Barack Obama was elected first African-American president of the United States. In talking to people about what the election meant to them, I began wondering about the reactions of Americans who'd fought to make the election possible. I wondered if Viola Liuzzo had left behind any family and how they felt, particularly as white Americans who'd lost their mother and wife to the civil rights movement.

From there began a journey to find Viola Liuzzo's family.

I learned that Liuzzo's death seemed to have had a negative domino effect. Her husband never remarried and died thirteen years after she did. One son became a conservative talk radio host in northern Michigan, and then went underground. Another son disappeared into the woods not far from where Viola Liuzzo was found shot to death. The three daughters all moved west, but seemed to be living quiet lives, except for some appearances involving a documentary about their mom called

"Home of the Brave."

I finally tracked down Sally Liuzzo-Prado through Facebook and I emailed her. After some months of communicating, she said she and her sisters would see me. I flew out to Medford, Oregon, near where Liuzzo-Prado and Mary Liuzzo Lilleboe live. Penn Ann Liuzzo-Herrington took the train up from Tollhouse, California, where she lives with her family. I spent several days with them at Mary Liuzzo Lilleboe's house in the Oregon woods—a far cry from Detroit—while they talked about their mom.

She was the wife of a Teamster's official who was watching TV one day when she saw coverage of the "Bloody Sunday" melee in Selma, Alabama, in March 1965. That was when 600 people set out to walk to the Alabama state capitol in Montgomery to demand equal voting rights for African Americans but were stopped six blocks into their trip by a wall of state and local law enforcement officers who attacked them with tear gas and billy clubs. The video is hard to watch. Liuzzo, like many other Americans, was horrified. She decided she would drive down to Alabama, by herself, and volunteer to work with the civil rights workers. It was the kind of thing she would do, her daughters said.

While Liuzzo was making her plans, the civil rights community was making plans too. It was decided that Dr. King would come in and he would lead a second attempt at marching to Montgomery. When Liuzzo arrived down South, she was enlisted to take care of all sorts of tasks. After marchers arrived in Montgomery, she shuttled them back to Selma in her car. During one of these rides, four members of the Ku Klux Klan followed her in a car and ran her off the road. She was fatally shot in the head.

Two of the Klansmen were convicted in the slayings on appeal, one died of a heart attack during legal proceedings and a fourth, an FBI informant, was acquitted for his role in the murder.

VIOLA LIUZZO was different and special, her daughters said. She was 5'1" with blond hair and green eyes and could hold her own with a group of men.

She would take her children blueberry picking and rock climbing in shorts and no shoes. When she squeezed into her girdle, she would do "the girdle dance" for her children, sending them into fits of giggles. Once, when the electricity was about to be cut off, she took the family's last money to buy Christmas gifts for another family whose home had burned in a fire.

"Probably the best things that I remember were how much fun she was," Sally Liuzzo-Prado told a group of tourists earlier this year as they stood near the monument at the site of the murder.

She was six when her mother died.

"She would do anything to make me laugh. She loved the holidays. She would dress up our whole house for every single holiday. On Easter, she would make a magic trail of sparkle dust from my bed to wherever she hid the Easter basket, and that's what I would like people to know," Liuzzo-Prado said. "The government, the FBI tried to put out there that she was a bad mother. She was the best mother I could ever have hoped for and she taught me more in those six years than so many parents could ever teach their children in a lifetime."

She was giving too, her daughters said. She took her children to museums and gave Liuzzo-Prado and her brother tap dance lessons while Liuzzo-Herrington studied music and ballet. Liuzzo-Herrington says one of her classmates told her, "I wish your mom was my mother."

Today, Sally Liuzzo-Prado is a jewelry maker who says she has many African-American friends because she feels most comfortable with African Americans. Penn Ann Liuzzo-

Herrington has a multicultural family. Mary Liuzzo Lilleboe was active in Barack Obama's campaign and travels and speaks about her mother's legacy.

During the same bus trip in which her sister spoke earlier this year, Mary Liuzzo Lilleboe told tourists that being called on to speak about her mother has helped her. Now, Liuzzo Lilleboe takes part in the annual civil rights tour sponsored by the Atlanta-based Southern Christian Leadership Conference/Women's Organizational Conference for Equality Now (SCLC/W.O.M.E.N., Inc.) and hosted by founder and civil rights leader Evelyn Lowery.

"I had everything I needed from my mother to be a woman who had a voice," Liuzzo Lilleboe told tourists at her mom's marker earlier this year. "But I hid for close to forty years until Mrs. Lowery invited us down here to join you. And it was through that I found my voice again. The most important thing out of all of this is if we don't vote and have a voice, we let everybody who we've seen yesterday and today die."

Willie Nell Avery's Advice

As a NATIVE NEW YORKER, I like being around African Americans from the South. On the outside, they are all hospitality and comfort. They always say and cook the right things to make you feel good. Being with them is like spa therapy. But on the inside, watch out. They are all backbone and smarts. They think and strategize before they act or say anything. They live by principles. They have a strong force of water at their core and they don't feel right when oil invades, like one of those scratchy clothing labels that makes you feel as if you won't be able to stop thinking about it until you rip it out.

I had become familiar with this fact about African-American Southerners when I traveled to Marion, Alabama, in March

2010. On the outside, the deserted downtown with its movie-set courthouse and wide, silent streets seemed innocent. But I knew better. I knew there was more beneath the silence.

Marion had been one of the places where of the late Rev. James Orange, an African-American minister and activist, fought for voting rights for African Americans. Orange liked to tell everyone that he met that they were a leader. In fact, a monument erected to him downtown by the SCLC/W.O.M.E.N., Inc. (Southern Christian Leadership Conference/Women's Organizational Movement for Equality Now) bears his favorite greeting: "Hey Leader." As an organizer in the 1960s, he was jailed when he tried to register African Americans to vote. Local African Americans protested this, and one of them, Jimmy Lee Jackson, was shot (and killed) by an Alabama state trooper during a peaceful demonstration. Jackson died eight days later. His death sent ripples through the African-American community in Marion and surrounding places and prompted the organization of the Selma-to-Montgomery marches.

Those days were violent, traumatic, and full of smoke, tear gas, and gunshots for the African Americans who lived in the South. This part of Alabama was known for its vicious attitudes.

Willie Nell Avery, 72, lived amid all that. Small, cute, and dignified, she told her story earlier this year from the podium at Zion Methodist Church, in downtown Marion. The prim and pleasant package on the outside belied the determination inside.

She is made of water. She didn't like what she saw happening in her part of the world forty years ago when local officials would order African Americans to guess the numbers of jelly beans in a large jar if they wanted to register to vote, or would simply tell African Americans that their tests had been lost.

Avery said life was harsh for African Americans back then. She took a voter registration test and repeatedly tried to get the results from the registration office. Each time the employees at the office rebuffed her, she'd make plans to go back. This happened in that movie-set courthouse, across the street from the church where she spoke.

"They knew my walk, and before I would even get to the door, they'd say, 'we haven't graded yours yet,'" Avery remembered in a voice that makes you want to listen.

The African Americans got motivated and riled up with what was happening, particularly after Jimmie Lee Jackson died. The twenty-six-year-old man was a model citizen, a deacon, and a business owner, and he had been shot in the stomach when he tried to intervene with state troopers who were beating his mother and eighty-two-year-old grandfather. Jackson fled the café where he was shot and troopers continued to club him. He collapsed in front of the bus station before being taken to the hospital, where he died.

African Americans in Alabama could not live with what was happening. They staged marches and sit-ins and became unified. Locals often met at Zion Baptist Church to figure out their next move, Avery said. They became ambitious and defiant.

Today, Avery is one of three voting registrars in Perry County, Alabama. She wants other people to respect their discomfort the way she did. This is what she told an audience of school children and adults visiting her town earlier this year.

"I'm begging you today, children, to stand up for freedom, to stand up for justice, and please register to vote."

Reconciliation Procrastination

By Kimeko Farrar

On a Sunday afternoon drive
I lose myself in remembering, and then hours pass
Memory Lane dead ends in front of home but I can't see it
The house is in the way
It's worn and tattered with falling shutters and chipped paint
Faint traces of the pristine whites and yellows of my childhood
remain
No roses, irises, or sunflowers though
No plum trees, no strawberry patches, no garden of collards
Bald spots in the grass indicate neglect
No man around I suppose
Children look in my direction but none rush to say hello
They don't know me
"You kids live here?"
My Alabama twang comes back
They nod their heads and I assume we're related
They fight each other over the porch swing
There, a sweet old lady used to smoke Viceroy 100's
The paper says she went on to glory a few days ago
I stand at the door and bat away old hurts
I knock because it's time
Fractures of our lives don't mend like broken bones
I say a prayer and hope that returning home is a splint

About the Authors

Jenne' R. Andrews is a published poet, memoirist, novelist and blogger in Fort Collins, Colorado. She is a Fellow of the National Endowment for the Arts in Literature, former Poet in Residence of the St. Paul Schools, and is retired from teaching writing at Colorado State and the University of Colorado. She earned the M.F.A. in Creative Writing/Poetry at Colorado State. She posts poetry, nonfiction and political commentary at http://loquaciouslyyours.com.

Shonell Bacon is a true wordsmith who works hard at writing stories that tap into the universal and at helping writers become better at their craft. She has published both creatively (novels, short stories, and essays) and academically (textbooks and articles). Taking up her first love, screenwriting, in 2007, a script of hers has placed in a contest each year since; she's working feverishly toward that first contract. Currently, while also finding time to write, Shonell is busy pursuing her Ph.D. in Technical Communication and Rhetoric at Texas Tech University. You can learn more about her writing and interests at http://shonbacon.com.

Lissa Brown is a retired, award-winning public relations and marketing executive who has been a columnist, a speechwriter and has ghost-written extensively for public and business officials over the span of her career. Now retired, she has turned her city-trained eyes on the nuances of mountain culture in western North Carolina, where, as Leslie Brunetsky, she wrote *Real Country: From the Fast Track to Appalachia*. *Real Country* was named Humor Book of the Year for 2009 by the High Country Writers of North Carolina. Lissa offers workshops on writing humor and media relations. Contact her at LJBMAU@skybest.com

Mollie Cox Bryan writes blogs, cookbooks, articles, and fiction. Her second cookbook *Mrs. Rowe's Little Book of Southern Pies* (Ten Speed Press) was named one of the best cookbooks of 2009 by All Foods Considered. Her first novel, *Maggie Rae's Scrapbooks*, will be published in 2012 by Kensington Publishing. She lives in the Shenandoah Valley of Virginia with her husband and daughters. Keep up with Mollie at http://www.molliecoxbryan.com.

Maureen E. Doallas has been a professional writer and editor for more than 30 years. She founded in 2008 her own small business, Transformational Threads, which licenses images of fine art originals for rendering into custom hand-embroidery by artisans in Vietnam. Ms. Doallas' poems have been published in *Rye Bread: Women Poets Rising* (1977), an anthology of poems by women from Maryland, Virginia, and Washington, D.C.; *Season of Somber* (1976), a two-volume anthology comprising the work of university students and faculty; and *Kalliope: A Journal of Women's Art: The Florida Issue* (1983). Her poem "Call Out" originally appeared in a different version at *Poets for Living Waters* (July 2010). Ms. Doallas writes daily about art, artists, and poetry at *Writing Without Paper*.
http://writingwithoutpaper.blogspot.com

Mylène Dressler is a novelist and essayist whose works include *The Medusa Tree, The Deadwood Beetle*, and *The Floodmakers*. She lives in Texas and in the canyon country of southern Utah.www.mylenedressler.com

Nicole Easterwood was born and raised in Ohatchee, Alabama and is the author of three books: *Rollercoaster Road: A Collection of Photographs and Poetry, Twenty Years of Snow* and *Into the Wild*. Recently, she has finished a novel, *Brand New Eyes*, and is working on its sequel and a new novel, which is currently untitled. She splits her time between home, writing and traveling.

Angela Elson lives in Louisville, Kentucky, where she spends her time pursuing an MFA in creative writing from Spalding University and drinking on her porch. From nine-to-five she works as a proofreader for an ad agency; her commas can be found on fast-food menus nationwide.

Melanie Eversley is a journalist based outside of Washington, D.C., who has covered politics and race relations for major newspapers. She has been a reporter at the *Atlanta Journal-Constitution*, *The Detroit Free Press* and now is on staff at *USA Today*. She is also a former winner of the National Association of Black Journalists' Ethel Payne Fellowship, a program that allowed her to report from and write about Ghana in West Africa. Her work also has appeared in TheRoot.com, TheGrio.com, *Essence* magazine, *The Miami Herald*, *Dallas Morning News*, *Philadelphia Inquirer*, *New York Daily News*, *Chicago Tribune* and *City Limits*. She is a graduate of the Columbia University Graduate School of Journalism and Oberlin College, and a native of New York City.

Kimeko Farrar is a poet, actress, freelance writer and journalist who possesses an unyielding passion for the arts. She has been writing for several years and both her creative and technical works have been featured by local television, print and online magazines, private businesses and Universities. Ms. Farrar, a popular spoken word artist and host, performs regularly at open mics. She spends her spare time sharing stories of her own personal growth while encouraging and entertaining others with insightful and humorous commentary about family, religion and relationships on her blog; http://chickunderconstruction.wordpress.com. She graduated from the University of Alabama in Huntsville with a BS in Mechanical Engineering and works as a Senior Intelligence Analyst. She currently resides in Huntsville, Alabama with her daughter.

Laura B Gschwandtner is married, the mother of three daughters, a writer, magazine editor, artist, and co-owner with her husband of an integrated media business. Her work has appeared in various journals including *Del Sol Review*. She has received awards for three different stories from the Writer's Digest Annual Competition in the mainstream literary category in 2004 and 2006, the Lorian Hemingway short fiction competition in 2007, and was short listed for the 2010 Tom Howard Short Story Contest. She also founded *TheNovelette.com* which offers free themed writing contests with prizes for emerging writers. Her first novel, *The Naked Gardener* is available at www.amazon.com in Kindle and print versions. She lives in Virginia.

John Klawitter is a true Hollywood hyphenate: a writer-producer-director and author based in Los Angeles. He writes novels, books and screenplays and develops projects for television through his indy production company Dancing Bear Ent LLC. His novel *HOLLYWOOD HAVOC: The Trouble with Fat Boy* won the 2009 EPPIE Award for Best Action Thriller, and his show business-based memoirs *Tinsel Wilderness* won a 2009 EPPIE Award for Best Non-Fiction Book. Learn more about his writing at http://www.johnklawitter.com

Mary Larkin is a native Alabamian and has lived and worked in Europe, Maine, California, New Mexico, the Carolinas, and Tennessee among other places. She's lived in Florida for more than seven years, and thinks of the Gulf as home and of its sea- and shore life as her family. Her work has been published in *Shenandoah*, *The Nebraska Review*, *The Chattahoochee Review*, *The Red Mountain Review*, *Cutthroat*, and in other publications. Her work has brought many awards, including a Fellowship at the Virginia Center for the Arts and nomination for the Pushcart. She earned her MA from the Creative Writing Program at Hollins, and her PhD from Florida State University.

Las Vegas-based **Linda Lou** is a Guinness-drinking humor writer, spirited blogger, and occasional stand-up comic. Her memoir, *Bastard Husband: A Love Story*, chronicles her experience starting over in Sin City after a mid-life divorce, threaded with reflections on the relationship that led her there. In addition, she has been a monthly columnist for www.Living-

Las-Vegas.com and has had numerous personal essays published in anthologies including *Chicken Soup for the Soul: Divorce and Recovery*. Linda Lou speaks frequently about writing, the creative process and topics related to the empowerment of women over forty. Visit her website at www.agingnymphsmedia.com.

Kelly Martineau is a writer of personal essays and memoir. She recently received her MFA from Spalding University, and her work appears in the online journal Public Republic. She lives in Seattle with her husband and daughter.

Patricia Anne McGoldrick, from Kitchener, Ontario, Canada, writes poetry, essays, and reviews with recent published work in the Christian Science Monitor, The Irish American Post and WOW – Women on Writing. Visit her website
http://sites.google.com/a/pm27canada.com/p-a-mcgoldrick
or her blog http://pmpoetwriter.blogspot.com

Ginger McKnight-Chavers is a native of Dallas, Texas and graduate of Georgetown University and Harvard Law, who currently resides in suburban New York City. After sixteen years of practicing law, a variety of life events, both challenging and wonderful, afforded her the opportunity to explore her passion for creative writing as a full-time pursuit rather than a part-time hobby. She was the 2008 recipient of the Kathryn Gurfein Fellowship Award at Sarah Lawrence College and recently completed her first novel entitled *Messages from Midland*.

Carl Palmer, president of the Tacoma Writers Club, nominee for three Pushcart Prizes and the Micro Award, from Old Mill Road in Ridgeway, VA, now lives in University Place, WA.
http://brightlightmultimedia.com/BLCafe/ShowcasedTalent-CarlPalmerPoemsStories.htm#Poems

Karen Pickell has lived in a suburb of Atlanta and vacationed on the Gulf coast of Florida since 2002. She is a stay-at-home mom and part-time freelance writer. Ms. Pickell is currently pursuing a Master of Arts in Professional Writing at Kennesaw State University.

Dania Rajendra is a writer, editor and social justice journalist. Her work can be found in the anthology *Knitting Through It: Inspiring Stories for Times of Trouble* (Voyageur Press, 2008) as well as a variety of left-leaning periodicals. Dania is at work on an MFA in at Spalding University in Louisville, KY and a certificate in culinary arts at Kingsborough Community College in Brooklyn, NY, where she shares a small apartment with her sweet Southern husband. She can also be found at www.daniarajendra.net.

Cherie Reich is a writer and library assistant in Virginia. Her works have appeared in the magazine *Emerald Tales* and the anthologies *All About Eve* and *Bloody Carnival*, and her ebook *Once Upon a December Nightmare* was recently published by Wild Child Publishing. She has short stories forthcoming from Wyvern Publications and Pill Hill Press. She was a third place winner in Roanoke Valley's BIG READ writing contest and is a member of Valley Writers and Virginia Writers Club.

Jarvis Slacks received his Masters in Creative Writing from UNC-Wilmington. He currently teaches Undergraduate English courses in the DC Metro area at Montgomery College and Trinity College. With the tiny speck of free time he has, he is working on publishing his first novel. He also enjoys donuts. Not too much. Just enough.

Tynia Thomassie has published four children's books, three about growing up in Louisiana (*Feliciana Feydra LeRoux A Cajun Tall Tale, Feliciana Meets D'Loup Garou,* and *Cajun Through and Through*). She won the 2000 Louisiana Young Reader's Choice Honor Award for *Feliciana Meets D'Loup Garou,* voted "favorite book" by 3rd, 4th and 5th graders after *Harry Potter.* She teaches English Literature and Broadcast Journalism at West Orange High School and is completing her M.F.A. in Creative Non-Fiction at Fairleigh Dickinson

University. Ms. Thomassie was selected 2010-11 Teacher of the Year in Essex County, New Jersey.

Amy Wise is a writer and artist in San Diego, CA, where she lives with her husband Jamie and daughter Tatiana. She is the creator of The Many Shades of Love where she writes about the ups and downs of being in an interracial marriage and family. She is also a weekly Contributing Writer and Featured Writer for TheNextFamily.com, which is a site about non-traditional families. Additionally, she writes for *The Standard* where her stories are about making it through financially hard times. She is currently working on a memoir.
http://www.themanyshadesoflove.blogspot.com

Dallas Woodburn is the author of two collections of short stories and a forthcoming novel. Her short fiction has been nominated for the Pushcart Prize and the Dzanc Books "Best of the Web" anthology and has appeared in numerous print and online publications. She is the founder of Write On! For Literacy, a non-profit organization that empowers youth through reading and writing. Learn more at
http://www.writeonbooks.org.

About the Editors

Nicky Wheeler-Nicholson Brown is the seventh generation to live on the Gulf Coast. She began her career in theatre, pursued an MA in Classical Greek Theatre and Myth and at the same time travelled across the United States and Europe to record Native American Elders on location and at gatherings. As part of that journey she produced *All My Relations* aired on National Public Radio. Nicky has written scripts for theatre, video and an interactive game for girls *Secret Paths in the Forest*.

Nicky has been published in magazines and newspapers writing about comic book history, mythology, Native American Elders and theatre including a profile of the actress Karen Allen. She has written articles in Gulf Coast newspapers regarding hurricanes, overdevelopment and the damage to wetlands. Nicky is currently an editor and ghostwriter for several publishing houses in New York and the Berkshires and following in the footsteps of her grandfather Major Malcolm Wheeler-Nicholson, founder of DC Comics, she is a publisher for Berkshire Media Artists studios producing audio that is distributed internationally. www.bmastudios.com. She is currently at work on a bio of her grandfather's extraordinarily adventurous life. www.majormalcolmwheelernicholson.com

Zetta Brown is a Texas girl now living in Scotland. She holds a B.A. in English/Creative Writing from Southern Methodist University in Dallas and is the author of several short stories. She has had a residency at The Writers' Colony in Dairy Hollow in 2002 as well as attending the Hurston-Wright Foundation's Writers Week. In 1998 she was a regional first-place winner for

The National Society of Arts & Letters (NSAL) Award for Short Fiction for her story "Black Water."

Zetta's experience in community theatre as a sound technician and sound designer led her to be nominated for Best Sound Design by the Denver Drama Critics Circle in 1998. In 1999 and 2000, her short stories were adapted for performance for *Letters Live!* at the Craft of Writing conference in Denton, Texas.

With over a decade of freelance editing experience, Zetta is editor-in-chief for LL-Publications, which she runs together with her husband, author and publisher Jim Brown. She was the editor of the 2009 EPPIE Award winner for Best Horror Novel, *PIT-STOP*, by Ben Larken. Her first novel *Messalina: Devourer of Men* is an erotic romance set in Denver and has received excellent reviews. She also does book reviews for New York Journal of Books. Her website is www.zettabrown.com

Publishing History

Each contributor to this anthology has asserted their right as copyright holder to their work. The following is the publishing history of titles that have been previously published and are reprinted with the author's permission.

Mollie Cox Bryan, "Renegade Vegetarian," [blog entry] Kitchen Queen of Fish Pot Road, March 25, 2010.
(http://www.molliecoxbryan.com/2010/03/renegade-vegetarian)

Maureen Doallas, "Call Out," Poets for Living Waters [Group blog entry]
(http://poetsgulfcoast.wordpress.com/open-mic-d-g).

Mary Larkin, "Where Luck Lies," *Shenandoah*, Fall 2002, Vol 32, No.3; Reprint as Award Finalist *Santa Fe Writers Project's Literary Journal*, SFWP.org, Nov, 2009.

Linda Lou, *Bastard Husband: A Love Story*, Copyright © 2009 Reprinted with permission of Aging Nymphs Media, LLC.

Amy Wise, "'Sewer' Candy Store," The Next Family [Group blog entry], July 14, 2010
(http://thenextfamily.com/index.php?s=sewer+candy+store) and
The Many Shades of Love [blog entry]
(http://www.themanyshadesoflove.blogpspot.com).

Other Charity Titles

A Blonde Bengali Wife
By Anne Hamilton

Published by LL-Publications
15 October 2010
www.ll-publications.com/bengaliwife.html

$16.99 (US) / £11.99 (UK/EU) / $7.99 (ebook)
ISBN: 978-1-905091-48-7 (print) / 978-1-905091-48-5 (ebook)

For Anne Hamilton, a three-month winter programme of travel and "cultural exchange" in a country where the English language, fair hair, and a rice allergy are all extremely rare was always going to be interesting, challenging, and frustrating. What they didn't tell Anne was that it would also be sunny, funny, and the start of a love affair with this often overlooked area of Southeast Asia.

A Blonde Bengali Wife shows the lives beyond the poverty, monsoons, and diarrhoea of Bangladesh and charts a vibrant and fascinating place where one minute Anne is levelling a school playing field "fit for the national cricket team," and then cobbling together a sparkly outfit for a formal wedding the next. Along with Anne are the essential ingredients for survival: a travel-savvy Australian sidekick, a heaven-sent adopted family, and a short, dark, and handsome boy-next-door.

Anne's adventures takes her to the dusty clamour of the capital Dhaka, the longest sea beach in the world at Cox's Bazaar, the verdant Sylhet tea gardens, and the voluntary health projects of distant villages, She amasses a lot of friends, stories...and even a husband.

A Blonde Bengali Wife is the "unexpected travelogue" that reads like a comedy of manners to tell the other side of the story of Bangladesh. It led to her manuscript being noticed by literary agent

Dinah Wiener. Anne says, "I think her first words to me were: 'This book is not commercial. I might never sell it, but I'm passionate about it, and it really makes me want to go to Bangladesh.'"

Between her travels, Anne currently lives in Scotland where she is working on a novel whilst studying for a PhD in Creative Writing at Glasgow University. She celebrated the birth of her first child in August 2010.

Royalties from the sale of *A Blonde Bengali Wife* will go to benefit Bhola's Children, a home and school for orphaned and disabled children on the island of Bhola (UK registered charity No. 1118345).

A Blonde Bengali Wife is available in print and several ebook formats and can found at www.ll-publications.com, www.amazon.co.uk, www.amazon.com, well as many other online retailers.

Other Titles by LL-Publications

The following titles are by our Southern authors:

Devil Don't Want Her – by Zetta Brown

Faith Darling is a young, spiritually righteous woman who must face the fact that you cannot escape from your family and the truth. When Faith's notorious great-grandmother Miss Sunny Vincent dies, Faith, as the only surviving relative, must arrange the funeral. However, Miss Sunny Vincent's remains are hard to dispose of because God won't have her and the Devil don't want her.

OOPS! – By Darrell Bain

Oops! is the third collection of stories by Darrell Bain. When Cupid and a Gremlin bump heads, the sparks fly in a rare

fantasy story by the author. Others stories in the collection include **"A Simple Idea,"** an almost ludicrously simple method of eliminating corruption and idiocy from the political process, one that has been around for centuries but gone unrecognized. **"Cure for an Ailing Alien"** finds a nurse who must come up with a cure for an alien, one whose bodily processes are completely unknown. You'll be amazed at her cure! **"Retribution"** is the story of unexpected consequences when alien meets human. **"Robyn's Rock"** is partially based on a happening in the author's life during a walk with his granddaughter.

Bark! - By Darrell Bain

Find out what happens when Tonto, a little, ADHD affected, one-testicled weenie dog, turns out to be the only thing standing between the Earth and accidental alien invasion! Pure comic genius from multiple award-winning author Darrell Bain. Also includes the autobiography of the real Tonto, the little dog who inspired the story!

Pillar's Fall: Book One of The Legend of Pillar Series

Detective Thomas Pillar had no premonitions of the day ahead. He didn't know he was about to clash with a sadistic lunatic on

Railston's only suspension bridge. In one gut-wrenching moment, Pillar was forced to make a life-or-death choice that left the entire city shaken and set a madman's plan into motion. Now, months later, it's starting again. This time, Pillar's investigating a string of rage-filled murders, and all the clues point to the most unlikely of suspects—a twelve-year-old named Seth Morrissey. The child seems nice, if a bit lonely, but something malevolent and demonic hides beneath his surface. While Pillar searches for answers, the thing inside Seth prepares for a showdown that will rip Pillar's life to shreds and pave the way the hell on earth

The Hollows: Book One – The Ticking – By Ben Larken

Former detective David Alders rents an apartment at a quiet unassuming place nestled in the outskirts of Fort Worth. Instead he finds terror, time travel, and murder—all for one low monthly rent. Welcome to THE HOLLOWS. Pray that the lease agreement expires before you do.
A finalist in EPIC's eBook Awards™ 2011 for Best Horror.

Pit-Stop – By Ben Larken

Welcome to the Pit-Stop Grill, a roadside attraction along Arizona's Route 66 where travellers kick up their feet while sipping a nice cup of joe. It's a cool oasis in an unforgiving desert landscape. It's also the last stop on the road to Hell. When ten people find themselves inside the eerie diner, unable to get out or remember how they arrived, all they know is what their waitress, Holly, tells them: a bus is coming. It will take them the rest of the way to a destination of unspeakable horrors.

2009 EPPIE Award Winner for Best Horror.

Available Now at LL-Publications.com

About the Publisher

"...taking the reader down a different path."

LL-Publications was established in 2008 and is run by the husband and wife team of Jim and Zetta Brown, along with editors Rachel McIntyre, Leslie Brown, and the sensational cover artist and graphics goddess Helen E. H. Madden. Based in Scotland, LL-Publications produces mainstream fiction in paperback and in multiple digital (ebook) formats. Our talented authors represent both sides of the Atlantic.

We are proud to be a small, independent press. Our aim is quality over quantity and our motto is "taking the reader down a different path" because the titles we produce are not recycled plots with reused characters in uninspired settings but compelling tales that readers will remember.

Visit us at www.ll-publications.com